WHAT

MONEY

CAN'T

BUY

MARCI GIEBELS

Misty Morn Publishing

"Your talent is God's gift to you. What you do with it is your gift back to God."

Leo Buscaglia

CHAPTER ONE

THERE WERE ONLY THIRTY-SIX PEOPLE in the club when Kaaber arrived, but the iconic Greenwich Village venue was pushing capacity. A shaggy-haired kid who looked too young to have a driver's license was the sole occupant of the dimly lit stage. As Kaaber negotiated for a vacant seat at an occupied table, the kid stumbled over one of two cords that snaked across the three-by-three-foot plywood platform. The boom of uncalculated steps on the hollow riser echoed through the club and a barely-legal blonde at a nearby table jumped at her chance to get attention.

"Careful up there!"

Kaaber turned and immediately zeroed in on the face of the proud, young heckler. She smiled coyly at him and raised her shoulders into a cute pose. Kaaber scanned her from head to toe and back again, then turned around unaffected. He knew the type— indifference would shake her confidence and deter another outburst.

The kid plugged in his cheap guitar and slipped the strap over his shoulder. He uttered a few "*yups*" into a rusty, dinged up Shure 58 microphone. It was plugged into a Peavey powered head that showed years of road wear, but the sound it produced was distinctively round and warm. Armored with second-rate gear, the awkward boy miraculously transformed into confidence personified.

"Hi there. My name is Kelly Bailey, not from the circus Baileys." He used the same opening the previous three times that Kaaber had come to see him. The small audience chuckled politely. "It's an honor to play this room—so many of my idols created the vibe here. I'm gonna play of few of my new songs for you tonight. I wrote twenty-three this week, but I only have time to play seven or eight, so I hope you like 'em."

The audience clapped. The acoustics in the small room were so good that the sound of the applause didn't reverberate.

Just like Kelly's previous shows, he played all brand-new originals. The songs were so well styled it would be reasonable to assume he spent years perfecting the phrasing and the composition. Kelly delivered the vocals effortlessly, feeling the meaning of each word while hitting the notes of the melody with such purity that it brought tears to Kaaber's eyes.

The thirty-minute set sped by too quickly, and Kelly sustained the root of the E minor chord while he riffed with his free fingers for his final flourish. He used no effects on his voice, so he made no adjustment to the board before he said, "Thanks for listening. Mad Dogs Unleashed is next. They're really good, so stick around. I'll get out of their way really fast."

Kelly Bailey didn't seem to notice the aggressive applause that his audience lavished upon him well after he had wrapped his last cord. He lovingly placed his guitar into a hard case, threw the mic and cords into a small leather bag, and grabbed the handle of the small head. The club was too small to have a backstage area, so he walked between the tables, through the crowd, toward the door.

"Excuse me, Kelly. Can I buy you a Coke?" Kaaber asked as he passed.

It took a second for Kelly to react. He seemed surprised that anyone was talking to him.

"Um, no thanks. My dad is probably waiting for me."

"Okay, then. Just wanted to tell you how much I enjoyed your set. I played in a band in college, but no matter how many hours a day I practiced, it never clicked for me."

Kelly laughed a little and smiled shyly. He looked at Kaaber's tailored Italian suit, his Breitling watch, and his expensive leather shoes. He noticed that an eighty-dollar haircut and a tanned face framed the man's perfect teeth. "It looks like you're pretty good at somethin' else though, so … at least what you do gives you a future. The greatest musicians in the world can't pay the rent some months."

"I just sold a fifty-million-dollar penthouse in Manhattan to a pop star who doesn't have half the talent you have. He paid cash. You're in the right city to get discovered. In fact, if you have a card, maybe I could pass it along."

Kelly laughed, "Oh, ah … no, I'm not the self-promotion slash YouTube channel type." Kelly set the PA head on Kaaber's table and reached into his pocket for his cell phone. He glanced at the screen. "Sorry, I gotta go. Dad's double parked on Bleeker around the corner."

"Nice talking with you, Kelly. Maybe I'll come see you again."

"Yeah. I play here on Tuesdays. I'll try to have some new songs by next week." Kelly put his phone back in his pocket and grabbed the handle of his PA.

"You're a lucky kid, I'd give anything to be able to do what you can do."

"Thanks, man."

Mad Dogs Unleashed was starting an earsplitting sound check and Kaaber motioned for the server to bring his bill.

"Did you mean what you said? That you would give anything to have that kid's talent?" The man from the table next to Kaaber's didn't have to lean over too far to make conversation.

"Sure, but lessons can only take you so far. I came to realize that you either have it or you don't."

"Talent is a gift. It can't be learned," the man agreed. "I'm Wesley Davis." He held out his hand.

Kaaber guessed that he was in his mid-thirties, about ten years older than he was.

"Wesley, I'm Sasha Kaaber. My friends call me Kaaber."

"Nice to meet you, Kaaber. I see you're settling up; you headed to another place?"

"No, I'm going home. I'm listing an apartment at six-thirty tomorrow morning. It's an older couple, they wanna do it right after breakfast."

Wesley laughed. "Sunrise is bedtime in this city, isn't it?"

"Not when you're eighty," Kaaber explained.

"I might as well make it an early night myself. I can't do these mid-week late nights anymore and still expect to be productive at the office."

The waitress brought the bills for both men, and they continued their conversation while they signed and made their way to the street.

"So, what do you do?" Kaaber asked.

"I'm in mergers and acquisitions for one of the big boys. Nothing exciting for me, but I like making connections and watching people thrive from new partnerships."

"Sounds fulfilling," Kaaber replied. "Well, it was—"

"You heading up town, Kaaber? My driver is … right there. I could save you some cab fare."

No thank you died on Kaaber's tongue as he watched the stretch Bentley pull up to the curb.

"Real estate is not doing as well as mergers and acquisitions," Kaaber said.

Wesley laughed. "It's not mine, unfortunately. It's a company car. I took some clients out to dinner earlier and they wanted to come to the Village. I figured one more stop wouldn't hurt anyone."

"I'm at Thirty-eighth and Eighth, is that out of your way?"

"Not at all. I have this car and no friends around to show it off to. It would be so much better if you were a six-foot-tall blonde with double Ds, but those are hard to come by."

Kaaber laughed. "All right. When am I gonna get another chance at a ride like this? I wanna feel the leather that covers the seats in a stretch Bentley." Kaaber took his cell phone from the inside chest pocket of his suit. "Would you mind taking a shot of me with this bad boy?"

"Same exact thing I did the first time I got next to her. That picture was my one and only post to Instagram."

Kaaber stood in front of the car with his arms crossed and a serious expression on his face. Wesley took pictures rapid fire. "Lean up against it," he instructed.

"I'm not touching anything I can't afford to fix. My luck, I'd scratch it."

Wesley winced. "Luck is bullshit made up by cowards who don't have the balls to take their destiny into their own hands."

"All the same. I'm sure you got a good shot." Kaaber laughed.

In typical New York style, a car that had plenty of room to go around the parked car blared the horn the whole time it did so.

"Better end the photo-session," Kaaber suggested.

"Welcome aboard," Wesley waved his hand toward the door that the driver held open for his passengers.

Kaaber slid into the Bentley and looked around at the fine appointments. Bright white leather seating dominated one side of the car. Across from the couch, walnut cabinets supported a marble bar top underneath an Apple TV in a custom mounting.

"Holy shit. This is amazing."

Wesley slid in and sat on the rear settee beside Kaaber. "The leather feels like baby skin, doesn't it? My boss has one of these for his personal use and the company buys three new ones every year. The resale is pretty good, but the cars are a big investment in our image."

"It's workin'," Kaaber confirmed.

"You're not doing too bad yourself. I heard you say you just sold a fifty-million-dollar property—you list it too?"

"No, not that one."

"So, what, you spilt the six percent commission, pay your broker and pocket almost three million, right?

Kaaber shifted in his seat. "Close enough."

"You gotta work hard to hustle those mega deals. That's a small percentage of the market. You must have a real passion for what you do."

Kaaber chuckled, looking out the window as the car floated up 8th Avenue. "No, I don't have a passion for real estate, but I do like depositing the commission checks."

"What would you want to do with your life if you could do anything?" Wesley relaxed deeper into his soft leather seat.

"I guess I would want to play music. Like that kid from the club. He doesn't know how lucky he is." Kaaber said, his voice softer than before.

"What is it with you and luck? Luck is a fairy tale. Weren't you paying attention when I told you that earlier?" Wesley became agitated.

Kaaber tensed up a little. "Right. No, I was listening. It's just an overused cliché, I guess."

"What if I told you that you could have that talent. Kelly Bailey's talent. You said you would give anything to be able to do what he can do. Would you really?"

Kaaber hadn't thought that Wesley was drunk when he accepted the ride, but it seemed that the alcohol had caught up to him now. "I think we're taking a hypothetical conversation too seriously."

"It's not hypothetical at all. It depends on the level of the commitment you are willing to make." Wesley was insistent and his voice raised with every word he spoke.

Kaaber's gaze darted between his host and 8th Avenue. Once they hit the twenties, the car slowed to a crawl. Madison Square Garden traffic stretched out ahead of them and the Bentley started to feel less like a choice and more like confinement.

"I took lessons for a long time. It wasn't a lack of commitment on my part, it was just a lack of natural ability." Kaaber tried to keep the conversation light as he looked for a place to tell the driver to pull over.

"Natural ability is like a shirt. Kelly has it on right now. But you could wear it tomorrow."

Kaaber nodded as his eyebrows indicated he was considering the concept. "That's a cool idea."

"It isn't an idea," Wesley said gruffly.

"Listen, I'm sorry. I'm not sure what I said to make you angry, but I apologize," Kaaber said. "I shouldn't have imposed on you like this. You were very generous to offer me the ride and I appreciate it, but we're getting close to my apartment, and I think I could use the walk, so if you—"

"Doesn't it bother you that he has no intention of using his talent? That kids writes two-dozen hit songs a week. Plays like a god," Wesley rolled his eyes at his own comment, "and has no intention of doing anything with that. He doesn't even carry business cards."

"He's just a kid, he'll find his way. Or someone will find him." Kaaber was trying to get the attention of the driver who seemed to be oblivious to the contentious nature of the conversation taking place just a few feet behind him.

"No. He won't. He has no intention of pursuing his music beyond his own selfish desires to write in his room after school and play at a dive club on Tuesday nights."

"I had no idea how I was going to provide for myself at his age, but my paychecks have a lot of zeros on them. The kid has time," Kaaber said, still trying to make eye contact in the oversized rear-view mirror.

"Look around. Really look at who has the talent. The intellect. The God-given abilities." Wesley made quote marks in the air. "Then ask yourself, what would I do if I had that? You're in your mid-twenties and you already own real estate in Manhattan." Wesley said this as if it was fact, but he hadn't asked Kaaber for that information. "You obviously worked to make things happen for yourself. So, does a do-nothing really deserve rewards? Ask yourself that."

The car was pulling up in front of Kaaber's building.

"Ask yourself that," Wesley repeated as the car came to stop. "Unlike that ungrateful brat, I have a business card." Wesley held it out to Kaaber. "Take it. When you can answer that question, give me a call."

Kaaber took the card, checked his pocket for his cell phone and opened the car door before the driver made it around. "Thanks for the ride, Wesley. I appreciate it."

"We'll see," Wesley replied as the door slammed shut.

CHAPTER TWO

MARY SAT ALONGSIDE THE HOSPITAL bed reading out loud from her tablet while her father studied her face.

Thad Newcombe was months away from his eighty-third birthday. Reaching the milestone wasn't guaranteed, and it pained his daughter to face the bleak reality. It had been easy to ignore the passage of time—it happened slowly, in twenty-four-hour increments, each day closely resembling the one before. Mary hadn't foreseen a time when Thad would no longer live with her family or spend his days in the painting studio they built for him. But the fall shattered his hip socket and the surgery to repair it revealed the aggressive cancer. Despite aging two decades in two months, Thad was at peace with his fate.

"Life will go on without me, you know," Thad said softly.

Mary stopped mid-sentence. She closed her eyes, removed the cheaters from her nose, and focused on her father.

"Don't talk like that, Daddy."

"Hospice is the last stop before Heaven. I think that slogan is printed on the stationery. I need to know that you are mentally prepared."

Mary cleared her throat before speaking. "I know that this injury has been very hard for you. But you'll heal. We didn't know the cancer was there before and since you aren't doing chemo, you can live somewhat normally, at least for the near future. No one knows exactly how much time they have. That's why we all have to live each day to the fullest. You can still paint, even if you need a wheelchair for a while. You can still mentor Matthew." Mary smiled lovingly at her father. "Your grandson idolizes you and you can still help him hone his artistic expression. Things might be a little different, but different can be good."

Thad Newton smiled at his only child. "I've always loved that about you, Mary. You never gave up hope. If your ship sank, you took a swim … and enjoyed it. That's a fantastic quality. Matthew has it too."

"So, are you ready to have him come in for a lesson? He could bring his paint box and some canvasses. I know he misses—"

"I've had such a good life." Thad interrupted softly but firmly. "Your mother's love made me a man. Having you as my daughter made me a proud man. I accomplished more than most. I enjoyed many sunrises and many sunsets. I have a grandson who will pick up where I left off, so the art world will not suffer my loss. I lived on my own terms, and for that, I'm mostly unapologetic."

Mary sighed, but the breath caught in her chest, and it turned into a sob.

"Please, honey, don't be sad. I'll always be watching over you. I know that David will take care of you and Matthew, but tell him I'm watching his ass too. He's a good man, but he's also an attorney and those two things can't coexist in the same human for too long."

"Stop joking, Dad. This isn't funny."

"Mary, Mary, Mary. It's all funny. It's all ironic. It's totally unfair … it's just life. Nothing more and nothing less. It's only a big deal if you make it a big deal." Thad patted a spot on the bed next to him. Once Mary was perched there, he put his hand over hers. "I want to know that you will not change. You'll be sad for a while, but your sunny disposition will want to take over—let it. Travel. Explore. Be happy." He kissed his daughter on the cheek. "I have a letter for Matthew in the nightstand. Could you take it to him?"

"Of course, Dad, but I don't have to leave yet. I wasn't finished reading you that article. Don't you want to hear the rest of it?"

"No thank you, my dear. I'm getting tired and the matters of this world don't matter enough to lose sleep over."

Mary kissed her father on the cheek and stood up to find the letter and slip it into her purse.

"Is there anything I can get for you before you turn in for the night?"

"Maybe just tell those nurses that I would love a few hours of uninterrupted sleep. I know I'm a handsome devil and they can't help sneaking into my room at all hours just to be near me, but let a man get some shut eye, you know what I mean? I'm in no condition to satisfy their needs." Thad smiled.

Mary leaned in for one more kiss on the old man's cheek.

"I love you, Daddy. See you tomorrow."

"I love you too honey."

Mary left the room, pulling the door closed behind her.

Thad Newcombe made the sign of the cross and sat in reverent silence for a few minutes. Then he clicked off the lamp next to his bed. He made his way to the walker—each step was excruciating, and his repaired hip burned like it was on fire.

The razor blade was in his shaving kit on the bathroom vanity. Thad lowered himself onto the shower floor, razor blade in hand, and went to work. He slit his wrists vertically and then cut both his femoral and carotid arteries on an angle. He rested his head against the shower wall and smiled. Thad Newcombe bled out in sixty heartbeats.

CHAPTER THREE

"H EY, MAURO. YOU SMELL LIKE—"

"Every fuckin' night, Will? I could go to any another bar for watered-down liquor and lousy happy hour food." Mauro settled onto his barstool, the one where no one else would think to sit because it belonged to him, and adjusted his Wickersham Waste Management ball cap.

"I wish you would, bro," Will smiled.

"What mystery meat are you servin' on a stick tonight?" Mauro wrapped his big hand around the rocks glass that Will produced in miraculously short order.

"It's Thai Chicken Satay with Peanut Sauce," Will said defensively.

"It's probably cat, but I don't give a shit. I'm hungry. I start at four a.m., work until four p.m., spend an hour in the shower, and by five o'clock Happy Hour, I'll eat anything."

"An hour in the shower and I can still smell you comin' every day."

"You smell something familiar? It's your sister." Mauro laughed.

"My sister? You would be so lucky to have a saintly woman like my sister to take care of your old, stinky ass." Will motioned for the customer waving at him from further down the bar to give him a second.

"Why would I mess up my perfect life by allowing a woman into it? Go take care of your patrons or no one will come back to this disgusting rat-hole."

"They come back for the cat. Gets 'em every time!"

Mauro helped himself to the free buffet and then returned to his seat at the bar. He watched the flat screen TV that Will mounted behind the bar well last year. The president of one of those tech companies, Mauro didn't care enough to keep track of which, was on the news. Instead of holding a press conference or making a new product announcement, he was sitting behind a piano and singing into a microphone. Mauro stood up on the rung of his stool and leaned over the bar to grab the remote from where Eddie kept it. He turned up the volume.

The female reporter was gushing admiration. "How have you been able to hide this incredible talent from us for all these years?"

"I actually started playing piano, writing music, and singing very recently." The cocky, young millionaire plinked melodies on the keyboard as he spoke. "I never really devoted any time to making music, but I've always been interested in it. I guess I just have a natural ability, but never knew it. All those hours I spent listening to Miles Joosten and Stevie Wonder—I guess it slipped in by osmosis!"

He laughed. The reporter laughed. Then she turned to face the camera. "Well, there you have it. Shelton Barr's album dropped on iTunes today and it's already number one. What can't he do? From San Francisco, this is—" Mauro pressed the mute button.

Will walked back from the other side of the long bar. "What the hell is wrong with you? Some woman propose to you or somethin'?"

Mauro closed his eyes and took a long breath. "Nothing—just a little déjà vu. I hope."

CHAPTER FOUR

Cassandra Marcot considered the only available seat on the LA Metro bus and repelled backward when she saw the half-dry puddle of vomit in the center of it. There was a pole with no one clinging to it in the back of the bus and she claimed it by leaning against it.

The other passengers stared at the floor, out the window, or had something to read. No one made eye contact and none of the other passengers seemed to notice Cassandra's arrival. She stood with her legs shoulder width apart, diligently watching the traffic so she would know when to shift her weight for the jerky stops and starts of the smelly, lumbering vehicle.

Had she boarded this bus six months ago, she would have stood out like a swan in a hen house. But she looked different now. Her Princess Kate hair was a violet bob, designer clothes had been traded for Goodwill finds, and generic sneakers took the place of her favorite Jimmy Choos.

She looked down at her Billy idol T-shirt and black leggings and laughed to herself about how the concierge at the Ritz-Carlton would undoubtedly greet her by name and tell her that she looked lovely. It was his job to recognize frequent guests and Cassie knew that he would see through her outward appearance to the heiress underneath.

When the bus reached the open-air terminal, Cassandra let several people disembark ahead of her. She found a clean-ish place to sit on a shaded bench and waited for her connecting bus. Cassandra clasped her hands in her lap to curb her desire for her old iPhone. In her former life, Cassie was constantly engaged with the device. She glanced around and noticed that everyone in the bus terminal, even people who appeared unhoused, had a phone. She sighed.

An older woman, who was wearing far too many layers for the weather, squeezed herself between Cassie and the person sitting next to her. Cassandra shifted as far as she could toward the end of the bench, and looked at the large, old-fashioned clock on the wall. In spite of the bars that crisscrossed the face, the glass was shattered. The second hand defiantly went about its business and Cassie knew to expect the bus within the next few minutes. She stood up and walked to the ladies' room but decided against going in when the door opened, and the stench wafted outside. Cassandra returned to the area where she would board the last bus in her hour-long journey and paced.

The bus arrived on time and was one of the newer ones in the fleet. The AC was pumping efficiently, and Cassie felt relatively refreshed when she got off at her stop. The mile long stroll was pleasant. She was in a familiar neighborhood now and she felt comfortable. The afternoon wasn't warm or cool and the walking was easy. Cassie felt a pang of anxiety when she started up the long driveway to the Ritz. She used to primp and prep to come here with her family, knowing that she would see friends and frenemies. After a few deep breaths, she was emboldened by her new appearance and the statement her life made against abundance.

Cassandra straightened her shoulders, lifted her chin, and walked without bouncing, the way her mother taught her by placing a hard-cover dictionary on her head. The doorman was disappointingly non-judgmental and treated her cordially as he opened the door. Once inside the palatial lobby, George, who had been the concierge at the hotel since Cassie was a teenager, greeted her.

"Miss Marcot, it is a pleasure to see you again. Your grandmother has chosen a table near the grand piano. Allow me to show you there."

"Thank you, George. And thank you for recognizing me," Cassie said with a laugh.

"I'm sure I don't know what you mean, Miss Marcot." George winked and motioned for Cassie to follow him.

They crossed the expansive, open lobby, which featured a wall of floor-to-ceiling windows, rendering the lit, planet-sized chandelier futile. The black carpet with white geometric design suppressed their footsteps as it absorbed superfluous noise. Cassandra spotted her grandmother perched on the edge of a wing-backed chair; one ankle tucked elegantly behind the other.

"Hello, my dear. I just had them pour the tea and I was waiting to give you first right of refusal on the finger sandwiches." Mrs. Marcot remained seated as she spoke. "Thank you, George. That will be all."

Cassandra smiled at George who handed her a full cup of tea on a saucer before he departed.

"You know how much I adore you, Gram. If I wasn't totally devoted to you, I wouldn't subject myself to this pretentious display of conspicuous consumption." Cassie settled in a chair across from her grandmother while eyeing the extravagant three-tiered tea service on the table between them.

"Don't be pejorative, Cassandra. These are good people. Just because they spend the afternoon surrounded by fine things rather than dumpster diving doesn't make them miscreants."

"I bet a family of four could eat very well out of that man's garbage." Cassie nodded toward a man reading a financial magazine on an art deco couch. "If he could elevate his awareness beyond his portfolio, he might even care to know that."

Mrs. Marcot looked north of her granddaughter's skin-tight leggings and baggy T-shirt and became lost in emerald eyes that displayed aggressive compassion. Cassandra's porcelain complexion was physical evidence that the world had not yet taken its toll.

"That's quite judgmental. You can't claim a superior mind-set while you're forming opinions based upon two seconds of observation." The older woman lifted her china cup from the saucer and took a slow sip. "Divine," she whispered, almost to herself. "At any rate, darling, I'm sure you didn't ask to get together today to debate the moral obligations of the one-percenters, a group within which you have privileged inclusion, I might remind you."

"Don't remind me," Cassandra said, brushing her newly colored violet hair from her eyes.

"One of the greatest luxuries that wealth provides is a wider range of choices. The choice you are currently trying out is anti-consumerism. Now, if I were going to be disparaging, I might describe Freeganism as living on society's excrement, but I am a well-mannered, Radcliffe educated woman, so I wouldn't voice such a vulgar opinion."

Cassandra couldn't suppress her smile. "I'm sorry, Gram. I don't know why I have a chip on my shoulder."

"You expected me to react your new lifestyle the way your parents have, I suppose. I'm quite insulted that you would lump me together with those idiots, Cassandra."

Cassandra laughed. "Gram!"

"We both know it's true, dear. That's not judgment, it's fact, and that is why the two of us have bonded so tightly together. Honestly, when was the last time that you had a conversation of any substance with either of your parents?" Mrs. Marcot waved away a server who was on the way to refill her teacup. "Even so, I knew it might take some time before you were ready to see me. I missed you while you were in Boston, and I was so glad that Mr. Weston hadn't romanced you into staying there once your graduate work was finished."

"You can call him Chris, Gram."

"If I ever get the chance to meet him perhaps I will feel more comfortable calling him by his first name."

"I want you to meet him as soon as possible. And I explained to you that he was working his way through school. He had two jobs and carried a full course load. When we had breaks, he took on extra hours to make more money, which shows how responsible he is. Chris was at Harvard on a full scholarship, but he still had to support himself."

"He sounds like a solid young man, but that doesn't excuse him from not extending himself now. Unless he is embarrassed about the path he led you down since graduation and plans to drive a wedge between you and your affluent family."

Cassandra shook her head so violently that a tsunami developed in her teacup. "This lifestyle was entirely my idea. Chris had job offers from several Fortune 500 companies. In fact, he accepted a position with Apple. They have a fantastic program that allows for a one-year sabbatical between graduation and your start date. They encourage their staff to become the best version of themselves, so they have more to offer. Chris was eager to get to work, but this was something I really wanted to do, and he was afraid I would do it without him. He said he would never be able to forgive himself if anything happened to me, so he put his goals on pause and here we are."

"I have been trying to assign a bodyguard to you for years. You know Cassandra, whether you want to admit it or not, your position does make you a target. Sadly, there are people who would use you to get to your family's wealth. I've told you from a very young age that you have to be careful about the company that you keep." Mrs. Marcot sighed and remained silent for a moment. "Chris was afraid that something might happen to you. Is this group you live with dangerous?"

Cassandra placed her teacup and saucer on the table next to her grandmother's. She looked around the lobby of the hotel and took a deep breath.

"Cassandra?"

"The Freegan Club in Cambridge promoted the lifestyle. They were hippie rich kids, and I liked their ideas. But, in the real world, the philosophy is a bit 'fringy', and it attracts some non-conformist types."

"Answer my question, dear."

"Well, our housemates are a blend of people we identify with and a few stragglers who would probably be on the street if we didn't have an open door policy. People I don't know come and go. Chris put a lock on our bedroom door, but the main door was jimmied a few weeks ago and hasn't been fixed. I feel safe when Chris is there with me, but his grandmother is in the hospital, so he is going back east for a few days. If I go to my parents' house, it would be like admitting defeat and I just wondered if—"

"Of course you can stay with me. The Marcot Estate belongs to all of us, darling. You never need an invitation to come home."

"Thanks, Gram. Chris doesn't leave until tomorrow, so I'll come on the late afternoon bus."

"I'll have Kane pick you up."

Cassandra laughed at the thought. "No, no, no. Thank you, but I don't want your chauffer coming to the house."

"He's more than a driver, Cassie, he is my Head of Security."

"Even worse, Gram. The people I live with don't have help with job descriptions like 'Head of Security'."

Mrs. Marcot reached for a petit four. "May I ask how much longer you plan to maintain this anti-consumerist lifestyle?"

Cassie selected a few finger sandwiches. "Look at these delicacies. I can't resist the temptation to try each one. I can see why you come here every afternoon for high tea."

"Hmmm. Well, I'm glad that you reached out to me and that I will have some precious time with my favorite person."

"Dad and Uncle Henry would be crushed to hear you say that," Cassandra teased.

"They know, dear." Mrs. Marcot giggled with her lips pressed together. She leaned forward to place her hand on her granddaughter's knee. "I'm very proud of you, Cassandra. You know your own mind. You are overwhelmed with passion, but you're twenty-three and that comes with the territory. You will channel that passion, balance it with good sense, and realize your tremendous potential."

Cassandra lowered her eyes.

"Don't cower Cassandra, it doesn't become you. Arrogance without grounds is the thing to avoid. Look at your mother for a living example of that."

Cassandra giggled with wide eyes. "What was in that tea, Gram?"

"Truth serum, my dear. Have another sip."

CHAPTER FIVE

KAABER STOOD ON THE SIDEWALK in front of Vivienne Haute Cuisine with his cell in his hand. His attention was on the screen, which allowed his girlfriend Charlie to sneak behind him.

"You're too sexy to be kept waiting," she said in a fake French accent.

Kaaber didn't look up from the screen. "Go inside. If she doesn't show in the next five minutes, I'll meet you for a drink at the bar."

Charlie smacked his shoulder with her tiny evening bag.

"Oh, it's you!" Kaaber turned around laughing. Once he allowed himself to focus directly on Charlie, his eyes devoured every inch of her. The red dress that she wore displayed the rewards of daily spin class and her wavy blonde hair fell to the middle of her back. Charlie's eyes were the same ethereal green-gold combination that framed a sunset. Kaaber once witnessed the phenomenon that lasted only a fraction of a second and he never forgot it. The first time Charlie gazed deeply into his eyes, he was similarly affected.

Kaaber opened the door to the French restaurant wearing the smile that always accompanied Charlie's presence. "After you, gorgeous."

The maître d' greeted them warmly and guided the couple to the table that Kaaber had reserved.

"We're celebrating tonight, Luc. Don't let a server come near our table without a bottle of Perrier Jouët Belle Epoque Blanc de Blanc in hand."

"Yes Sir, Mr. Kaaber, right away."

"I love this place," Charlie cooed once they were alone.

"I know you do. That's why I love it."

"Good evening Mr. Kaaber, mademoiselle." A server material-ized and popped the champagne cork. He poured two glasses and disappeared.

Charlie raised her glass, "To New York's present-day Rockefeller," she toasted.

"To his mademoiselle." Kaaber laughed.

"That does have to be some kind of record, doesn't it? How often does an agent list a property with a ten-million-dollar price tag and deliver the owner a full price offer the same day?"

"Selling a property before it hits MLS is somewhat common, but I expected this one to sit on the market for a while. When I walked in, I felt like I had gone back in time. It was like a perfectly preserved tribute to 1970. They had plastic runners on top of shag carpet."

"You're kidding!" Charlie laughed.

Kaaber shook his head. "Dark wood paneling on every wall. The kitchen had olive green cabinets. I have the pictures on my phone if you want to look at it."

"I'll take your word for it."

"The unit had good square footage though, and the building has a doorman and an elevator. Still … a tough sell. So, I got back to the office, and I was typing up the listing, using every euphemism in the book, and I got a call from a representative from this corporation in Brussels. She said that they were in immediate need of a temporary residence for a new hire executive, but they wanted to buy a place because they're expanding their New York office. She said they want something close to an address across the street from the apartment I just listed. I told her about the place, she asked me to email the property details and they made a full price offer within thirty minutes. Craziest thing ever. We close Friday." Kaaber raised his glass again.

"You're on a hot streak, for sure." Charlie touched her champagne flute to Kaaber's.

"Well, I could be …" Kaaber nodded to someone standing behind Charlie and violins began to play a song called Marry Me. Charlie turned to look at the musicians, then looked questioningly at her boy-friend. Kaaber stood up from his place at the table and took Charlie's hand before kneeling in front of her. "Charlie, you will always be out of my league, but I know that I can give you a beautiful life. I will make you feel appreciated and loved every day. I will never take you for granted. I will never stop looking for ways to make you smile. I want to make all your worries go away. I want to have a family with you and grow old with you. You can keep me on a hot streak if you say you want the same thing, too."

Charlie stared at Kaaber with an expectant look. "Say the words, Sasha! A woman waits her whole life to hear the words!"

Kaaber laughed. "Charlie Thomas, will you marry me?"

Charlie leaned forward to kiss her fiancé. "Yes!" she whispered in his ear.

Kaaber fumbled in his suit jacket pocket while they kissed and laughed. He found the ring box, opened Charlie's hand, and placed it in her grasp.

They kissed a little more before curiosity got the best of her and she opened it. The three-carat emerald was surrounded by two carats of baguette diamonds. Charlie inhaled sharply again and mouthed the words, "Oh my God!"

She sat in stunned silence for a moment before whispering, "Kaaber, how ... much ...?"

"I know you wanted something like Princess Diana's ring, but I loved the idea of the stone matching your eyes."

"This is ..." Charlie was speechless.

"It's over two hundred years old. I imagine it was worn by some interesting women, so it belongs on the hand of someone magnificent."

Kaaber slid the ring into place, and it fit perfectly.

"It's stunning! I don't think I've ever been this happy."

Kaaber laughed and kissed her left hand before standing up and going back to his seat. "I don't think I've ever been this happy either. I know you're dying to take the Instagram photo. See how many likes I get by the time dinner is over."

"You glory hound!" Charlie laughed.

"I want everyone in the world to know that you're off the market. I just closed the deal of a lifetime. All I do is close."

Charlie rolled her eyes and giggled.

CHAPTER SIX

T HE FUNERAL HAD BEEN WELL attended by friends, colleagues, media, and more than a few curious art patrons who eluded security. Thad Newcombe's death made headlines in Miami, New York, and Los Angeles. As the only child of the man considered the greatest living contemporary artist, Mary's statement to the press extended her sincere appreciation for the nation's outpouring of love and admiration. Thanks to HIPPA and the fact that Thad had opted out of the Hospice directory, she managed to keep the real cause of death out of the press.

Mary was touched by how well respected her father had been by so many, but she was ready for the condolences to stop. She, David, and Matthew lived a very normal existence despite her father's celebrity, and she wanted to grieve in peace. The man standing in her driveway was the last straw.

"Mary Newcombe-Drake?" He asked as she pulled the large garbage can to the curb.

Mary pulled her bathrobe tighter around her torso. "My husband's law firm, Drake, Collins, and McKinney are handling my father's estate. You can contact them with any inquiries."

"I would rather speak to you, if that's okay."

"It's not okay. In fact, you're trespassing." Mary left the can near the street and started up the drive to the house. The man hurried to walk beside her and then stepped in front of her, blocking her way.

"Get off my property," she said slowly, looking the young man in the eyes. He couldn't have been much older than Matthew, but he was dressed in an expensive suit and had a far more mature manner than her teenage son.

"I'm sorry. I don't mean to be aggressive. I knew your father and we have some unfinished business—"

"As I said … my husband's law firm is handling the business. Please get out of my way."

"I understand, but your father had something of mine in his possession at the time of his death and I'd like it back."

Mary tried to step around the young man, and he sidestepped to stop her.

"It would have been something he kept with him all the time. He lived here before the accident and I have reason to believe that it's still in the house."

"You aren't listening to me. Get the fuck out of my way and get off my property or I'm calling the cops!" Mary realized that her conversational tone had become a shrill scream.

"Calm down, Mary there isn't anything—" the young man was mid-sentence when Matthew grabbed the back of his suit jacket.

"What do you want?" Matthew spun the guy around. Mary was aware that her son was growing into a man, but she was surprised to see how Matthew towered over the intruder.

"It's just a misunderstanding." The suited man displayed a movie star grin.

"My Mom asked you to leave, and you didn't. Seems straight forward to me." As Matthew talked, he placed himself between the man and Mary.

"I'll call your husband's office, Mrs. Drake. My boss hoped that we could settle this out of the press—just trying to be respectful to Mr. Newcombe's memory, but I'll go."

"What are you talking about? Who are you?" Mary yelled from behind Matthew's back.

"He's obviously just another Stan." Matthew said, eyeing the intruder. "He just has better drip and is more high-key than the others."

Matthew pulled an iPhone out of the pocket of his slacks. "You goin', or am I calling Miami PD?"

The suited man laughed good-naturedly. "You have a wonderful son, Mary. I'm sorry that our first meeting was such a disaster. I promise to make a better impression next time."

The suited man walked behind the tall hedge that surrounded the Drake's property and disappeared down the sidewalk.

"C'mon, Mom." Matthew walked toward the house and Mary followed. "What are you doin' taking the garbage out when I'm home anyway? I don't want you touching the garbage."

"You haven't been sleeping well and you were finally getting some rest. I didn't want to miss the pick-up," Mary explained as she fell in step.

Matthew put his muscular arm around his mother. "Instead, I have to wake up hearing you scream the F-word in the driveway, Principal Drake? What would your elementary school students say?"

"Stop teasing me," Mary said defensively. "Who do you think that guy was, and what do you think he wanted?"

"What everyone else wants—guap, which can be your young person vocabulary lesson for the day. Guap means money. Everyone assumes Gramps had trunks stuffed full of money. Hell, I thought he had trunks stuffed full of money."

The twosome entered the kitchen and Matthew locked the sliding glass door behind them. Mary spun the Keurig carousel and waited for a coffee flavor to jump out at her.

"Can you make me a hazelnut?" Matthew got two mugs from the cabinet.

"Yeah." Mary spun the carousel three more times.

Matthew walked over to her and placed his hand on the top of the coffee rack, stopping it. "Which one do you want?" He removed a hazelnut and popped it into the coffee machine.

"I knew that Dad didn't have a lot of money," Mary said, distracted. "He and Mom only carried catastrophic medical insurance and when Mom got sick it put a major dent in their savings. His money came spurting in, you know? He'd make seven figures one year and then take five years to finish his next work. And Dad lived beyond his means most of the time. Of course, he never accepted a dime from us—too proud. We found ways to secretly subsidize him, but ..."

"Why are you telling me this?" Matthew asked softly.

"Because, if I was you, I'd be wondering where my windfall was. Some people don't know the day or the hour, but the person you held in the highest esteem planned his departure. At least you got a note—more than I got."

"You got to kiss him good-bye," Matthew said in a whisper.

The hazelnut coffee filled the cup and Matthew held up another hazelnut Keurig cup. Mary nodded. Matthew focused his attention on setting the machine up to make a second cup of coffee.

"What did the letter say, Matthew? Can I read it?"

"You can read it, but it isn't what we wanted. There's no satisfying explanation. No apology. His hand wasn't steady, so it isn't even the artful script you'd recognize. It was upsetting to see, so I thought it was better if you didn't. I wish I hadn't."

"I think I need to read it."

Matthew climbed the stairs to his bedroom and returned to the kitchen with a folded sheet of blue stationary.

Mary mumbled the text out loud as she read in a monotone voice, void of the emotions that the words were bound to release.

Dear Matthew,

I hope you are never in a circumstance that allows you to understand the choice I made. Please trust that I thought it through, and it was the best course of action for all considered. My decision does not reflect on anyone other than myself, so when my suicide is covered in the press and this footnote is added to my biography, do not feel ashamed. I am not ashamed. I am vindicated. I am set free. Allow the gossips to say what they must—it doesn't matter. My death does not define my wonderful life. I am a proud father and grandfather, and my love goes with you forever. Your work will surpass mine, and I am proud to have played a small role in mentoring your ability as a gift to the world. Take care of your mother.

Love, Gramps

Mary stood silently for a moment staring at the letter. "Well, at least I was able to save his reputation and any further grief we would have been subjected to if the press had gotten wind of his suicide."

"Yeah. That isn't anybody's business, but it's kind of sad that he thought it would be part of the news cycle and part of his legacy."

"Then why did he do it?" Mary said angrily. She cleared her throat. "Sorry. I guess a psychiatrist would call my behavior Displacement. I'll be myself again sometime soon, I promise."

Matthew handed a coffee cup to Mary. "I'll drink to that. Cheers."

Mary clinked her mug against her son's and then set it on the counter. "I better get ready for work. I have a thousand elementary school kids to princi-*pal* today. You better get to school to squeeze every dime of our investment from those private school educators."

Mary left the kitchen without tasting the coffee.

As Matthew watched his mother walk away, he felt slightly guilty about not showing her the second page of the letter, but his grandfather's instructions had been very clear.

Matthew emptied his cup in three swigs, then washed both mugs and put them away. He unloaded the dishwasher and moved some chicken from the freezer to the fridge. He planned to make Chicken Parmesan for dinner, so he checked to see if he needed to bring any ingredients home with him from Publix. He used a stainless wipe to clean the fingerprints from the appliances and left a cheerful note on the kitchen island for his mother to see before she left for work. Matthew placed her car keys on top of the note so she wouldn't have to look for them. He jogged ten blocks to school, closing the door to his homeroom just as the bell rang.

He hadn't noticed the black BMW that shadowed him and parked on the street in front of MCA Academy School.

CHAPTER SEVEN

MAURO DIDN'T LIKE THE FREE buffet at this bar, and he missed his daily banter with Will, but it was important that his meeting be as private as possible. He sat at a two-top table in the rear corner of the watering hole and watched the entrance. The door to W 115th Street opened and closed, but his man hadn't arrived. Twenty-five years passed since Mauro last saw him. He hoped they would still recognize each other.

After his third beer, and before he broke down and ordered chicken and waffles, his colleague walked through the door, pinpointed Mauro's table, and walked over to take a seat.

"It's been a long time, Mauro."

"You look exactly the same. Jet black hair, corporate cut, pearly whites— always flashing, shit-brown eyes, dark circles underneath …" Mauro smiled. "A hundred ninety pounds of pure muscle and perpetual look of confusion."

"You should write my Match.com profile. That's me to a T." Wagner laughed. "You still look like the goombah you used to be. Maybe even more fit now."

"Working twelve-hour days lifting garbage cans over your head is good conditioning." Mauro chuckled.

"You're still doing that?" Wagner closed his eyes and shook his head. "What you coulda been …"

"If you hadn't come along."

Wagner opened his eyes and saw that Mauro was smiling.

"I'd be bitter as hell if I was you."

"Nah. I'm doin' good, honest work for good pay. If you'd asked me right after it happened, though—" Mauro shook his head and Wagner nodded his understanding. "I did a bodyguard gig. Spent ten years protectin' a guy who didn't deserve protectin'. I was happy as hell when he got arrested. That was a dirty job. At least the dirt from this job washes off. I been through too much stuff that I can't wash off."

"I hear that." Wagner rapped his knuckles on the wooden tabletop.

"You been watchin' the news? You see that story about the tech CEO who released a record this week?"

Wagner raised his eyebrows. "Yeah. I saw."

"You think I'm being paranoid?"

"Yes. Those kinds of guys, they learn differently than most people. It doesn't mean anything."

"You heard about Thad Newcombe dying? He would be ripe for the pickin'."

"Lots of stories written about how he was the Undisputed King of the Art world, but no evidence that he cashed in on it. There wasn't much of anything in his name when he died. He was livin' with his kid."

"Yeah, but someone like that. You said it, *'Undisputed King.'* That's money in the bank."

"Keep your eyes open, but there's no evidence at this point. The man died nearly penniless according to all accounts."

"If he saw the end coming, maybe he had the chance to pass it on to someone," Mauro suggested. "I mean, if he knew he could."

Wagner shrugged. "We shouldn't concern ourselves with things like this, Mauro. There's nothin' to gain and lots to lose."

Wagner took a swig of his beer while Mauro handed him a menu he plucked from the basket of condiments on the table.

"You hungry?" Mauro asked.

"I think I'm drinking my dinner tonight."

"Could be nothing,'" Mauro said, replacing the menu.

"If you believed that, you wouldn't have called."

"But you said it; I'm paranoid."

"Men who know too much often are." Wagner finished his beer in one long swig. "Keep in touch." He slapped Mauro on the back and walked out the door onto W 115th Street.

CHAPTER EIGHT

T HE SMALL CLUB WAS FILLED to capacity again, but the doorman recognized Kaaber and pointed him toward a couple that cashed out. The minute they stood up from their places at the bar, Kaaber grabbed a stool. He ordered a scotch on the rocks and looked around the room for Kelly Bailey. As Kaaber scanned the crowd, the geeky kid flew through the front door in a frenzy. He whipped his gear together on the stage, made his way to the bar, and leaned over the generous slab of oak right next to Kaaber's stool.

"Hey, Kelly." Kaaber held out his right hand.

"Oh, yeah, hey." Kelly shook hands but didn't show any recognition.

"Jeff!" Kelly shouted at the bartender.

"What ya need?" The bartender walked down the length of the bar so Kelly didn't have to shout.

"Can I put a tip jar out?"

"No, you can't put a fuckin' tip jar out! Customers' money goes in my pocket, not yours. You have a problem with what I'm paying, go play in the Subway."

"Sorry, man. I'm really thankful for the job. I didn't mean anything, I just wondered …"

"You're late, so I'm already docking your pay tonight. You better get started."

Kaaber turned around to face Jeff. "It's none of my business, but why can't the kid have a tip jar? Every musician in New York has a tip jar."

"It *is* none of your business, Suit and Tie, but if you gotta know, when you put ten bucks in his tip jar, that's one less beer that you're ordering from me."

"If he wasn't playing here tonight, I wouldn't be here. I'm good for about three scotches in a half hour and your place empties out when his set is over. The kid's a draw. Why not let him make some extra bread?"

Kelly's face turned purple. "It's no big deal. No big deal. I'm sorry, Jeff."

"Get up there!" Jeff yelled, pointing at the stage. "And how 'bout if I come to your job tomorrow and tell you what to do all day? Sound good, Suit and Fuckin' Tie?" Jeff walked back down to the other end of the bar and Kaaber decided not to order another drink. It would have been a spitter for sure.

Kelly's voice filled the room, "I'm Kelly Bailey. Not from the circus Baileys. Sorry I'm late."

He started playing a song that Kaaber had never heard before. It was full of sad chords and the lyrics were about losing someone. The rest of the set was new material, just like all the Tuesdays before. Twenty-five minutes flew by, and then the set was over. Kaaber left a twenty on the bar and headed to the stage.

"I'm sorry if I made things more difficult for you with the bartender. I just thought he was being a dick." Kaaber talked to Kelly's back as he wrapped his mic cord.

"Don't worry about it," Kelly replied without turning around.

"I'd like to give you a tip. I'm ashamed that it never occurred to me to do that before, I've seen you several times, so I kind of owe you."

Kelly turned around. "All right Suit and Tie. I'll let you tip me," he said with a grin.

Kaaber pulled a hundred dollar bill out of his wallet and handed it to Kelly.

"I can't take that, man. That's too much."

"What if I gave you a twenty?"

"That's very generous."

"Okay, so I'm giving you twenty for every time I've seen you and throwing in next week's tip for good measure."

Kelly laughed.

"Just take it. You make my Tuesdays, so I'm happy to pay it forward."

Kelly glanced at the bar, quickly grabbed the money, and shoved it deep into his jeans. "Thanks."

"Can I help you carry your gear out?" Kaaber offered

"I can get it in one trip. It's okay."

"I'm leaving anyway. I don't think Jeff and I are going be very good friends."

"All right. Thanks." Kelly handed Kaaber his powered head, which was heavier than it looked.

"So, you said you played a little in college?" Kelly asked.

"You do remember me." Kaaber laughed. "Yeah, I played in college. I had a Fender Strat and Fender Deluxe."

"The yuppie starter kit!" Kelly laughed as they walked through the crowd to the door. Kaaber held the door open, and Kelly followed him through.

"September in the City is a good smell," Kelly observed. "Not as good as November, but better than August."

"You're a weird kid." Kaaber laughed.

"Yeah."

"Your Dad coming to get you?"

"He's supposed to, but I might have to take the train tonight. My Mom's pretty sick. Dad stayed with her earlier. Said if she was better, he would come get me, but if he isn't here by now, he probably isn't coming."

"So, you haul your gear on the Subway?"

Kelly laughed. "I'm not the only guy on the train with a guitar."

"Wouldn't it be easier to take a cab?"

"It would be easier to have a tour bus, but I'm not quite in that arena."

"Is that what you want to do? Become a recording artist and tour?"

"For now, my music is my sanity. I don't know if I ever want it to be my job because then it's a job, you know? Then I have to play what they tell me to play, and I can't be creative anymore. I'd be a puppet."

"Maybe for the early years, but you'd be writing your own ticket before too long." The door to the club opened and the sound of the next band came bursting through. "They don't have to worry about getting a deal because it will never happen. A guy like you could have a deal on his own terms."

"I don't know. I'm a junior in high school. I don't know what I want to be when I grow up. My Mom would like to see me get rich and famous. She says my music moves her, but she probably won't live to see it, so ... what's the point even thinking about it?" Kelly suddenly looked like he was going to cry. He looked up and down the street then checked the cell that he pulled out of his pocket. "Looks like it's the train."

"Do you want me to go with you?" Kaaber offered.

"You goin' to Chinatown?"

Kaaber shook his head. "No, but I'd go with you, just to make sure you're okay."

Kelly laughed. "Me and my guitar have been ridin' the train together since I was six. I appreciate it man, but I'm fifteen. I'd be on my own by now if my mom wasn't sick."

"Hardly an adult at fifteen," Kaaber observed.

"Depends on the fifteen," Kelly countered logically.

"All right, then. I'll probably come see you next Tuesday. If Jeff doesn't fire you during the week for your asshole friend at the bar."

"Nah, don't worry about that. He likes to make a fuss, but he's a decent guy."

"Okay, good. If you, ah, need anything, you can always give me a call." Kaaber held his business card between two fingers.

Kelly took it. "I'm not really in the market for a house, but I'll hang onto it in case I meet someone who is."

Kaaber said good-night and watched Kelly walk to the corner. He was an only child, but he had younger cousins, and he felt the same protectiveness toward Kelly that he did with them. The City could be hard on even the toughest souls. It demolished the tender ones. Kaaber decided not to hail a taxi. He took the train uptown instead.

CHAPTER NINE

THE BUS STOP WAS AN epic hike away from Mrs. Marcot's Bel-Air residence, but Cassandra enjoyed being in the open air. When she got to the imposing wrought iron gate with the large "M" in the center, she touched the call screen and the face of her grandmother's head of security appeared.

"May I help you?"

"Hello, Mr. Kane. I'm here to see my grandmother." Cassandra lifted her face toward the light coming from the posts that lined the driveway.

"I'm so sorry I didn't recognize you, Miss Marcot," Mr. Kane stammered. "I will send someone to bring you up to the house immediately."

"Thank you, Mr. Kane."

Cassandra looked above her head at the massive gate. When she had a Porsche and a gate opener, she drove right through. Now she stood outside and waited for the oversized golf cart to come down the long driveway to get her. Several cars passed traveling very slowly. Professionals who wouldn't dare remove their eyes from the road drove the vehicles in this neighborhood, but Cassandra felt stares from passengers behind tinted windows. Finally, the gates began to noiselessly swing inward, and Cassandra walked toward the stretch golf cart waiting on the driveway.

"Good evening, Miss Marcot. It's nice to see you again," Mr. Kane had come for her himself.

Cassandra sat on the seat beside him, and he shifted a little toward the outside edge. She smiled to herself at his visible discomfort.

"Mrs. Marcot has just finished dinner, but I'm sure Mrs. Wade will be happy to put a plate together for you. It's my pleasure to ask her."

"That's okay. I stopped at a restaurant on the way here. I had my fill from what they tossed outside. Some of it was still warm."

Mr. Kane didn't speak again until he pulled the cart under the portico in front of the stately mansion. "Here we are."

Mrs. Marcot was standing at the top of the front steps looking as though she had just returned from the salon.

"Thank you, Kane," she called with a wave.

"Of course, Mrs. Marcot."

"See ya, Mr. Kane," Cassandra said as she jumped off the cart. She took the steps two at a time and thrust herself into her grandmother's hug. "It's so good to be home—I feel more at home here than my parents' house. Isn't that weird?"

"Home is where your heart is, so I'm happy to hear you say that."

The two made their way through the sixteen-foot double doors and into the grand foyer. Mrs. Marcot's voice bounced off the ivory marble cave that formed the open room.

"You know that you make Kane uncomfortable when you sit in front with him, so why do you do it?"

"Someone has to break the mold."

"Why? The mold works."

"Mold smells, Grandma."

"You don't smell like a day at the spa yourself, young lady."

Cassandra bit her lower lip. "Sorry."

"You didn't bring a suitcase."

"Our house might have bedbugs, so …"

Mrs. Marcot sighed through her smile. "Go upstairs and take a long bath. Use every sinfully luxurious beauty product that you can find. I promise I won't tell anyone. I haven't touched the bedroom you always used. Find something to wear and meet me in the library."

"Using stem cell cream and shampoo tested on animals goes against my beliefs."

"Allowing you to sit on my twenty-thousand-dollar couch while you smell like garbage and have insect hitchhikers goes against my beliefs." Mrs. Marcot gave Cassandra a gentle nudge toward the triple width staircase.

"All right, but I'm not going to enjoy it."

"Yes, you are," Mrs. Marcot called after her.

Nearly ninety minutes later, Cassandra floated down the staircase and entered the library where Mrs. Marcot was sitting on the couch reading a book.

"Look, we match." Cassandra pointed out that she had chosen cashmere drawstring pants and a long-sleeved cashmere T-shirt, very much like the set her grandmother was wearing. The two women had petite frames and bob-style haircuts, one white and one violet.

"We have always been kindred spirits." Mrs. Marcot motioned for Cassandra to sit on the other end of the long sofa.

"Can I have Mrs. Wade bring anything for you?"

"No, thanks. I feel perfectly content."

"It's so good to have you here. My world feels balanced again with you under my roof." Mrs. Marcot smirked playfully. "I'm glad to see that you can maintain your newfound beliefs and your former lifestyle simultaneously."

Cassandra blushed.

"Don't be ashamed. We all want to be pampered every now and then." Mrs. Marcot placed her book on the nearby coffee table. "So, let's get this out of the way so that we can enjoy our time together. I have never received a satisfactory explanation as to why you have withdrawn from civilization. It's me, Cassandra. No one else knows you better, and you can't bullshit a bullshitter. I want to know why."

Cassandra began to inspect her fingernails.

"It's perfectly normal to mourn once you advance from the excitements of collegiate life, but you had so much to look forward to and that is why your current lifestyle doesn't make sense to me. Something triggered this radical life-change, and I don't believe the explanation you gave to your parents. So, out with it."

Cassandra pulled her knees to her chest and folded her fingers around her ankles.

"Sometimes, a bright future is intimidating—you're afraid to disappoint people. You know, when I was seven years old, they told me that my IQ was in the Profoundly Gifted range. Genius is a heavy label for a second grader."

"Do you consider your intellect a curse?"

"Not at all. It's a blessing."

"Blessings must not be wasted, so how are you utilizing your exceptional intellect?"

"Well, I have a master's degree in biology from Harvard—"

"That you aren't using."

"I want to show that sustainability and consumption are entirely out of whack in today's society and my life demonstrates the extreme alternative to show that if we all make small changes, we can have a productive planet rather than one deteriorating because of our selfishness."

"That's very admirable, darling, but no one is paying attention. The only people witnessing your life project are the ones in the dumpsters next to you. So, my question to you, again, is, why have you dropped out of society? You can point to your *cause*, but if you were really trying to effect change, your platform is ineffective. You are thumbing your nose at the rest of us. We're doing it wrong—I get that. With your education and your family money, you could be heading up a nationwide organization churning a PR machine that could reach every citizen in this country. So, what are you actually doing?"

Cassandra leaned her head back and let it sink into the pillowy soft couch cushion.

"Why can't I just live a life that I believe in? Why is that too small for you?"

"It's not too small for me. It's too small for you. You have never been a cog in the machine. You design the machine. What are you hiding from?"

"You think I'm keeping information from you. But I feel like you're trying to get me me to confess something you already know."

"Fair enough. Why didn't you tell me that you were tested at Harvard and your IQ was immeasurable ... twice. Your IQ is likely to be 200. Right around the time that you found that out, you started eating out of dumpsters."

Mrs. Marcot studied her granddaughter's face. When she spoke again, her voice was very gentle. "I'm sorry dear. I am passionate about your happiness and well-being and sometimes I wish you would share that passion."

Cassandra smiled.

"When you are ready to talk about this, you know that I will be available to listen. Or, if you are more comfortable with your peers, maybe you could talk with Mr. Weston."

Cassandra pursed her lips. "I feel like Chris and I aren't as close as we were in school."

"Have you asked him why that is?"

"Yes. He denies it, but there's a distance. I'm afraid he resents me for pulling him away from what he wanted to do."

Mrs. Marcot drummed her fingers on the sofa cushion. "When will Mr. Weston return from seeing his family?"

"Thankfully, his grandmother is doing well, so he'll be back later this week."

"What do you think about inviting him to stay here with you for a while? Maybe a break from your current circumstances will give you both the perspective that you need to plan your next step. I have to go away on business for a few days, so you would have the estate to yourselves. Until I depart, though, I would like you to keep up the pretense of occupying separate quarters."

Ten years evaporated from Cassandra's face and her eyes brightened at the suggestion. "I'll ask Chris. I think that would do us a lot of good. Thanks, Gram."

"Whatever you need, dear. Whatever you need."

CHAPTER TEN

MAURO'S FACE RELAXED AS HE dreamed. It was the same familiar dream that combined all his favorite memories into a highlight reel. He was in his college football uniform. The white number 4 stood out against his red Boston University jersey. The stands were alive with people chanting "Gre-co, Gre-co, Gre-co …" That had been Mauro's last name when his first name had been Salvatore. He didn't need to look at the play clock to know that there was time for one last play. A touchdown would win the game; a kick would tie. Most college coaches would call a running play to get the kicker a little closer and try to win in overtime, but Boston University's coach had Salvatore Greco, and he was going for the win.

In the huddle, Mauro called all the jersey numbers while his receiving core laughed and shook their heads. They knew to be ready on every play. Greco could thread a tighter needle than the top NFL quarterbacks. Receivers buried in coverage were open targets for him. "Let's get this over with and get in the locker room. My mom's making tortellini and gravy. I wanna get on the road. Touchdown on three. One, two …TOUCHDOWN!" The offensive unit shouted in unison and lined up across from a line of hungry defensive linesman.

In the dream, as in real life, it didn't matter who they were, they were irrelevant to the outcome. Greco lost only one game at the helm of the BU offense in the three years he was the starting quarterback. The loss had come on his first outing, and he hated the feeling so much that he never let it happen again.

The home crowd hushed, and Greco's cadence could be heard in every section of the stadium. "Thirty-four, Twenty-two, tortellini—" It didn't matter what he said, the play was *get open and I'll get you the ball.* "Hike!"

The center snapped the ball to Greco who took a few steps back in the pocket. He surveyed the field. To him, everything seemed to be moving in slow motion. He had three good options, but his favorite receiver was in double coverage. Greco waited. The pocket was closing in on him. He rolled left, still looking for his favorite target—three men wide open, but none of them had the wheels Greco trusted in moments like these.

A flash of red jersey—Greco's man had a step on his coverage. He released the ball before most of the defense had seen his arm pump. The receiver didn't have to break stride; the ball appeared six inches in front of him and he plucked it from the air on his way to the end zone.

Greco got hit before the play was completed and he asked the dude on top of him if it was a touchdown. The stadium noise was deafening; of course it had been a touchdown, but Greco liked asking the other team for confirmation.

Greco felt the elation. He smelled the sweat. He felt the adrenaline. He heard the chant "Gre-co, Gre-co, Gre-co!"

The defensive lineman took his helmet off and Wagner's face was revealed. The football stadium changed to an empty warehouse and Wagner's voice replaced the cheering crowd.

"Listen to me, Sal. We've come too far for you to back out of the deal now."

"I never told you I was sellin'—"

"You didn't believe that the agency I work for could compensate you fairly for the ability you possess. I proved that we could. We revealed our operation to you in good faith."

Mauro threw the man off him and got to his feet. "No amount of money can replace the experience of doin' what I can do on a football field. I don't care how many zeros you add to the number, I ain't takin' it and I only came here today to make that clear."

Wagner closed his eyes and opened his shirt. He was wearing a wire. "You're not going to be able to just … walk away. You know too much, Salvatore. These people … they'll kill you and take it anyway."

"You fuckin' asshole. All that bullshit about admiring me and worshiping football like it was your religion. The whole time you were diggin' my grave."

There was banging on the only door in the empty room as men shouted at each other to get it open.

"That's them. If I can't make a deal, they're gonna harvest the skill. Take the money, Salvatore. It's the only way out of this."

The young football player shook his head.

Wagner made a guttural growling noise. "Fuck! Fuck!" Wagner pulled a Glock from his waist and a 9 mm from an ankle holster. He handed the smaller gun to Greco.

Mauro started breathing heavy as he watched the scene play in his dream just as it had in real life. The door swung open and the sound of his first shot echoed off the cement in the empty room. Once again, everything moved in slow motion. He struck his first target twice before he fell. There were four men with him and two more were down before they could identify where the shots came from. Return fire came in bursts, causing Mauro to flinch.

"Let's go!" Wagner was shouting at him as he sprinted toward the door. "Salvatore, move!"

Mauro shot straight up in bed, his hand reaching for the loaded Walthers pistol on the nightstand. The cool steel brought him back to reality. He was more out of breath than he had been when he had lived the scene from his dream. Mauro Giordano dropped the gun in the pocket of his sweatpants on the way to the bathroom. He splashed cold water on his face and shuffled to the kitchen. He knew from experience that there would be no more sleep tonight.

The clock on the stove told him that he had two hours to kill before it was time to leave for work. The tortellini from the first part of his dream came to mind, and he portioned some of the frozen pasta into a pot of water on the fast boil burner. He ladled some of his homemade gravy into a saucepan and set it on a small burner set to LO.

Mauro went from the kitchen to the living room. The entire tour of the apartment spanned only a couple dozen steps. He sat in the oversized chair, picked up the TV remote and pressed "power" then "mute" so the sound wouldn't wake his neighbors. He figured the smell of the gravy might do that anyway, but he needed the comfort. Rather than watching television, Mauro's eyes continually scanned the room, looking for anything that might be askew. From where he sat, he could see his gray front door and the four deadbolts that were all slid into place. The tiny kitchen was perfectly in order—the way he always kept it. His kitchen accessory caddy had the can opener hanging straight forward and the pizza cutter was ninety degrees to the left, just as it should be. The laminate floor reflected only shine, no footprints. His chair, the only piece of furniture in the small living room, was lined up with the planks, just the way he had placed it. From where he was sitting, Mauro could see that his bedroom and bathroom were in order.

The gravy started to simmer, and the apartment began to smell like home. He closed his eyes to pretend he was home. Where he had lived with his parents when Boston University still had football. Where he could use his real name and when he could play in front of a stadium filled with fans.

Mauro knew that home was far away, and it was never coming back.

CHAPTER ELEVEN

THE WEEK DRAGGED FOR KAABER. Every time his cell rang, part of him hoped that it would be Kelly Bailey checking in to say that he was all right. As irrational as it seemed, Kaaber felt a connection with the kid whose talent he admired. Knowing his depth as an artist made Kaaber want to know the person. Especially if he needed a big brother figure, which Kaaber thought he might.

When Tuesday rolled around again, Kaaber arrived at the tiny club in the Village and looked for a table so he wouldn't have to talk to the surly bartender, but the only open seats were barstools.

"Hey, Jeff. How ya doin'?" Kaaber greeted him with more enthusiasm than he felt.

"Suit and Tie! It must be Tuesday." The bartender nodded in Kaaber's direction. "Scotch rocks?"

"Yeah, thanks."

Less than a minute later, Jeff slid the rocks glass across the oak toward Kaaber's seat. Not a drop sloshed over the side when the drink came to a stop.

"Impressive," Kaaber observed. "If I had done that, half of it would be all over the bar right now."

"Bartender skills, Suit and Tie. Just like having a long memory for drinks and a short memory for asshole behavior." Jeff winked.

"So, you've forgiven yourself for last week? Good for you, man." Kaaber raised his glass before he took a sip and Jeff laughed.

"Maybe we should start over. I'm Jeff Adams. I own the place."

"Sasha Kaaber. My friends call me Kaaber."

"I like Suit and Tie, but I can call you Kaaber." Jeff held out his hand. "Is Kelly a friend of yours, Kaaber?"

"Not really. I stumbled onto him here. I think he's a talented kid. If I was as good as he is, I'd be an arrogant asshat, so I think I kind of admire his disposition as well."

"He's a nice kid. Too bad about his mom, and I know that makes it hard for him, but I'm runnin' a business here. I can't have him showing up late throwing off the line-up, and I have a no-tip policy—can't make special rules for him. I pay everyone fifty bucks for a thirty-minute set. Some of these bands split that four ways, at least he gets to keep it all for himself. When I was fifteen, I made that much after cleaning my uncle's filthy bar seven nights a week."

"He told me his mom was sick. Is it serious?"

"If you call stage four lung cancer serious."

Kaaber shook his head. "Damn. I'm sorry to hear that."

"Yeah. She taught him to play. In fact, she used to play here when my uncle owned the bar. She brought Kelly in on open mic night when he was thirteen. He tore the place up, so I let him have a set. He has his mother's talent and then some. She's his biggest fan."

"That's rough. He's still a kid. Is the dad gonna get him through?"

"Never met him." Jeff raised his chin in the direction of the door. "Speak of the barely-on-time devil."

Kelly didn't bother to look toward the bar as he made his way to the stage. Anyone could tell by the look on his face that his mind was three steps ahead of his body. He picked up the main speaker cords and popped them into the back of his P.A. head, ran his mic cord, adjusted his stand, strapped the guitar on, and plugged in while he greeted the packed house.

"Hello. I'm Kelly Bailey. Not from the circus Baileys. I have some new songs this week. Some are sad, some are angry … which are you in the mood for?"

"It's New York, kid. We're all sad and angry!"

Kaaber unconsciously rolled his eyes at the guy who had appointed himself the "witty" spokesperson for the room.

"I bet I got 'ya beat on that, Sir, but some of the greatest music comes out of the most difficult times, so ..." Kelly started an aggressive, fast song with a surprisingly sweet melody line. The hook was *I'll never let you go*. Kaaber felt closer to the material now that he knew the backstory.

Kelly played eight songs before he ended his set. Kaaber looked at his watch—it had been exactly thirty minutes.

Kaaber cashed out with Jeff and left him a generous tip.

"See you next week, Suit and Tie."

Kaaber nodded and went to the stage where Kelly was packing up.

"Great set, as usual."

"Hey, thanks. Not my typical stuff. Glad you liked it."

Kaaber grabbed the P.A. head that he had carried the week before and headed toward the door.

"Is your dad coming for you tonight?"

"No, man, he's staying with Mom. One of us has to be with her at all times now. That's this week's new thing."

"I'm really sorry, Kelly."

"Yeah, well sorrys in a sack and all that bullshit. I better get goin'. I guess I'll see you next week?"

"Are you in a hurry? I mean, you wanna get something to eat? It's only nine-thirty."

Kelly shrugged his shoulders.

"I spent the whole week beating myself up for letting you take the train home last week. I pictured you getting robbed by drug-addicted musicians who roughed you up for your gear."

Kelly laughed. "Hardly likely."

"I'll save you the train ride. Have a slice with me and I'll get you a taxi."

"So, this is kind of your way of tipping me?"

"Exactly."

"All right, then. There's a really good pizza place on Bleeker."

"John's?" Kaaber asked.

"Is there any place else?" Kelly laughed.

"My favorite too! Let's go ruin some pizza."

"So, you said you're a real estate agent?" Kelly asked as they walked down the sidewalk.

"I'm a broker, yeah."

"I hear the market's coming back—that true?"

"Showing strong signs of recovery."

"So, you make pretty good money?"

"Yeah, I do okay."

"So, where's your supermodel? Doesn't every rich guy in this city get a supermodel? Unless you're … oh, …"

Kelly stopped walking and looked at Kaaber.

"No!" Kaaber shook his head and laughed. "No." He took out his cell phone and hit the on button, showing Charlie on his lock screen.

"She's freakin' beautiful, man! Is that your wife? Sorry about …"

"It's fine. You never know—not that there's anything wrong with that."

"No, there isn't anything wrong with that, I'm just not … anyway, is that your wife?"

"My fiancé as of a few days ago. We've been together three years now. She's the kind that you never want to let go."

"Congrats, man." Kelly smiled as Kaaber held the door open to John's pizza. Oven smoke filled the small dining room, but the smell of scientifically perfected pizza overruled the unpleasant by-product.

The man behind the counter shouted at them, "What can I get ya?"

Kaaber held up two fingers to Kelly, who countered with three. "Three cheese slices."

"It'll be a minute. Sit down."

Kelly stacked his gear on a chair by the wall and sat down at a small table with Kaaber.

"Where do you go to school?"

"I'm taking a semester off. I want to be with mom every second, and dad has to work, so it makes sense for right now."

"Do you do any other gigs?"

"No, right now I'm only at Jeff's."

"I'm sure you won't have a problem booking yourself every night of the week when you're ready."

"I don't know if I want to be a full-time working musician. My mom did that her whole life. Probably why she has lung cancer now—being in all those smoky nightclubs night after night. Did you know back in the day, they could smoke in public places?"

Kaaber laughed. "So I've heard."

"Anyway, it was a hard life for her. She never had a W-2 job. Nothing withheld, no benefits, no paid vacations, no raises … forget about medical insurance. You don't know what you're going to make from one week to the next, one month to the next. It's a hard way to live."

"You could say the same about real-estate to some extent. You have to be hustling all the time, but the good part of that is you have your destiny in your own hands."

"I guess."

The man behind the counter yelled at them, "You want drinks?"

"Two Cokes," Kaaber answered with one eye on Kelly who nodded his approval.

"Twenty-five bucks. Come and get it."

Kaaber went to the counter, paid the man, and carried a tray back to the table.

"Eat up!" Kaaber surprised himself by saying what his mother used to say when she set dinner on the table.

"So, is college in your future? Lots of music scholarships available. I bet you'd be a shoo-in for one."

"I don't think so. I think it's gonna take Dad and I both working full-time to pay the outstanding medical bills. I don't want my dad to kill himself pulling three shifts to pay it back. We're already in collections all over the place, but we're paying what we can slowly but surely."

"You know, I might be able to help. We could organize a benefit—you could play."

Kelly laughed. "My old man would never hear of it. He's not going to take anyone's charity. Warren Buffet could hand him enough cash to get us even and he would give it right back. He has a hard time accepting the casseroles that my mom's friends bring over. He's a proud man and he doesn't want to be in anyone's debt."

Kaaber nodded. "How much are we talkin'—if I'm not prying."

"Deep six figures and climbing," Kelly took another bite of pizza.

"What if an anonymous benefactor paid the debt for you? Then your dad wouldn't know where the money came from and he couldn't pay it back. If the debt was paid directly, the hospital or the doctors or whatever would just send a notice that the balance was paid off."

Kelly smiled. "You gonna pay my mom's medical bills, Suit and Tie?"

Kaaber shrugged.

"As easy at that would be, I have too much of my dad in me to allow it. You bought me the most overpriced pizza and Coke in the Village, so I'm already in your debt."

"Don't forget about the cab."

"And the cab! You *are* a good Samaritan!" Kelly laughed.

"What if you got a record deal? That pop star I told you about—the one I just sold an apartment to—I could call him and get him to come see you and he could tell his people about you."

"My mom went through all of that. She wasted tons of money recording demos and trying to get signed to a label. Industry people made promises that they never intended to keep. It's just a big racket. Every decade or so they give someone a genuine break, but the ones who get the big deals with advances and loads of money powering the machine come from the inside. Somebody's brother-in-law's nephew." Kelly took a swig of Coke. "Thanks for putting yourself out there though. Funny thing is, you're the second person this week to approach me about helping to pay off the debt." Kelly wiped his mouth with his napkin. "Last Tuesday, this guy in a stretch Bentley pulled up alongside me as I was walking to the train after the gig. He rolled the window down and called me by name, so I stopped to see if it was anyone I knew."

Kaaber went cold inside. "Wesley Davis?"

"Yeah! You know the guy? He said he'd been to see me at the club."

"I met him a few weeks back. Seems like a total douche. Anyway, what happened?"

"He offered me a ride home. I know better than to get into a stranger's car, but how many billionaires are out kidnapping teenagers in the Village, right? And when am I gonna get the chance to ride in a car like that again?"

Kaaber nodded. He had the exact same thought when he was asked to go for a drive in that car.

"So, his driver put my gear in the truck, which made me a little nervous because that made me feel trapped. I couldn't just jump out without my gear if it went south, but everything seemed okay at first. I got in and told the driver where we're going. The guy started asking me about my life and what I plan to do with my music … the usual stuff. But then he asked about my parent's financial situation—in a way that made me feel like he knew the answer. Asked what I would give to make my mom well, stuff like that. Stupid questions. He told me that there's a doctor in Sweden that cures stage-four lung cancer like doctors here clear up an ear infection. Gave me a web address for the study and everything. He said that one unselfish act on my part could save my mom and he could pay me enough to cure her and pay off all the debt."

"That's crazy."

"That's kind of why I came with you tonight. I was wondering if he would be waiting for me in his fancy car again. Of course, for all I know you could be partners and you could be working me into your scheme together."

"That's the second time you misjudged me tonight," Kaaber assured him.

"Good."

"So, did he ever say how he was going to get you this money? What is the unselfish act you have to do? Does he want you to sleep with his haggard old wife, or what?"

"He never said directly. He implied that I had something in my possession that people would pay a lot of money for, but I can tell you right now, that's not true." Kelly took a swig of Coke. "Dad and I sold everything before we slipped into debt. My grandmother's china, our TVs, Mom's wedding ring … anything we could pawn. Mom wouldn't let me sell my gear and it wouldn't have gotten much anyway. It's her old stuff—not worth much. But I can tell you, Suit and Tie, I don't have anything that anyone is going to pay me hundreds of thousands of dollars for."

Kaaber tried to take a deep breath, but as he inhaled, he felt like all the air was being expelled from his lungs. A chill settled over him again as he recalled Wesley Davis's words. "Natural ability is like a shirt. Kelly has it on right now. But you could wear it tomorrow."

CHAPTER TWELVE

MATTHEW WATCHED THE MAN GET in his check-out lane behind a young woman with two kids and an overflowing grocery cart of food. He wore the same flashy suit he wore the morning he confronted Matthew's mother in the driveway. The man held a coconut water and an energy bar. If his presence at Matthew's workplace had been a coincidence, he would have checked out in the "10 items or less" line—it was empty. Matthew consciously went about his business, acting like he didn't recognized the man.

"Can I have one of those?" The little boy was focused on the ice cream sandwiches that Matthew was putting into a plastic bag. He looked at the woman who shook her head sternly.

"Sorry, little man. Frozen stuff has to go in the chill bag so that it won't melt before you get home."

"Awwwwwww! How about the cookies? Can I have a cookie?"

Matthew's hands worked at bagging the groceries, but his mind was occupied with how to handle the stalker in his check-out line. He stacked two hundred dollars' worth of groceries back into the shopping cart, waited for the transaction to be completed, and started rolling the cart. "Which way to your car?"

"This way, thanks." The stressed woman wrangled kids and explained that they were about to go out into the parking lot where cars would be moving back and forth.

Matthew got the SUV loaded up while the woman got her kids buckled into car seats. He discreetly looked over his shoulder to see where the guy in the suit had gone as he placed the shopping bags. Matthew rolled the cart back into the store without catching sight of him.

There were forty-five minutes left on his shift and his stomach grew queasier as each one passed. Matthew had the feeling suit guy wanted to be seen and wanted to unsettle him, which had worked.

He usually enjoyed his short walk home, but as the sun set, and darkness overtook daylight, Matthew felt like an anxious child. His backpack bounced as he started to jog. He was two blocks from home when the car pulled up behind him. The interior light was on, and he saw that the driver of the BMW was making his third appearance of the day.

Matthew considered taking a short cut through the neighbor's yards, but then he remembered his grandfather's letter. He picked up his pace and ran directly at the car. The driver slammed the brakes, and the car stopped inches before connecting with Matthew's knees.

"What the fuck do you want, man?" Matthew yelled. He pulled his cell phone out of his pocket and started taking video of the driver. "What do you want? Why are you following me? Why did you trespass at my house this morning, and why did you come to my work today? I have evidence that you're harassing me and my family now, you prick!" Matthew started laughing.

The driver of the BMW scowled and put the car in reverse, going from 0-60 in a period of time that would have satisfied Bavarian engineers. Matthew ran with it, trying to hold the camera still. The car was registered in Florida, so it didn't have a front license plate—only one in the back. Matthew tried to capture the image of the plate when it spun around and took off at a speed that was very dangerous for a residential neighborhood. He couldn't get close enough and there wasn't enough light to read the plate. All Matthew could see was that it was, indeed, one of the six thousand or so license plate styles designed for the state of Florida.

"Don't come back ass-clown!" Matthew shouted after the car.

"You okay, son?" A man around the same age as Matthew's dad was standing on his front lanai.

"Yes, sir. Someone was following me, but he took off."

"You were screaming like a maniac, and I have young kids, so I actually came out to kick your ass, but then I saw that you might be in trouble." The man laughed. "You sure you're okay? Wanna come inside? Maybe you could call someone for a ride."

"I'm just two streets behind you, actually. I might cut through your yard if that's okay."

"Have at it." The man turned around and went back inside.

Matthew walked across two xeriscaped yards, crossed a street, and cut through one lawn before he reached his property line. As a little kid, he didn't mind jumping through the hedge boarder, but it had been a lot shorter then. He turned his back to the bushes and pushed his way between two, entering the perfectly manicured maze that his father crafted after over many years. The well-tended greenery added an English garden flavor to the Spanish-style house, and connected the main house to the guest house. Matthew navigated the towers of bush, popping out where the interior lights of his home were casting a glow into the back yard. The sight of home calmed him, but he hesitated to go inside. He had never been one to keep secrets … before his grandfather died anyway. Now he was holding a few. He decided that he wouldn't tell his parents what just happened to him. Not until he could answer the questions they were bound to ask. He took a deep breath and shook off the unsettling experience. He started up the pavered walkway and opened the back door—it was unlocked, as usual. For the second time that day, Matthew locked the door behind him.

CHAPTER THIRTEEN

M AURO CLICKED THE STORY FROM the Huffington Post's entertainment page. The headline intrigued him, "*Miles Joosten Retires: Cancels Remainder of North American Tour.*"

One of the most prolific songwriters and performers of our time has decided that enough is enough. After five decades of creating trends, Miles Joosten is ready to leave the stage and join the audience.

Joosten released the following statement. "I realized that this tour was a very ambitious commitment for a man in his early seventies. I regret that I was only able to make it halfway through and I am truly sorry to disappoint ticket holders."

Those disappointed ticket holders will receive refunds but missing the opportunity to see the music legend perform one more time would have been priceless.

"I was surprised when he released a new album and announced tour dates. I was online the second tickets went on sale and bought a block for my friends and family. I was really looking forward to seeing him live one more time," Sam Walker said. "I'm sorry he won't be finishing the tour."

Industry insiders expressed surprise at the news of Joosten's retirement. Brad Taylor, a former band member, told USA Today that he spoke to Joosten last week and retirement never came up. "He said that he was enjoying playing the new material and that the audience was responding more enthusiastically than ever. He said he felt great physically and was happy to be on the tour bus again."

Joosten spent most of the last decade as tabloid fodder as his fifty-million-dollar divorce played out in headlines. The music icon also lost a high-profile lawsuit against his former record label where he claimed that he was due several million dollars in unpaid royalties. Joosten filed bankruptcy eighteen months ago, and owed several million in back taxes.

"If anything, this tour was a Godsend for Miles. He needed the income, and the tour introduced his music to a new generation of listeners. His third album, from 1970, was number eight last month. The world was his oyster, it doesn't seem right that he would hang it up now," Taylor said just before ending our phone interview.

Mauro had read enough. He picked up his cell and dialed Wagner.

"Hey Goombah." Caller ID hadn't told Wagner who was on the other end—it was either a random solicitor or the only person on earth who had his number.

"I think I'm right. You see the news about Miles Joosten?"

"Yeah. I think they're getting sloppy again."

"Greed and arrogance," Mauro said. "You get away with something for so long, you get a false sense of security. We've talked about this before, but do you honestly think we are the only ones who ever got away from Davis?"

"I don't know. While I was brokering for him, no one left the company on their own terms. A few had sudden heart attacks, there was one fiery car crash ... you know."

"I've had this on my conscious for too many years, Wagner. Knowing is a burden. Doing nothing makes me feel like a coward. And even though I still have what he wanted from me; he stole my life anyway. I think this might be the time we've been waitin' for. There's a chink in the armor."

"We're two people. Two people against an organization with more resources than the US Government. We're not Batman and Robin."

Mauro sighed. "What if we went to the media?"

"Who in their right mind would believe us?"

"I don't know. That guy from the Ancient Aliens show. He believes a lot of weird shit."

"Aliens would be easier to prove than this."

"What if we go right to the source?"

"With what?"

"I can call Davis and tell him that I want to sell. I regret the past and I want to sell now. Then I can meet with him and wear a wire."

"Davis would find a way to kill you through the phone. Maybe not literally, but it's suicide. How would that change anything?"

"This has to stop and who's gonna stop it if we don't?"

"We were lucky to walk away once. Maybe you don't remember it the way I do. I was supposed to acquire football skills from a poor Italian kid who was supposed to jump at the money. That kid felt taking one snap in the NFL was worth more than the millions on the table and tried to walk away. At the point the deal was going sour, despite me telling you that you weren't going to be allowed to walk away knowing what you knew, you refused the offer. I had compassion for you because I knew I was a piece of shit to be brokering God's gifts. When the clean-up crew arrived, we killed five men in cold blood. Not only are we twenty-five years older now, we're twenty-five years wiser. We beat the house once. We beat every odd to do that once; it ain't gonna happen twice."

"What they're doin' is unthinkable and inhumane. It's gonna keep going on for as long as good people stand by and do nothing. It's safe to keep our noses down and stay off the grid, but I don't know how much longer I can rationalize doin' that."

"We made the right decision. We did the right thing back then and we're free of it now."

"Are we? How's your wife doin'? Your family? Oh, that's right, you don't have any relationships in your life because you can't risk it. The consequence of what we did isolated us from the rest of the world for every miserable minute of the rest of our miserable lives."

"Listen, I gotta go, I got stuff to do. Talk later." Wagner hung up and resisted the urge to throw his cell in the river.

CHAPTER FOURTEEN

ASSANDRA APPROACHED THE DOOR TO the gatehouse, and it opened before she could knock. She pulled her hand back and a surprised sound escaped her lips.

"I'm sorry to startle you, Miss Marcot. I saw you coming. We monitor the property around the clock."

Cassandra laughed. "Right, of course. I should have … anyway, I came to ask a favor. Would it be possible to borrow your car?"

"I would be happy to drive you anywhere you'd like to go. The estate car is far more comfortable than mine."

"I don't want to impose on you or take you away from what you're doing, I just wanted to go to Whole Foods to grab some things for a guest who's coming to stay with us."

"Have you discussed this with your grandmother or Mrs. Wade?" Kane put his hands behind his back and took a more relaxed stance. The six-foot tall, salt and pepper-haired man wore his business suit like a military uniform and looked "at ease."

"Well, no. Why do you ask?"

Kane's eyebrows raised. "Mrs. Marcot prides herself on being an exceptional hostess and Mrs. Wade has her own fiefdom inside that kitchen. I'm afraid that your attempt to be low maintenance could be mistaken as a hostile coup, or taken as an insult at the very least."

"Seriously?"

"I know you're independent, Miss Marcot, but that isn't the way it works around here. Those of us who perform duties on the Marcot

Estate take great pride in our contributions." Kane's expression was friendly, but serious.

"I understand and I wouldn't want to overstep. Thanks for the advice, Mr. Kane."

"Of course. Put a list together and take it to Mrs. Wade. She will make sure that Mr. Weston has everything he needs to make him feel welcome. I'm sure she would be happy to have your input."

Cassandra smiled. "So, you know that my boyfriend is coming to stay with us."

"Who do you think is picking him up at LAX this evening?"

"I thought I would?" Cassandra's pitch went up at the end of her statement, transforming it to a question.

"No need to bother yourself with airport traffic, Miss Marcot. I will have Mr. Weston at the estate in time for dinner. If you want the menu to reflect Mr. Weston's taste, you had better get to Mrs. Wade as soon as possible." Kane's eyes scanned the property behind Cassandra.

Cassandra smiled at Kane. "Thank for you for guiding me away from the mine field."

"As Head of Security, it's my job to keep you safe and interfering with Mrs. Wade's kitchen might be dangerous." Kane came close to smiling. "And you are welcome to my Tahoe at any time in the future, Miss Marcot."

"Thanks."

Cassandra turned away from the gatehouse and walked toward the stately main residence, passing the guesthouse on her way. She looked longingly at the perfect little cottage and sighed, thinking of the privacy that she and Chris would have if they were staying there. Cassandra hadn't told him that they were expected to remain in separate bedrooms for the first few nights. She didn't think he would have agreed to come if he'd known that in advance.

Cassandra left a grocery list with an uncomfortably eager Mrs. Wade, spent the afternoon at the pool, and took her time getting ready for Chris's arrival. He hadn't seen her wearing trendy clothes or make-up for a while, and she wanted to take his breath away.

Once her violet bob was styled and her tanned face was highlighted to glow in all the right places, she paced the floor in the foyer waiting for the Rolls.

"You're going to wear a path in the marble, dear," Mrs. Marcot teased as she came down the staircase.

"I don't know why I'm so nervous. I felt great in this outfit, but then I wondered if he would show up dressed in repurposed clothing. I think maybe I should change, but I don't know if I have time. I could call and see where they are, but Chris doesn't have a cell phone anymore."

Mrs. Marcot considered the white, strapless Michael Kors jump-suit and the platform wedges that had been among the items delivered by her Personal Shopper at Neimann Marcus. "I could call Kane to satisfy your curiosity, but I wouldn't let you change. You look beauti-ful. You're so angelic that I'm tempted to color my hair purple."

Cassandra laughed. "If anyone in your generation could pull it off, it would be you, Gram."

Mrs. Marcot nodded toward the portico. "They're here."

The white Rolls eased to a stop in front of the main staircase. Chris sprung from the back door as if he were making a jailbreak. He waited at the rear of the car for Kane to retrieve his luggage from the trunk.

"I will make sure that your bag is taken to your room, Mr. Weston, if you'd like to proceed inside."

"I'll carry my own bag, Jeeves," Chris joked. "I wouldn't want to get used to being spoiled."

"You seem a good fit for Miss Marcot, Sir," Kane said amicably, handing the single piece of luggage to Chris.

Chris looked toward the front doors of the grand home for the first time and saw Cassandra standing on the landing waiting for him. His smile started out wide and then grew larger. "Cassie!" He took the steps two at a time, set his bag on the landing, and wrapped her up in his hug.

After a long kiss, he whispered into her hair and Cassandra self-consciously looked around for her grandmother. "Gram was here just a second ago, I guess she thought we needed some privacy."

"You look ..." Chris made the sound that a hungry man makes at a buffet.

"And you look very handsome in your 'back-east' clothes. I didn't know if you'd think I had sold out dressing like a consumer." Cassandra laughed.

"I had to show up here looking like a Harvard man. How'd I do?" Chris did a lopsided pirouette to show off his dove grey suit and crisp white dress shirt. Cassandra noted the Cole Hahn loafers and his freshly cut hair.

"You went to Cristophe's and got that pomade that you like," Cassie observed.

"My family is worried enough about me taking a hiatus from a job I haven't started yet. I couldn't let them see me in my Captain Freegan attire. Would have killed them."

"Is your grandmother still doing well?"

"She's back in action."

"Did you tell your family that I wanted to come?"

"They know me. This could have been an emotional trip and I handle that stuff better alone. I'm just glad you know me as well as they do."

Cassandra stole one more kiss. "Are you ready for this?"

"You always say that she's your favorite person in the world— 'other than you, Chris' is what I'm sure you mean to say. It's about time I meet her."

"Here we go." Cassandra opened the tall glass door.

"What, no butler?" Chris teased. "Pretty ghetto, don't you think?"

Cassandra laughed and the sound echoed through the foyer.

"In here, dear," Mrs. Marcot called from the library.

Cassandra watched for Chris's reaction to the house, but he seemed unphased by the ostentatious display of wealth. That was a good sign. Cassandra thought back to middle school when many of her friendships changed after her twelfth birthday party at the Marcot estate.

"Gram, this is Chris."

Mrs. Marcot was sitting on a couch reading her iPad. She quickly set the device down and crossed the room with her hand outstretched. Chris took it gently and planted a kiss on her cheek.

"Thank you for inviting me, Mrs. Marcot. I'm very pleased to finally meet you."

"I'm sure the pleasure is mine, Mr. Weston. How was your flight?"

"Long and unpleasant," Chris said smiling.

"Commercial air travel is a half-step above the buses you two have been riding lately."

"I couldn't agree more," Chris nodded.

"Dinner will be ready in a half hour. Can I get you something in the meantime?" Mrs. Marcot asked.

"How about a glass of Pom juice and some salted cashews?" Cassie offered.

"That's an insult to the room. That would be like ordering a cheeseburger and fries at La Coupole in Paris," Chris countered.

"But it's your favorite snack," Cassie said.

"I'm fine, Cass. Unless you ladies want something, I can wait until dinner."

Cassie shrugged and smiled sweetly. "I'm fine."

"Please have a seat, Mr. Weston, and tell me about yourself." Mrs. Marcot gestured toward a grouped seating arrangement of comfortable, oversized chairs in front of a large plate glass window. The threesome sat down, and Chris took in the view of the perfectly landscaped and tended garden.

"This is a beautiful estate, Mrs. Marcot."

"Thank you. My father built this house during the Great Depression. The deed restriction for East Bel-Air at that time required that landowners spend at least twenty thousand on construction. He far exceeded the minimum, but not to be vulgar. He did it because so many people were out of work. Construction lasted several years and fed many families."

"That's very noble," Chris replied.

"Cassandra can give you a tour tomorrow, if you like."

Chris looked at Cassandra. "That would be great."

"I hope you will be comfortable here and use the time wisely." Mrs. Marcot said, maintaining eye contact with Chris.

Cassie leaned over and touched Chris's forearm. "What Gram means is she hopes we will indulge in some rejuvenation during our stay. I know it was stressful for you when your grandmother was sick and with the stuff going on at the house —"

"No, Cassandra, what I mean is that I hope you use this stay to regain your focus. You have had the time and luxury of making a statement. Perhaps you can reflect on what you've learned and decide how to use that experience to move forward."

Chris cleared his throat. "If you're suggesting that we start building our resumes, I'm all for it," he said.

Cassandra's chin dropped towards her chest, and she stared at Chris with an incredulous expression.

"Come on, Cassie, don't act surprised. The Freegan thing was your idea, not mine."

"You agreed with the philosophy, and I didn't coerce you."

Chris smiled. "That's true, that's true. When a man loves a woman, he'll eat out of a garbage can ... isn't that how the song goes?"

"Mr. Weston, I understand that you have a job waiting for you. Is it lucrative?"

Chris laughed so hard his shoulders shook. "Mrs. Marcot, if you are going to ask such personal questions, I insist that you call me Chris. And yes, I'll be making six solid figures to start, plus an annual bonus and salary increase. There is also potential for upward mobility within the company."

"Your parents must be proud."

"Worried is more like it. I had a full scholarship and I worked full-time while I was at school, but I racked up some debt too. They can't afford to get me in the black, so they would like to see me earning."

"We talked about this," Cassie said softly.

"Cassandra has a trust fund, as I'm sure you know. Her income doesn't concern me much, but she has rare gifts. She will have more opportunities than someone with the last name of *Jones*, but holes in your resume do concern people in high places. If you were serving in the Peace Corps, that would be easily explained. I'm not sure this lifestyle choice will be."

Cassandra folded her hands in her lap and inspected the fingernails she had carefully painted pink for the occasion. Her voice was barely audible, shaky, and capable of producing only one syllable, "Gram ..."

Mrs. Marcot rose from her chair and brushed the hair from Cassandra's eyes.

"Darling, I'm so sorry. I certainly didn't mean to hurt your feelings. I'm the queen of the back-handed compliment, I suppose. I was only trying to point out how gifted you are."

Cassandra forced a smile for her grandmother.

"When did I turn into the old lady incapable of censoring herself? You are the most special person in my world, and you've invited someone very special to you into our home. I don't know how the conversation went so askew. Please forgive me, Christopher." Mrs. Marcot bent down and kissed the top of Cassandra's head. "I think a change of scenery and a wonderful meal will do us some good. Let's go into the dining room."

Chris stood up and held his arm out for Mrs. Marcot.

"What a gentleman. I can certainly see why you fell for this one, Cassandra." Mrs. Marcot smiled sweetly at her granddaughter. "Right this way, young man." Chris took long strides to keep up, and Cassandra watched as the two people that she loved the most walked far ahead of her.

CHAPTER FIFTEEN

WHEN YOU'RE LOOKING OVER YOUR shoulder, other people who live the same way walk inside of a spotlight. Mauro always thought his situation must be similar to what American travelers experience abroad—they can pick each other out. Without hearing an accent, or having any direct contact, they're aware of their own.

Mauro became bar buddies with Will, but he had no real friends. Every now and then, he would encounter someone whose mannerisms he could identify with and, from a distance and just for a moment, he felt connected. One such person changed her hair color often, sometimes dressed in preppy clothes, and sometimes dressed like a street rat. In the early spring through late fall, she would show up, alone, in the park across from Mauro's apartment. On Saturdays and Sundays, she would sit on a blanket or on a bench in the early morning, late in the afternoon, or around sunset. Mauro imagined that she was soaking up as much fair weather as she could before the brutal Northeastern winter descended on the city. The only constant thing about her was the MacBook that she held onto like a loved one. He wasn't sure that this girl was a gateway for him, but he had a strong hunch.

Mauro had almost given up looking out his window for her when he zeroed in on a platinum blonde girl with an unmistakably short stride. Years ago, Mauro noticed that she took twice as many steps as most people. Her posture was perfect, her gaze never deviated from the space six inches in front her, and her fast-moving feet gave her a cartoonish quality. Mauro watched her spread out a small blanket and sit down underneath a giant oak tree. He grabbed his laptop, tapped his pocket, locked all four deadbolts behind him, and walked to the park.

As he approached the girl, his heart began to race. He rehearsed what he was going to say and practiced smiling. A passing woman returned the friendly gesture, which gave Mauro confidence. He approached the girl from behind, sneaking a peek at the laptop screen she crouched over. The text displayed was encrypted. Bingo.

Before he could say anything, she sensed his presence and looked over her shoulder.

"Hi. Good evening. I hope I didn't startle you. I, uh, see that you're working on your computer there and I have the same one." Mauro held up his laptop. "I wonder if you could help me—I would be happy to pay you for your time." Mauro thought he sounded like a sixth-grade boy asking a girl to dance.

The girl refocused on her screen. "I'm not, like, an expert or anything." She started typing again.

Mauro was taken back by the sight of her face. She was pretty from a distance, but she was flawlessly beautiful up close. Long, dark eyelashes framed her vibrant blue eyes. Her skin was translucent, and her full lips were painted a frosty pink color that Mauro preferred to see on girls when he was in college.

"It seems to me that your age group is generally better with technology. I'm right on the cusp. I had a bag phone when bag phones were cool, you know what I mean? They say this stuff is intuitive, but I think it only comes naturally for people under 35."

Her eyes lifted from the screen, but the rest of her face remained unconvinced. "What kind of problem are you having?"

"I don't know if it's really a problem as much as not knowing where to look for something." Mauro crouched down so that he didn't have to speak loudly. "I'm looking for the type of eBay that a guy would go to if he wanted buy something that eBay isn't allowed to sell."

"Why do you think I would know anything about that?" The girl snapped.

"There's a Wi-Fi connection at O'Connell's pub over there. It reaches into the southernmost quarter of the park. Where you always sit. Whatever you do for a living, you can't be away from that computer for the forty-five minutes that you spend here, and you keep some pretty weird office hours."

"Who are you? You a cop?" The blonde pursed her lips together hard.

"Nope. Just a guy who wants the kind of information that I can't get from a tattooed twenty-year-old at the Apple Store." Mauro took out a roll of bills from his pocket. "And I'm happy to pay for it."

"Fuck off." The girl went back to typing. "Go away."

"All I'm asking for is information. If you don't know, I'll give you a hundred bucks anyway."

"Listen, there's plenty of porn on the Internet and if you want something more up close and personal, action isn't hard to find."

"No, no, no, nothing like that. It's more a general market that I'm looking to tap into."

"Dude, I don't know what you're into, or what you think I'm into, but whoever told you I could help you is mistaken."

"Really, I'm just looking for someone to answer some questions about how to access certain things online."

"Sorry."

Mauro's huge hand swiped the laptop in one quick motion. The page on the screen looked like an account statement, but the currency wasn't familiar.

The girl growled through bared teeth, "Give that back to me now, or I'm screaming rape."

"What is this? What is XBT?"

"Fuck you. Give me my laptop."

Mauro held the laptop in one hand and peeled off a hundred-dollar bill with the other. He let it fall on the blanket beside the girl. "What is XBT?"

The young woman considered the Benjamin, and Mauro saw the moment she decided to take it. She grabbed it and shoved it into her pocket. "It's an abbreviation for bitcoin. It's an Internet currency."

"So, if you were doing some form of Internet business, why would you use this currency?"

"Because it isn't easy to trace."

"Explain."

The young woman held out her hand and Mauro peeled off another hundred. She waited for him to deposit another hundred into her palm before she spoke again. "When you are conducting confidential business online, you need to be in a location that is untraceable, and you want a means of collecting payment that is unregulated. For example, if you were selling a reserved commodity, you could acquire payment through Bitcoin, but they are operated by PayPal and Western Union types, so they follow government regulations to prevent fraud and money laundering. In order to get to the Bitcoin, you would need to open a Dwolla account. From a Dwolla account you could deal with a Bitcoin exchanger like Coinbase, Binance, Kraken—there are a plenty to choose from. Then you can transfer the money in whatever currency you prefer to a global bank with less restrictions than US banks."

Mauro looked at the computer screen. "It says here your balance is 1XBT. Why do you need to launder that? The amount isn't going to red flag the IRS."

"That's ninety-eight thousand dollars as of five minutes ago. But it's not like I can go to an ATM and make a withdrawal."

"See, you sold yourself short, you sound like an expert ..." Mauro laughed.

"Give me my laptop and leave me alone."

"In a second. So, you're getting paid for goods or services, I don't care which, through a web site? How is that untraceable? Even if the transfer of funds is underground, the web site must be a risk to operate. Do you change domains every week or what?"

"The web site is underground, grandpa. It's the Amazon.com of the black market. There's a whole under-line economy going on and the feds can't keep up with it, even though the US Navy developed it for secret communications. Isn't that ironic?" The young woman laughed. Mauro thought she was even more beautiful when she was laughing.

He peeled off five more hundred-dollar bills. "I need to know everything."

"You gotta install a Tor Bundle Pack. It'll cost you, but you don't seem to mind throwing money away. I know a guy who can help you. I'll arrange an introduction."

"Do it now," Mauro put the laptop on the blanket next to her.

"Right now?"

"Now."

She rolled her eyes and inhaled deeply as she lifted the machine to her lap. A few keystrokes later she stopped typing and nervously tapped her forefinger and pinky finger against the section of the laptop next to the mouse pad.

"Well?"

"I'm waiting. Be patient."

Mauro heard the chime of a tiny bell.

"He says we can come now. I'll be happy to take you there for another hundred bucks."

"I've given you eight hundred already," Mauro said.

"I've made more than that just sitting here, but I can't take Bitcoin to the club tonight."

"This guy can get me on the black-market Internet?"

"Guaranteed."

Mauro reached in his pocket and peeled off another hundred.

"Never show your hand, Grandpa. If the type of people you're about to mingle with see a wad of cash, they're going to know you're good for triple that. They'll take you and your grandchildren for every penny. This is the Wild West. You gotta pay to play and they don't play nice."

"I can handle myself, just lead the way."

"Dead man walking," she said under her breath as she shoved the blanket and her laptop into

her duffel bag. "Follow me."

CHAPTER SIXTEEN

IT WAS SEVEN-THIRTY ON A Friday morning. Cars inched down the streets in the Grove while Matthew made better time enjoying the sun on the sidewalk. He walked to school using the same route every morning, but when he saw the black BMW, he regretted not changing his routine. He knew that it would be easier for him to change direction on foot than it would be for the car to make a U-Turn on the traffic-filled residential street, so he simply turned and walked the other way. He would be late for school now, but he took pleasure in toying with Mr. Bimmer.

Matthew looked over his shoulder. The car was using a driveway to turn around. When the BMW finally pulled up alongside him, Matthew darted between two houses. Safely on the next block, he started walking in the opposite direction.

There were very few cars on the side street and Matthew suddenly felt very much alone. His heart was starting to pound and his mind raced. Matthew considered walking up to the front door of one the residences to ask for help—something his mother taught him when he was six. She told him to look for a house or business with the poster of the hugging arms in the window.

"No. Fuck this." Matthew suppressed his fear and let anger take over. Why was he running from this guy? Any time he had challenged Bimmer Boy before, he had backed down. Matthew stopped walking and stood still on the sidewalk, checking the street to the right, then to the left. He heard the tires squeal around the corner and saw the

BMW race toward him. Matthew walked out into the street and faced the oncoming car. The 7 series threw on the brakes and stopped in the distance that the commercials said it could.

The driver slammed the transmission into park and threw the door open. As he rushed to Matthew, rage burst from his reddened face and Matthew realized that the occupant wasn't the same guy he encountered previously. "Are you trying to get yourself killed? What kind of stupid game are you running here?"

"Why are you following me?" Matthew shouted back.

"If someone hasn't called the police yet, they will soon. Get in the car and I'll explain everything."

Matthew laughed. "I'm not going anywhere with you, but you're right about the cops. I called them myself while I was waiting for you."

The man studied Matthew's face for signs of a lie. When he spoke, his voice was even and confident. "My company had business with your grandfather. The transaction hadn't been completed at the time of his death. He had something very valuable in his possession when he died, something that now belongs to me. And I have an awful lot of money to give you in return. It's what your grandfather wanted."

Matthew didn't say anything.

"You are entitled to an obscene amount of money … once I get what's mine. This doesn't have to be difficult."

"I can't imagine what you're talking about." Matthew started walking toward the man who stood his ground. "If you have business with Gramp's foundation or his trust, my dad's law firm is handling all of that. I'm sixteen. I'm not a lawyer. I'm not the person you need to talk to."

"I think you are exactly the person that I need to talk to you. As Mr. Newcombe's favorite student and his grandson, I think you are the person he would trust with his most prized possession."

Matthew stopped his advance. He looked down his nose at the slick-looking businessman. "You'll be as surprised as I was to know that my grandfather left me nothing in his will. Nothing at all, let alone some valuable asset that he treasured. Fucking. Nothing. Got it?"

"Where would he hide it, then?"

"I'm so sick of your cloak and dagger bullshit! You have a fucking question, ask me, man. Let's get this over with—tell me exactly what you're looking for and I'll tell you if I've ever seen it."

"How's your painting lately?"

"What?"

"Your study—how is it going? Has your grandfather's death inspired you to stretch your gift in ways you never thought possible?"

"I'm doing okay."

"Do you notice any sort of sudden … improvement in your ability or technique?"

Matthew's face scrunched up. "It's a process, Cuh. Nothing happens suddenly."

"I'd love to see some of your work."

Matthew shook his head. "Are you an art dealer? Did you commission something from my grandfather?"

"No, it isn't the art that I deal."

"Okay, more cloak and dagger shit. I'm trying to talk to you straight, but you wanna act out some film noir, so I'm going to school." Matthew walked past the man.

"Can you paint like your grandfather?" Bimmer boy called to Matthew's back. "Since he died, can you paint like him?"

"You're crazy, man. It's not like he could will me his talent." Matthew yelled back, still walking away.

"He did though. He left it behind—sold it for millions. Some very dangerous people think you have it."

Matthew shook his head and kept walking, one hand on his cell. He was starting to think that he should have called the police when he had the chance. He grew up thinking he should be afraid of people with nothing to lose, but he had a crazy, well-dressed, Bimmer driving, rich guy at his back who was terrifying him.

"I can help you prove that you don't have it. Once you do that, your life won't be in danger anymore."

Matthew stopped walking. His scalp tingled and a chill snaked through his body despite the South Florida heat.

"If what you're saying is true—that you your grandfather didn't leave anything to you, no one from my company will ever bother you again. I promise. Come with me, cooperate, and all this could be over in an hour."

Matthew turned around and looked into the man's eyes. "You want me to trust you? I'm supposed to believe all this bullshit and get in a car with you? I don't even know your name."

"Davis. William Davis. One of my men contacted you previously, but his approach was embarrassingly remedial, and I apologize for that. That's why I came myself. Out of respect for your grandfather, and to make sure that this was handled properly."

Matthew looked up and down the street again—there were no open arms offering refuge and no neighbors in sight.

"Fuck you, man." Matthew started running through another yard. He didn't look back, just kept going. He tried the door of a neighbor's pool cage, but found it locked. Matthew decided that he was safer on the street where he would be in plain view of morning commuters. He ran to the front yard and waved at a white cargo van that was slowly making its way through the narrow street. The minute Matthew made eye contact with the driver he knew he was in trouble.

The man behind the wheel and the passenger jumped out of the van. Matthew tried to outmaneuver them, but they were strong and quick. Matthew felt a sharp pain in his side; his mind reverted to his fear of inoculations at the pediatrician's office when he was a child. His body went limp before his mind went numb. Matthew's last conscious thought was of his mother.

CHAPTER SEVENTEEN

KAABER CALLED CHARLIE TO SEE how her Tuesday had gone. She was looking forward to her Soul Cycle class and her post-workout cocktail with the girls. Kaaber observed that the two events seemed to cancel each other out, but Charlie said he was overthinking.

Kaaber walked from Midtown to the club in the Village, enjoying the crispness in the fall air. Spring and fall in New York were the best times of the year—the balance was perfect and Kaaber reveled in it.

When he got to the club, his mood quickly changed. Three guys were on stage setting up a drum kit, bass rig, and a guitar amp. Kaaber checked his watch—he was right on time for Kelly's set. He walked up to the bar and waved at Jeff who was talking to two cute young girls. The bartender nodded and finished his conversation before greeting Kaaber.

"Hey there Suit and Tie—scotch rocks?"

"Ah—I don't know. Is Kelly playing tonight?"

"No, man. Kid left me in a bind. Called yesterday and said he couldn't play here anymore. Less than twenty-four hours' notice. I found these guys, but the fact that they were free at the last minute, and needed two hours to set up has me a little worried. I hope this isn't amateur hour."

"Did Kelly give you a reason? Is his mom worse or did she ..."

"He didn't give me shit. Didn't even call my cell, he left a message on the machine here when he knew we were closed. Just said he couldn't come anymore and that he was 'sorry'."

"I hope he's okay."

"One thing I've learned in this business is that musicians are irresponsible and fickle. He probably found a guy to pay him twenty bucks more for a Tuesday, so he took the gig. Or he thinks he found a room to play that will give him more exposure. I'm sure it's something like that—same old story. You need a scotch?"

"I don't think so. Do you have a number or an address for Kelly? I'd like to check on him. Make sure he's okay."

"I don't. His schedule never changed, so I never needed to call him. I paid him cash under the table, so I don't have a W-9 for him."

Kaaber thought for a second. "Okay. I'm going to leave my card with you if that's okay. If he shows up here, would you have him give me a call?"

Jeff raised his eyebrows and tilted his head to the side as if that was the most ridiculous thing he had ever heard. "I'll try to keep track of your card Suit and Tie, but I'm not a secretary."

Kaaber patted the bar a few times where he had placed the card—almost as if he was saying good-bye to the only connection he had to Kelly and walked out onto the street.

He found himself walking in the direction of the Subway, but then came to his senses. What was he planning to do—take the train to Chinatown and walk the streets looking for Kelly Bailey?

Kaaber sat down on a bench and took out his cell phone. He searched for "Kelly Bailey NYC." There were 112 hits on Spokeo. He clicked a few IG accounts and a Tik Tok account, but none were the Kelly Bailey he was looking for.

There was someone who knew exactly where Kelly Bailey lived—Wesley Davis had dropped him off at home. Kaaber took his wallet from his pocket and looked in the section where he kept miscellaneous receipts and business cards. It was there. He pulled the card out and dialed the number. It only rang once.

"Wesley Davis."

"Wesley, this is Sasha Kaaber we met a few weeks ago in the Village—"

"Kaaber! Nice to hear from you."

"Oh good, I'm glad you remember me."

"Of course I remember you; the guy who believes in luck and unicorns," Davis said pleasantly.

"Yeah, that's me. Listen, I'm looking for someone and I think you might be able to help me ... Kelly Bailey, the young musician who was playing at the club where we met."

"Sorry, Kaaber. I remember seeing him that night, of course, but I never saw him again. Never even knew his name."

"So, you didn't give him a ride home after the gig one night? Because he said—"

"You guys buddies now?"

"What?"

"You seem to know things about his life. If you're buddies, shouldn't you know how to connect with him?"

"Listen, I'm not trying to be confrontational. I'm worried about the kid. I know his mother is very sick and he didn't show up for work tonight ..."

"Oh, right. It's Tuesday. That's your night to lust over his talent in the Village."

Kaaber started walking uptown with a purposeful stride. "Kelly told me that you drove him home a few weeks ago. Can you please tell me where you dropped him off?"

"I don't feel comfortable giving out that information, but maybe I can get a message to him."

"Yeah, sure, that would be great. Could you have him call me?"

"What will I tell him this is in reference to?"

"I just want to make sure he's okay."

"I guess it isn't a breach of contract for me to tell you that he's just fine."

Kaaber took a deep breath to steady himself and slowed his pace. "What do you mean, a breach of contract?"

"I'm writing down this number and I promise to pass it along. If I happen to cross paths with Kelly again, I'll give it to him."

"I thought you said—"

The line went dead.

Kaaber pulled the phone from his ear and saw the phone screen had reverted to the Safari page he last used. "Fuck!' he growled, eliciting little to no reaction from his fellow pedestrian New Yorkers. He shoved the phone into his pocket and replayed the conversation with Davis in his mind. Kaaber had only been in the man's company for about thirty minutes, but that was enough time to hate him.

Feeling lost, Kaaber continued to walk familiar streets, but he was no longer aware of the perfect temperature or the crispness of the air. He didn't care what shade of amber was streaking across the horizon. When his cell vibrated, he answered using muscle memory. The voice on the other end of the line got his attention.

"Hey, Kaaber. I'm sorry I was abrupt before—got a lot of balls in the air today. I talked to the kid, and he said he'd like to see you. I can have my driver pick you up and take you to him." Wesley Davis's voice dripped with sweetness, but not the genuine variety. The so-sweet-this-has-to-cause-diabetes variety.

"That's a nice offer, but totally unnecessary. Just give me an address or a phone number and I'll find my way."

"No, no, no. I insist. In fact, why don't you just stay where you are? My guy will be there in a minute."

Kaaber stopped in the middle of the sidewalk, causing a three-businessman pile-up. He sidestepped the angry pedestrians and scanned the street in both directions. "What do you mean, just stay where I am?"

"Go to the corner and turn right on East Twenty-third. The car will be right there." Wesley Davis hung up again.

Kaaber hadn't noticed what intersection he was at, but Twenty-third Street was the next corner. He walked slowly toward it, his head on a pivot, trying to deduce how Davis knew his exact location. Edward Snowden popped into his mind, and he cursed his cell phone.

When Kaaber got to the corner, he stayed in the wave of traffic that was crossing the street. He looked off to his right but didn't see the stretch Bentley. He crossed East Twenty-third and tried to blend into the scene on the North side of the busy corner. The traffic light turned red, and the cross traffic started to make headway, but there was no sign of Davis's car. Kaaber didn't know which scenario would make him more nervous, the one in which the car shows up, or the one where it doesn't. Was he getting in the car? Last time he accepted a ride from Wesley he had been looking to escape. But if he didn't get into the car—if it showed up—he may jeopardize any chance of seeing Kelly Bailey again. The fact that Kelly had somehow aligned himself with Davis concerned Kaaber.

Within two minutes, the stretch Bentley rounded the corner and pulled over on the right side of Twenty-third Street. At that moment, Kaaber knew his greater fear was that the car wasn't coming. He crossed the street and approached the driver's window. The blacked-out glass began to slide down before Kaaber reached the middle of the road.

"Is Davis back there?" Kaaber pointed to the rear of the vehicle.

The rear door opened, and Davis stepped out. "I just happened to be in the neighborhood, Sasha. I'd be happy to take you for a little ride to see our mutual friend. I called him. He's expecting us."

Kaaber didn't move. "What's your relationship with the kid?"

"I'll explain everything on the way."

Kaaber hesitated, then felt his feet moving before his brain agreed to the decision. Davis got back into the car and slid over to make room.

"What is your relationship with the kid?" Kaaber repeated once the car was underway.

"First, I'm a little suspicious of why you feel that you have a right to insert yourself into Mr. Bailey's business. You aren't family. You aren't a close friend. He has both, you know. He is well looked after."

"I'm sure that's true. I've gotten to know him a little and I like him. He's an impressive young man. That's all. I guess you could say that I admire him."

"Do you admire him or his talent?"

"Both. Not that you can separate the two."

"There you go again ... stating your opinions as if they are facts."

"Miss me with your condescending bullshit, okay?"

"I'm merely trying to determine if you are a candidate for my intermediary services. I've run your financials—you have some means, you have the desire, but I'm trying to ascertain if you have the stomach."

Kaaber exhaled loudly through his nose and laid his head against the buttery leather headrest.

"What would you give to be able to stand up on stage and perform with the same confidence that Kelly did? Knowing that your music is genius in its composition and style? Trusting that your execution will be flawless? Knowing that you could captivate an audience of 100 or one hundred thousand by delivering the essence of what they perceive as perfection? What would you give to do that? Could you put a price tag on that?"

Kaaber closed his eyes, trying to shut out what he feared would come next.

"Kelly was able to out a price tag on it. And in doing so, he saved his mother's life. He provided himself a college education. He made it possible for his parents to live anywhere in the world, in far more luxurious accommodations than they are used to. If they're wise, none of them, or the children Kelly might have someday, will ever have to work again. They could live quite well off the interest of their newfound wealth and should be able to accrue future wealth through smart investments. So, Kaaber, I assure you that you don't have to worry about your little friend. He made a very wise choice enlisting me to do his bidding. I changed his life. And I can change yours."

Kaaber opened his eyes and focused on Davis. "You're doing it again."

Wesley laughed. "I know what this must sound like to you. You are having a hard time accepting what I say as the truth, and I understand. It's the same every time. The general population doesn't have the means to realize ability as a commodity. Even if they could fathom that the possibility exists, only one percent of the one- percenters could afford it anyway. For you, it's a bit of a reach. You have just over five million in assets, which is respectable considering your relatively young age. Still not quite enough to sit at our table as a buyer, but we have made some interesting deals recently. Talent management has a long history of splitting up the pie and, when you consider that all the talent is already proven, it's a very small risk on our part."

"I'm one of the top salespeople in Manhattan and even I can't decipher what the fuck you're trying to sell me."

"Maybe Kelly can explain better than I can," Davis said as the car came to a stop.

Kaaber looked out the window. They were on Bowery just North of Canal. Apartments were stacked on top of grubby storefronts. Kelly Bailey stood on the sidewalk and reached for the car door handle before the car came to a complete stop. The car was still locked, so he had to try again after the driver unlocked the doors. He crawled in and sat on the seat adjacent from where the two older men were already seated.

"Hey," Kelly said as the car eased out into traffic again. Kelly untied and retied his shoelace, not looking up at Kaaber.

"I told you I could help you with money." It was all Kaaber could think to say.

"I didn't need anyone's help. I got it done. Felt good to take care of things myself."

"You got what done?"

"I paid for my mom's treatment. She's in Sweden right now. They gave her a virus that eats cancer. The doctors said she'd be in remission in six weeks. Six weeks after that the cancer will be gone completely, and there's no reason to think she won't live to a ripe old age." Kelly was still fiddling with his shoes.

"And how did you pay for this?"

"I sold something valuable," Kelly attempted a convincing laugh. "I didn't even know I had anything valuable, but it turns out, I did."

"Fortunately for Kelly, my company brokered a deal. Unfortunately for me, that deal fell through. My business with Kelly is complete. He has been compensated, quite generously, but I was not able to close the deal with my buyer. I am left holding the bag and I'm writing in red ink. Kelly and I came up with an idea that might please all parties involved."

"Mr. Davis, can I tell him?" Kelly looked up for the first time since he climbed into the car.

Wesley Davis nodded and extended his hand to formally give Kelly the floor.

"Things started happening pretty fast with my mom. She had a scan the day after we went to John's, and the cancer spread at an alarming rate. Even the miracle cures were looking like a long shot, but there was this study in Sweden that got shelved a few years back due to lack of funding. They introduced a virus into animals with cancer that attacked and killed off the cancerous cells. The virus hasn't been tested in a clinical study on humans, but the daughter of the biochemist who worked on the study contracted the same type of lung cancer that Mom has, or had. He injected the virus last year and she is totally cancer-free now. That was all Dad and I needed as proof. I don't care what the FDA says, I want a healthy mom. We contacted the doctor and he said that we could bring Mom over there, but it was going to cost a million dollars. Then I remembered my conversation with Mr. Wesley and, well, I'm millionaire now."

"You sold your … talent?" Kaaber asked.

"All of it," Kelly laughed awkwardly.

"How is that possible?"

"It's actually as simple as giving blood. Took a few hours to identify the genome and … drain me? I guess?" Kelly looked to Davis for the right words.

Davis shrugged.

"Well, whatever they did. The hardest part was figuring out how to receive the money and all that business. Dad and Mom are stopping in Switzerland on the way home because that's the hard part."

"What are you saying?" Kaaber's outburst filled the car. "You gave away a God-given gift? How—"

"You don't have to worry about the how!" Davis's voice drowned out the rest of Kaaber's thought.

"Mr. Davis, please …" Kelly interjected. "Kaaber, God understands. Believe me. He gave me something that I could use to help the person that I would do anything for. I'm so thankful to Mr. Davis for turning my talent into a mountain of money. This is nothing but good news for me. And it could be good news for you too."

Kaaber leaned forward and put his head into his hands. "I really need to get off this crazy train. Please stop the car."

"But Kaaber, it can be yours now. The deal fell through. The Bitcoin rate dropped overnight, and the buyer doesn't have the funds. So now, you could have it! You could have the thing you wanted so badly in college. The lightning you tried to catch in a jar—you can have the jar!" Kelly's eyes were alive with excitement, and he was displaying a smile that Kaaber had rarely seen him wear. "The only thing that could make this any better for me is if it was you who had my gift. I would love you to have it. I know you would really use it and appreciate it."

Kaaber's head snapped to the man sitting next to him. "Can I buy it back for him?"

Davis laughed. "Oh, God. You really are a choir boy."

Kaaber spoke slowly through his teeth, "Can I back it back for him?"

"I don't need it Kaaber. It's been a few days and it's almost a relief to not be trapped in my room writing. I reenrolled in school. I went out with friends. I feel like I got my life back. I don't have to worry about my mom and I'm not a slave to the curse of expectation any-more, you know what I mean? Like, it's great to be able to do what I used to be able to do, but then people expect it. And they expect you to be brilliant all the time, and be knocking down doors and market-ing yourself and chasing the business … I feel free, man. Like I set down the heaviest backpack ever!"

Kaaber looked into Kelly's eyes, and he could see that the young man believed what he was saying.

"I've been fifteen, Kelly. If every decision that I made at your age was permanent, I'd be very sorry today. You are a very mature teen-ager, but, at your age, the future seems so far off and it's hard to see the ramifications of what you do now."

"My mom and dad worried about that too, but we talked about it a lot. There's nothing you could put on the other side of the scale that could equal Mom's life. There was really nothing to think about."

"Have you tried to play? Or …"

Kelly laughed. "No desire at all."

"But do you remember? You must still know the chords and how to play your instrument."

"We have had clients regain some form of muscle memory, but it's kind of like speaking after having a stroke that affects speech. I gener-ally advise my clients not to try." Davis smiled.

"I don't want to anyway," Kelly assured him.

"You don't want to today. This is like a vacation. But next month or next year, you're going to look at a guitar or sing along with the radio, or have an experience that you want to relate through a song, and you are going to miss that part of yourself so much. God, I feel like someone in my family died." Kaaber sighed.

"This is why I want you to have it, Kaaber. You'll treasure it."

"I'll buy it back for him."

Davis shook his head. "Doesn't work that way."

"Please, Kaaber. Buy it for yourself. Realize the dream you had in college. You could call your rock star friend and have a demo for him next week!"

"You would need to have a career that could support the rest of your payments. You don't have enough money to buy Kelly's ability. We would manage you."

"I don't even understand this conversation. I feel like I'm in the Twilight Zone."

Kelly laughed. "So did I, but it's all legit. I promise you. Sometimes it's not too good to be true. Think of it, '*Sasha Kaaber*' in lights at the Garden. Playing your songs all over the world. Having all that attention and privilege."

"Why don't you want that?"

"I don't know. I just never did. The one thing I wanted more than anything is happening though. My mom is going to be okay. Take this. Take this opportunity and run with it. You're good looking. You're the right age. There is no reason not to do this."

"Well, money is one thing that might get in the way," Davis said. "You'd have to tour a lot to repay us. I would accept five million up front, but you'd have to be making us about three mil a year for the next five years. It might be more than that. I'd refer you to our legal department for the details."

"I don't have five million liquid," Kaaber laughed.

"We're carrying paper for some cases. The real attention whores can't help being on the road and generating income. And if they default, we just go get 'em, but it's only happened twice. Once they get a taste …"

"How many?"

"Enough to ride around town in stretch Bentleys. Enough. You don't want to know."

"Can I acquire this talent and hold it for Kelly somehow? He's going to miss it someday and I'd like to know that he can have it back."

"You don't listen very well, do you? I thought salespeople had to be fantastic listeners. Kelly's talent no longer belongs to Kelly, nor will it ever again. A fact that he weighed very carefully. The opportunity to possess his talent has been presented to you. You will give me an answer right now. Our verbal contract is binding, and it includes an ironclad confidentiality agreement. You will be truer to this agreement than you are to that saucy little fiancé of yours ... what's her name? Charlie?" Davis raised his eyebrows when he said the name. "You have been invited into a very exclusive society. An invitation that you are expected to accept. It makes things easier. The details can be hammered out tomorrow, but I need you to accept my offer now."

"Doesn't the buyer usually make the offer?"

"No. He who has the gold makes the rules. In this case, that's me."

Kaaber couldn't help laughing. He looked from Kelly to Davis and back again. Kelly nodded his head in encouragement. "Say yes, Kaaber. You have far more to gain than what you have to put out."

"How am I supposed to explain my sudden genius?"

"You say you've been taking lessons, you've been renting rehearsal space, you got struck by lightning, I don't care ... make something up that fits and can't be disproven. It's best if you write your own fiction, then you'll remember the details. And give as few details as you can—that's where you'll get tripped up."

"And where am I supposed to record this demo of mine? Should I hire studio musicians and make it a full band thing, or should it just be me?"

"That's your problem. I have nothing to do with that. I'll make sure you get a year to make your first payment. You just be ready with the funds when they're due. There is no grace period for payments."

"I have one year to make five million dollars? Is that even possible? I thought it took a while to get established in the industry before you start getting paydays."

"You're going to have to be smart. And you have a nice in with your superstar client. You'll make it happen because you have to."

"That sounds like a threat."

Davis took a deep breath, as if explaining himself suddenly became exasperating.

"We are partners now, Kaaber. You have certain responsibilities in exchange for the incredible life that you are about to inherit. You will never be sorry that you made this decision."

"Someone else was sorry or you wouldn't have Kelly's talent to offer me."

Davis smiled a slow, wide smile, but his eyes were cold. "He certainly is sorry now. If he had kept his word, his future would have been charmed, but there is no tomorrow for those who don't keep their word to me."

"And what if I don't want to do business with you?"

"You do though. You've already considered the make-up of your act—whether you are a solo artist or a band leader. You're a solo artist, aren't you? The headliner with a band that stands in the shadows while you're in the spotlight. You already decided that didn't you? You want to play, Kaaber. So, let's play."

Kelly clapped his hands together. "This should be a celebration. C'mon ditch the talk about what could go bad—this is the best thing that ever happened to you, and you didn't even know it was possible this morning! This is a happy occasion, so let's just agree to move forward and you could be in the studio by this time tomorrow."

Davis tapped a panel on the bulkhead of the car and tray ejected a tablet in the way that a DVD player would eject a disc. He tapped the screen, and it lit up. He placed his palm on the surface and it unlocked, revealing a contract with Kaaber's name on it.

"Place your hand there and we have a virtual handshake and a binding agreement."

"I'm not signing anything until I read it and have my attorney read it."

Davis laughed. "Attorney client privilege isn't ironclad enough for a contract as confidential as this one." He grabbed Kaaber's right hand and pressed it forcefully to the tablet screen. There was a look of pleasure on his face, but it wasn't pleasant to witness. After twenty long seconds, the tablet made a wind chime noise and Davis released Kaaber's hand.

"You will have a copy of this contract in your new email inbox. Show it to anyone and you're dead. Talk about it to anyone and you're dead. Miss one of the scheduled payments and you're dead. Other than that, show up at the designated place and time and you are on your way to an amazing new life."

This is how you will communicate with us and how we will communicate with you. Don't give us a reason for a face to face. You won't like that. This method will suffice if you follow directions. I do not recommend that the two of you ever see each other again. It's best if there is no further contact, so wish each other well and forget this meeting ever happened."

Davis handed Kaaber a business card with a domain name that ended in .onion. There was a username and password. Kaaber looked at it and then looked at Kelly. He wore an *"I just won the lottery"* smile.

The car slowed down and Kaaber noticed that they were in front of his building.

"Nice doing business with you, Mr. Kaaber. Our meeting is over now."

The driver was opening the door on Kaaber's side of the car.

"Have fun, Kaaber, I'm really happy for you," Kelly said.

The driver reached in the car and grabbed Kaaber's arm. "Can I help you out of the car, Sir?"

Kaaber tried to maintain eye contact with Kelly as the car door closed leaving him on the outside. He couldn't find the words to express everything he was feeling, so he said nothing. The car pulled away and Kaaber watched it go. He felt violated and terrified. He was wound up, but he was also excited. He checked his watch and pulled out his phone. Sasha Kaaber dropped a pin on the closest music store and started walking in that direction.

CHAPTER EIGHTEEN

MATTHEW BLINKED A FEW TIMES but opening his eyes didn't transform the darkness. He was aware that he had a headache, and he felt a burning sensation in his nasal passages. He tasted vomit.

Matthew reminded himself that panic wouldn't serve him, so he consciously calmed himself and tried to gather information. He was lying on his back in a moving vehicle—probably the van that he encountered on the road. His hands were bound at his sides. When he tested the confinement, he felt tension in his inner thighs, which made him think his hands were tied to his legs. His feet were bound together.

"Lay still, kid." The voice came from beside him and the accent sounded like New York, but Matthew hadn't heard enough words to be sure.

There was a blindfold of some variety over his eyes, but his mouth and nose weren't covered.

"Where am I? Who are you?" He asked the voice.

"Shut up, kid. I didn't want you choking on your vomit, so I didn't gag you, but I will." Definitely a New Yorker. Matthew had a friend at school who transferred from Staten Island, and he would bet money that his kidnapper was from the same borough.

Very softly, Matthew asked, "Why did you take me? What did I ever do to anybody?"

"Kid, I'm gonna tell you one more time to shut up and then I'm gonna have to tape your mouth." The New Yorker muttered to himself, "God damned stuff isn't supposed to wear off that fast."

Matthew tried to take deep, steady breaths, but his heart was racing, and fresh air was in short supply inside the rank smelling cargo van. It smelled like the science lab at school when they used the Bunsen burner to identify chemical compounds. Matthew fought to stay conscious—he didn't want to pass out and become totally defenseless, so he refocused on his surroundings. He heard traffic and they weren't stopping at red lights or stop signs, so he assumed that they were on the highway. He didn't know how long he had been out, so he couldn't guess how far they traveled from Coral Gables.

There was no conversation in the van, so he couldn't tell if there were more people present than just him, the driver, and Staten Island. There was no music coming from the radio.

Matthew decided that the best he could do was to try to time how long the drive was from this point. He started counting. Seven minutes later, they exited the highway. The driver cursed in Spanish as the van slowed to a crawl.

"It's bumper to bumper, man. If anyone saw us take the kid, they'll catch us on foot before we get to the office." The speaker had a Cuban accent.

"Shut. Up," Staten Island growled.

Matthew decided that if there was a third kidnapper in the van, he was the silent type, but it felt like Cuban and Staten Island were alone. Two men jumped out from the van to grab Matthew, so maybe they were being followed by another car. Maybe it was the 7 series BMW. Matthew thought it was likely.

After eight minutes, the van made a right turn and heaved itself up an incline driveway. It sounded like the bottom hit the pavement. Matthew heard a crunching sound underneath the tires and guessed that they were in a shell- paved parking lot. They were only four minutes from the highway. Matthew reminded himself that so many communities cropped up along the 95 corridor; he couldn't possibly be aware of all of them, or the various businesses that would have followed. Regardless of his attempt to get his bearings, Matthew knew he could be anywhere in South Florida.

The van slowed to a crawl and began a turn.

"Go around to the back, Estupido!" Staten Island yelled.

The van stopped and Matthew could hear the wheels turning in the loose parking lot surface. They slowly moved forward and then made a wide left turn, rolling over three speed bumps.

"When I tell you to sit up, you're gonna do that for me nice and slow, Matthew."

Staten Island knew his name.

"Where are we going?"

"My boss wants to meet you and I suggest that you be real polite to him and answer any questions he might have for you. I'm gonna untie your feet so you can walk by yourself, but your hands are staying put and so is the blackout mask. My helper and I are gonna lead you where you need to go."

"My dad is a lawyer you know. Every judge in Dade, Broward, and Palm Beach County knows him. This is a really big mistake you're making."

"I'll worry about me, kid. You worry about you."

The van parked and the engine stopped, cutting off the AC. Matthew hadn't considered whether the temperature was comfortable until the sweltering heat completely consumed the parked car. Matthew felt the binding on his feet loosen and remained still until he was told to sit up. He heard the back doors of the van open—they squeaked and groaned as the doors swung out and hot, stagnant air filled Matthew's nose. There was a familiar fragrance outside. It wasn't pleasant, but it was comforting. As the men guided Matthew from the back of the van and started walking him inside, he identified his surroundings—he was in a dry cleaners. There was a dry cleaners in the shopping plaza that Publix anchored, and it smelled exactly like this.

Matthew counted his steps from the time he left the van. Fifteen steps, right turn, then twenty more. He didn't hear voices, but he heard the soft hum of machinery.

"Stop," Staten Island ordered. Matthew heard a soft knocking sound, and a voice told them to come in.

Matthew heard the door open—another squeaker—and he stepped through. He felt thick carpet beneath his feet. The air was cool now and he smelled no cleaning solvents, just vanilla.

"Sit him down, leave the mask on him," a man's voice said softly. There was no discernible accent. "Did he get a good look at your faces?"

"No, boss. No way," Cuban said.

Matthew didn't correct him.

"Good. Here. Go."

Matthew thought he heard the rustle of paper and imagined the man passing out envelops filled with money as a reward for pulling off a successful kidnapping. He heard the door close, and the felt the man walk past where he sat. The lock clicked into place and Matthew felt the man walk past him again. When he spoke, his voice came from its original location in the room—in front of Matthew.

"Is your name Matthew Newcombe-Drake?"

"Yes. My father is David Drake of Drake, Collins, and McKinney."

"That's nice. Answer the questions without embellishment. Was your grandfather Thad Newcombe?"

"Yes." Matthew slowly explored the area around him with his feet. The chair he was sitting in had legs and there was a solid piece of furniture about twelve inches from his toes—probably a desk.

"Did your grandfather leave anything to you when he died?"

"No."

The slap came across Matthew's face like a bolt of lightning on a clear day.

"That was an open-handed reminder not to lie to me. Your next lie will be dealt with more harshly."

Matthew wondered how the voice got around the desk so quickly; then he realized that there must be another person in the room. He slowly pulled his feet back under his chair. For the first time since this ordeal began, he fought back tears.

"What about the letter that your grandfather wrote to you? What did it say?"

Matthew wondered if the man already knew what it said.

"It said that he loved me and was proud of me." Matthew willfully did not brace himself for another blow—he didn't want to give the impression that he had lied.

"Have you ever heard of a polygraph test, Matthew?"

"Yeah."

"This is a type of polygraph. It will tell me if you're lying about not receiving anything from your grandfather. It will only hurt a little."

Someone freed Matthew's right arm and turned it over, resting his forearm on the chair's armrest. He felt something tighten around his lower bicep.

"You're pretty athletic for an artist, Matthew," His interrogator commented.

There was a piercing sensation in the crook of his elbow. Then another … and another.

"What the fuck?" Matthew tensed his arm against the assault.

"I'm sorry. My man isn't a nurse. Get it right this time."

This attempt struck the target and Matthew waited for the effect of whatever they were injecting into him. He prayed for help.

After a minute, the needle was removed. Matthew didn't feel any different.

"Do we have what we need?"

Matthew didn't hear an answer, but there must have been silent affirmation.

"You'll be our guest until we have the results of this little test."

"What happens to me after you get your results?"

"That depends on the result."

CHAPTER NINETEEN

WITH INSTRUCTION AND MUCH TRIAL and error, Mauro learned to navigate the Dark Web. Once home, he didn't waste any time setting his plan in motion.

He searched the Tor Directory for goods first, but didn't find the type of the listings he was looking for. He tried modifying his search under "Services," but struck out there as well. He searched for The Davis Agency, but there were no hits. Finally, he typed "quarterback skills" into the search and four links popped up. He was very excited, but he stopped himself.

Mauro set his laptop on the floor next to his chair and walked into the kitchen. He poured ¼ cup of ground coffee into a filter and filled the coffee pot with tap water. He filled the coffee maker with water, slid the filter into place and leaned against the countertop while the Mr. Coffee did its job. As always, the aroma comforted him and, just like in college, seemed to grease the wheels of his idea factory.

He didn't want to tip Davis off to his identity. Getting back into the sports division might be too risky. Besides, why would a guy his age want to acquire the ability to play a sport that his body was too old for? It had to be something else in an area where the story of Salvatore Greco wasn't legend. He remembered the name of another legend and it sparked a plan.

He poured the coffee and went back into the living room. Mauro took a sip of steaming perfection and set the cup on the floor next to the laptop that he scooped into his huge hand. He tapped the mouse pad and typed "Newcombe-like painting ability." One hit. He clicked the link.

> *The death of world-renowned contemporary artist Thad Newcombe left a hole in the fabric of the art world. Comparable ability would ensure that similar works of art would still be brought to life. There are masterpieces left to paint, and to deprive the world of such work would be shameful. If you are conscientious enough to assume the responsibility, please come forth.*

Must transfer bitcoin equivalent of $1M USD as a deposit upon notification of winning bid. Must provide account information with bid submission.

Mauro's bitcoin account had about ten-thousand USD in it at the moment.

Afraid to Bookmark the page, Mauro wrote down the URL and took a photo of the screen. He was through the gates, but he was trapped inside his Trojan horse.

CHAPTER TWENTY

KAABER PICTURED THE RECORDING STUDIO to be much larger. On TV shows and in movies, recording studios were depicted as vast, open spaces behind soundproof glass. The engineers always sat in front of forty-eight channel boards in huge controls rooms lined with leather couches. He was disappointed.

"This is it? This isn't where the label's artists record. Is it?"

The very young music producer laughed as he zeroed out the board. "Actually, Pitbull left about five minutes ago. He laid down some vocals for his new project."

"But where is everyone? Where's the band gonna be?"

"You and I are laying down the vocals and the guitar today. Adam wants to take a listen to what we have. He said, depending on how raw it is, he would take it to the label himself, or put some studio musicians on it. You're putting the cart way in front of the horse, Bruh. Let's see if we can get through a song or two."

"I have fifteen songs ready to go. I want the energy of a full band behind me when I record. If I need to come back tomorrow, I can do that. You know, give you a chance to hire the big guns for the session."

The producer took a deep breath and faced Kaaber. "Go ahead and tell me how this should work, Mr. Real Estate Agent. I produced eight of the iTunes top twenty downloads for this week. You are a newb. Why don't you not waste any more of Adam's money trying to take charge? The studio bills by the hour and I make more guap per year than a dirty hedge fund manager. The way I see it, you're getting a huge favor from one of the most relevant guys on the scene today. Show him he isn't wasting his time on you."

"If you're making so much money, you should dress better. Get some pants that don't drag on the floor when you walk. And a belt. And a jacket that doesn't have a zipper—"

"Dude, I don't know who the fuck you are or how you got Adam to owe you a favor, but if you don't get your ass in there and start giving me a sound check, I'm leaving right now."

Kaaber picked up his guitar case and opened the door to the small recording booth. The soft glow of a floor lamp made the space feel intimate. A stool was sitting beside a mic on a boom stand with a windscreen set up in front of it. A cord was run for his guitar. He plugged in, found headphones hanging on the wall behind him, and sat in front of the mic. He heard a popping sound and then the producer's voice came through. "Your Eton of Sweden shirt is pretty loud, let's see if we can get your vocal dialed in to drown it out."

"Fine, you don't like my clothes either," Kaaber said into the mic.

He heard the popping in his ears again, "Sing. Don't talk. I need you to sing."

Kaaber already knew which song he was going to start with, so he began to sing it a cappella. He could see the producer through a very small window, and he locked eyes with him for a second. The producer sat down behind the board, grabbed the neck of the lamp that had been illuminating the mix and turned the cone of light toward the wall. He closed his eyes for a second while Kaaber delivered the song, adjusted a few knobs, and then told him to play the acoustic. Kaaber didn't get through the first verse before the voice in his ears cut him off.

"Let's go ahead and take a pass at the first song. Don't be nervous, we have plenty of tracks to work with. We can do it as many times as we need to. Just relax, pretend I'm not here, and go for it."

Kaaber took a deep breath—he heard it amplified in his ears. He filled his diaphragm less aggressively and counted off, "1, 2, 3, 4 ..."

The sound of his guitar filled his headset and Kaaber closed his eyes. He loved the warmth of the instrument, and the fact that he was causing it to produce such beautiful chord progressions. His fingers knew where to be and when to be there. His timing was perfect. The chord progressions and changes were interesting and beautiful. He was almost afraid to open his eyes—the sight of himself playing guitar freaked him out when he did it for the first time in front of the mirror in his apartment.

The song was probably about some latent feelings leftover from childhood. He hadn't deliberately written the song—it just flowed out of him. When the songs first started forming in his mind, he labored to get them down—to record the lyrics and the melody into his phone, and to write down the chords that he was playing on guitar. It didn't take long for him to realize that once he heard the lines in his head, they were settled there. He didn't need reminders or prompts to reproduce the song again. He knew it. Once he figured that part out, writing became a lot easier. In the last week, he wrote fifteen songs and rehearsed them daily. Not because he needed the practice, mostly for assurance that the songs were still there.

He dreamed music now. He dreamed melodies and lyrics. He dreamed of guitar arrangements and when he woke up, he could play anything he dreamed. If he heard a commercial jingle on TV, he could pick up the guitar and reproduce it. It wasn't like the last time he had tried to play guitar—he didn't need to find the key. He didn't use a capo. He didn't need to practice the fingering until it flowed. It was just there.

Kaaber finished the song. The last chord he played rung in his headphones. When the last whisper of the music faded away, he opened his eyes. The engineer's eyes were closed, and he was nodding his head. The headphones popped. "That was … fucking awesome."

Kaaber laughed. "It felt good. Do you want another pass?"

"Nope. Let's move on to the next song."

Kaaber recorded fifteen songs in fifteen takes. Before the session was halfway finished, the record producer made four phone calls to four very important music executives. When the session was finished and Kaaber turned his phone on, he had messages from Adam, Adam's agent, and three record execs who had begun a bidding war for the album already being called *Kaaber.*

CHAPTER TWENTY-ONE

MATTHEW'S CAPTORS LAID HIM FACE down on the concrete floor. He was blindfolded and hogtied. Matthew willfully calmed himself by recalling his grandfather's warning and his reassurances.

He had memorized both pages of Thad's letter and he could envision the fountain pen lettering against the light blue paper. The second page was the one that predicted his current situation. A small key was taped to the top of that page and below it, Thad wrote:

The attached is not to be used until your fortieth birthday. I hope that the world will have come to its collective senses by then. I'm afraid that my decision to dance with the devil may cause you difficulty. Remain vigilant, but do not be afraid to confront anyone who questions your lack of inheritance. You can honestly say there was none. When they come looking for it, do not be afraid. They will find nothing, and no harm will come to you, although they might test you mentally, physically, and emotionally. Stay strong. The sooner they find out that you do not have what they are looking for, the better. Do not tell anyone about this, not even your mother. Hide the key in a safe place. What I'm asking of you requires copious self-control, which is a trait that all great artists master. I count you among the greats.

Next to an address at the bottom right-hand corner of the page, Thad added his own flourish. Matthew marveled at the intricate ink doodle made by the world's greatest contemporary artist, and he passed the time now by tracing it in his mind. The shake of Thad's hand had been evident in his writing, but it was imperceptible in the artwork.

Trusting his grandfather came naturally to Matthew, and he trusted him now. He knew that he wasn't in any real danger. Thad Newcombe knew his captors and his grandfather had known that this moment would come.

Matthew heard footsteps walking across the concrete floor. It was an A-B pattern—only one person was approaching, but the echo filled a very large space.

"We got your blood test back." It was Staten Island. "You have gonorrhea, but we weren't looking for that." He chuckled at his joke as he lifted Matthew from the floor.

"So, are you finished with me? Like, can I leave now?"

"We're gonna have a little talk."

Staten Island rammed a chair into the back of Matthew's knees, and he sat down hard. Matthew was overwhelmed by the smell of cigarettes and coffee, and he sensed that Staten Island's face was very close to his own. "You can go as soon as you and I have an understanding. I need to know that you're not going to say anything to anyone about what happened this morning.

Boss's secretary called your school. She told them she was your dad's sister, Auntie Meredith. She explained that you would be absent this morning to attend to some family business. Considering everything that happened recently, the school was more than willing to oblige an excused absence. So, you're gonna go back to school like everything is everything, but you're still gonna see us around. Know why? Because if we see any cops or anything unusual, we're gonna have to punish you for opening your mouth. You say nuttin' to nobody and this unpleasantness is as bad as it gets. You make a bad choice and start yakking about this and that … well, then we're gonna have to pay a visit to your mother."

Matthew's breath became ragged at the mention of his mom.

"She's not hard to find. Leaves the house at 7:30 am Monday through Friday, takes the same route to school in her little VW Bug convertible. Comes home to an empty house at 4:10, and she rarely stops to lock the door behind her. Even if she remembered, those sliding glass doors pop right off the track. I don't know why people bother having those things. They're such an easy point of entry into a house. Anyway, you saw how fast I knock someone out. Don't make the mistake of thinking that just because I was nice to you today, I'm a nice guy. My job description is about the opposite of that. This Miami crew … I don't know where they got 'em. None of these wanna-be gangsters have the stomach for it like I do. I could do your mom up good." Staten Island's voice descended an octave. "I know you don't want your mother to disappear. I know you don't wanna think about me having my personal way with her before I beat her to death with a hammer. Ah, but you probably just did think it—you know, power of suggestion. What an image, huh? Anyway, I guarantee that's what would happen. Cops might watch over you for a week, maybe a month because of your famous Gramps, but they can't keep you under surveillance for an extended amount of time without being able to justify the expense, so … be assured, I'm patient."

"Doesn't do me any good to talk to the police—I don't know shit. I don't know what you want. I don't know who you are or where I am. I tell the authorities about this and they're gonna think I'm nuts. I'd be crazy to try to get anyone to believe this. I'd look like a kid trying to get attention in the midst of a family crisis. I can't prove anything."

Staten Island didn't reply.

"I'm telling you I'm not going to talk. How do I know you won't go after my mom?"

"We already sampled her. She tell you anything about passing out in the kitchen yesterday? She was making coffee in that fancy machine, so I grabbed her from behind, kept her under until I had my sample, and she woke up on the floor probably thinking she had fainted. Probably thought the stress got to her. That your little painted handprint on her coffee cup? Cute she still uses it."

Matthew gasped.

"Oh, so she didn't mention it? I already been to your house. It's nice. We could have gone that way with you too—saved all of us the trouble of having to bring you here, but you were always runnin' around the neighborhood, talkin' to people, makin' a scene … you didn't leave us much choice but to do this the hard way. That's okay with me though. I like the chase."

Matthew felt something pouring over his feet. He instinctively tried to pull away, but his movements were extremely limited. He smelled gasoline.

"I want you to understand how important it is that you not talk about this, Matthew. I want you to know me. Know that I don't mind hurting people. Maybe there's something wrong with me, but I really love it. I love the terror, the screams—I love it all. I love looking into a pair of eyes that just realized they now know how they're going to die."

Matthew smelled the sulfur from a recently lit match.

"Oh my God, no. Please, no." Matthew started to cry. He felt intense heat right in front of his nose.

"No, no, no, no … please!" He screamed.

"See that? I love that! I have all the power right now. Don't piss your pants, Matthew, I'm not lightin' you up today, and you gotta go back to school. I got a nice gas can here, but that's water on you. It'll be dry by the end of the day. Your shoes might be mushy for a while, but that will be a good, solid reminder to keep your fuckin' mouth shut. Right?"

Matthew was crying now.

Staten Island was satisfied. "Okay, time to go to school."

CHAPTER TWENTY-TWO

MAURO'S PLAN REQUIRED FINANCING. SINCE he had already gained entry into the underground market, he figured he would fish in that pond to find it.

He signed on to the Tor Server and searched for "Financial Partnerships." He got 3,017 hits. He began to read the listings. Some were very specific. All wanted to launder money.

He scoured page after page of listings seeking to front nail salons, car washes, convenience stores—all businesses with low average unit sales. Experienced people who knew exactly what they were looking for placed the ads. Mauro didn't feel confident enough to dive into a pool with known sharks. Finally, on page thirty-seven, he found his listing.

> *High volume revenue earner seeking a front. One million USD for the New Yorker willing to take the risk.*

Mauro typed his reply.

> *Let's talk. Today at five o'clock at Nico's on East 93rd between 1st and 2nd. Bring the upfront. I'll be wearing a Wickersham Waste Management ball cap. Call me Fred.*

Mauro pressed "send" and his stomach started doing its own Cirque de Soleil act.

The reply popped up within seconds: *I'll be there.*

Mauro accessed the listing for the painting ability and was proud that he remembered how to proceed through the detailed log in process. The bid was still open, and the reserve had not been met. Mauro had no doubt that his offer would be the highest. Once he had a million in his Bitcoin account he could submit, and he would aim high because he wasn't planning on finalizing the transaction anyway. Mauro smiled and dialed his cell.

———

Wagner and Mauro sat behind a table at Nico's with their back to the wall leaving two empty chairs opposite them.

At five o'clock sharp, two men walked in and scanned the room. The lead guy, a tall lanky blond who could have been on break from walking the runway, made eye contact with Mauro, and nodded. Mauro nodded back. The blond made his way across the room, followed by a behemoth of a man that Mauro assumed served as a bodyguard.

"Fred, yeah?" The blond model had a British accent.

"Yeah," Mauro answered. "Have a seat."

The blond looked around the room. As he assessed his surroundings, Mauro evaluated him. He was over six feet tall and lean. His thick hair was styled with lots of product to make it look like he had just come from the beach. He wore black dress pants with a light blue button-down shirt. A presidential Rolex peeked out from under the sleeve of an expensive-looking leather sport coat. This was not the face Mauro had expected to represent the Black-Market Internet. He looked like a Yale Law graduate on his way to pick out a new Range Rover.

"Can I get an ale, then? Do you mind?" he asked Mauro and Wagner.

"I'm sure you can get the waitress's attention. Get her over here and we'll all order," Mauro said.

The second guy was definitely a bodyguard. His head was on a swivel. Mauro guessed that he carried about two hundred eighty pounds of meat. He had taken many hits to the face. His right ear looked a little chewed up. Sitting next to model-boy, he looked especially grotesque.

The smiling waitress sashayed her way over to the handsome patron.

"What do you want there, Sam?"

"Nothing Mr. Churchill," the big man replied.

"Mates?"

"Two Miller lights."

Mr. Churchill nodded and relayed the order to the waitress.

When she went to fetch the libations, the blond turned his attention to the table. "My name is obviously not Mr. Churchill and I'm sure you're not called Fred, but that will work for now, won't it?"

Mauro nodded.

"Do you have a name?" Churchill asked Wagner.

"Nope."

"Fine. I imagine you gentlemen have a fully operational system in place?"

"Yeah. Our letter of recommendation is that we're still alive. That tells you we haven't screwed over any of our business partners. What kind of volume are you talking about?"

"Could be as much as a mil a week."

Mauro intentionally did not react. "That's fine."

"How do you wash that?"

"First things first. We get forty percent of everything we clean for the risk we take and because we know something you don't."

"Forty percent? Fuck off, forty percent! My ad said a mil for your services. You're wasting my time." The Brit was riled, but he regained his composure as the waitress dropped off their drinks.

"Is there anything else I can get for you?" She only looked at Churchill.

"Thanks, babe, I don't think we'll need another round."

"I'll leave this for you, then. Whenever you're ready." She went to set the check wallet on the table, but Churchill handed her a hundred-dollar bill. "I don't need any change."

She batted her fake eyelashes and pulled her shoulders back. "Thank you very much, baby."

Churchill hadn't made eye contact with her during the exchange. She got the message and went to work another table.

"We're done here as far as I'm concerned," Churchill announced.

"Sorry to take up your time. I thought you were a major player," Mauro took a swig of his beer.

"I am a major player. That's why I'm not falling for giving you half of my profits."

"It's not half, it's forty percent. Of course, your tax liability will be about five percent, but you're still keeping fifty-five percent. Good luck finding a better alternative. I don't need your business—I'm plenty happy with what I got goin'."

Churchill watched Mauro drink his beer and the group sat in silence for a few minutes.

"I thought you were leaving," Wagner prompted.

"What is it?" Churchill asked, his eyes still on Mauro.

"The cleaner?" Mauro raised his eyebrows. "I'm not telling you shit, 'cuz we ain't doin' business."

"Listen, I got a meth lab cranking out product and guys on the street selling it faster than I can make it. I'd like to be able to spend some of my profits, and I don't want five million dollars stuffed into the appliances of my apartment anymore."

"I don't like how jumpy you are. You're too emotional," Mauro looked at Wagner who nodded agreement. "You might as well go. We're done here."

"You've already seen my face. You could call the authorities and turn me in."

"Your face doesn't do nothin' for me like it did for the waitress. And I'm not a rat. You got no worries. Go ahead and find another cleaner."

Churchill laughed quietly to himself. "I see who has control of the conversation. I need you, but you don't need me. I get it, mate. Can we talk particulars?"

Mauro looked at Wagner who nodded again.

"Here's how this is going to work. Online casino winnings are going to be around thirty-nine billion dollars this year across twenty-five thousand gaming sites. We're gonna set up a legit online casino for you. You're gonna have lots of cash flow and no physical product, which makes virtual profits hard to track."

"I don't think ..."

"Don't think ... listen. You got an offshore bank account where they don't exchange info with anybody?"

"No."

"Jesus, you are new at this. First, you get that bank account. We set you up with an online casino owned between letterbox companies. You're gonna hire a staff, buy the software, and go live with real casino games and legit customers. Then we set up fake accounts to generate fake revenue. You declare the winnings and pay the taxes because we'll have you in a haven where you'll only pay about five percent. You take care of me upfront, starting today, and you have the rest of your business profits all nice and clean."

Churchill's eyes shifted back and forth between Wagner and Mauro.

"Or you could continue hoarding cash money in your apartment where it has probably already been seen by your cooks and your dealers. You can trust those guys, though. No reason to think anyone would turn on you for money. Nobody would bite the hand, right? Who's gonna notice you wearing designer clothes, carrying bodyguards, and giving waitresses hundies on a twenty-dollar bar tab? Probably no one. You pay your rent in cash every month? Probably not a lot of land-lords in Manhattan getting paid in cash every month. What did you put down for a place of employment on your lease?" Mauro swallowed his last gulp of beer. "Never mind, none of my business." He stood up from the table and Wagner followed.

"Gentlemen, please ... sit. I'm sure we can work something out," Churchill pleaded.

Mauro and Wagner obliged and informed Churchill how their business partnership would proceed. Fifteen minutes later, Churchill shook hands with his new partners and followed his bodyguard to the door.

Mauro removed the cell phone from his shirt pocket, took it off speaker and held it up to his ear.

"You get all that?"

"Yeah, it'll be easy, but I'm going to have to charge you a lot more than what it cost you to get the Tor Server installed on your laptop."

"I don't care. You can keep the Limey's forty percent if you want. He won't know if it's you or me on the other end of the emails. I have the upfront and that's all I need for now. If I need cash, I'll take a commission later."

"Yeah, man. Whatever you need."

Mauro ended the call. "Internet criminals are very civilized," he told Wagner.

CHAPTER TWENTY-THREE

AFTER AN HOUR IN HIS air-conditioned classroom, Matthew's wet shoes and socks refrigerated his feet to the point of numbness. The chill served as the reminder that Staten Island predicted. Matthew tried hard to focus on his Calculus teacher, but his insides still felt jittery. He replayed the events of the morning over and over in his head. He tried to imagine the chain of events that might be set in motion if he told his parents what happened. In every scenario, members of his family seemed to be in greater jeopardy than they were now. If Staten Island kept his word, he would leave them alone to pay for Matthew's silence. Could he trust a criminal?

Matthew was jolted from his inner dialogue when he realized that Mr. Fulton had stopped talking and was looking directly at him. He had the look on his face that the whole faculty had worn for him since his grandfather's death.

"Um … I'm sorry, Mr. Fulton. I missed the question."

"I asked if you would like a hall pass to visit the men's room, or to take a lap."

"No. I'm sorry. I, ah, drifted off for a second. Sorry."

Several people in the class laughed.

"Okay, okay. Eyes on me. Let's walk through this one more time with everyone following along, yes?" Mr. Fulton turned his attention to the white board.

Matthew struggled to push the morning from his mind and pretend that this was just another school day. There were only a few minutes left of class when the principal poked her head through the classroom door.

"Mr. Newcombe, please come with me."

Matthew's heart began to race. As he gathered his books, he imaged the news he was about to receive. Had they found his mother dead of an apparent heart attack? Or was it an accident of some sort? Matthew could feel vomit rising in his throat. His expression must have revealed his fears.

"You do remember that you were one of the students chosen to sit on the dais today when our benefactor presents the school with the scholarship funding?" She asked.

"Oh." Matthew's voice came out in a rolling wave of relief. "Oh, yeah. I forgot that was today." He tried a little laugh.

"Sorry to pull you away from Mr. Fulton. I can see that you were completely under his spell. That man has a way of drawing you in, doesn't he?"

"Yes. Ma'am. Mr. Fulton is a great teacher."

The two walked down the hallway to the auditorium where the stage was already set. The president of the student council, Angie Willis was there. The Dean, Assistant Principal, and the most famous alumnus of the school, a Hollywood actress, were on hand as well. They called in the big guns. Thad Newcombe's grandson was the perfect piece to complete the collection. Matthew noticed that all the local Miami TV stations were vying for real estate near the podium that was set on the stage.

"Go ahead and set your books down backstage and then join everyone out front. There are pieces of paper on the chairs that tell you where to sit." The principal patted Matthew on the back to get him moving.

He lifted his frozen feet up each step leading to the stage, stacked his books behind the curtain stage right of the action, and then went to find where he would be sitting. He wasn't nervous about the ceremony—he was just an ornament. With all the TV cameras present, his greatest task was not looking the way he felt.

The benefactor arrived and all the school's figureheads went to meet her. The students remained in place.

Angie took her seat next to Matthew. "Hey."

"Hey." He smiled and wondered if the gesture was convincing.

"What a circus, huh? Did you see all those finger sandwiches and all those teas in the back of the auditorium? Who is this chick, the resurrected queen of England?"

Matthew laughed more genuinely this time. "From what I hear, she has more money than the Royal Family. Look how happy they are to be getting some of it."

"I hope I don't turn into a complete money whore when I'm finally classified as an adult. Principal Evans is practically washing her feet," Angie said.

Matthew watched the well dressed and perfectly coiffed woman greet the school faculty. "She looks like she would rather be somewhere else right now."

"Nah, I think she loves being fussed over. Wouldn't you?"

"I don't know. It looks a little predatory from here, you know? Like vultures circling a dead thing in the road."

Angie laughed. "That's how it is at my house every Christmas when my grandparents come to visit. All my aunts and uncles—" She stopped talking. "Oh, shit, Matthew, I'm sorry. I didn't mean to bring up grandparents."

He laughed. "It's okay. No big deal. You don't need to apologize because you have living grandparents."

"Sorry," she said again. "So, did he leave you, like, millions? Are you set for life now?"

"I said not to be sorry before, but now, you should be a little sorry. 'Cuz that's just—"

"I'm sorry. God, I always say the wrong thing."

"He didn't have any money to leave us. I think he spent most of it trying to save my grandma when she got sick, and then his medical bills ate up a lot. He didn't have good insurance. Anyway, I'm still gonna have to work for a living."

Angie made a face. "That sucks. I don't ever want to have a job."

Matthew laughed.

The AV department had popped up something that looked like a crest on all the screens around the auditorium. Something about it, caught Matthew's attention and he studied it.

"Do you think I'll ever have to?"

Matthew studied the crest intently. He took each of the four sections apart one by one in his mind's eye.

"Matthew, do you think I'll have to work?"

"Hmm? Oh, yeah, probably," his focus was still on the closest screen.

"So, you don't think I'm pretty? Pretty girls never have to get jobs. And you're saying ..."

Angie's words weren't reaching Matthew's consciousness any longer. He was stunned by the realization of what he was looking at. The top right-hand corner of the crest was the same symbol that his grandfather had drawn on the letter he wrote to Matthew. It was exactly the same.

"Matthew?"

He looked at Angie.

"What?" He snapped.

"Oh, sorry, again. Didn't know you were too busy sitting here doing nothing to have a conversation."

"Quiet, everyone, quiet. The student body will be coming in any second, so if we could have a few photos before they make their way in, that would be great." Principal Evans was using her principal voice. "Students and faculty, if you could stand on the stage in a semi-circle behind Mrs. Marcot, that would be fantastic.

The news crews began filming and Matthew could hear still shots being snapped.

Mrs. Marcot made her way to the stage and greeted each person she passed. She walked beyond the center of the line and said hello to Angie and Matthew.

"Thanks for taking the time to be here, Mrs. Marcot," Angie said.

"You're quite welcome, Miss ...?"

"Willis, Ma'am."

"Nice to meet you, Miss Willis."

The beautiful elderly woman stood in front of Matthew. She was almost a full foot shorter, yet she made him nervous.

"Matthew Newcombe-Drake, Ma'am."

"Yes, Matthew. My condolences on the recent loss of your grandfather. I was a fan and a collector of his work."

"Thank you, Mrs. Marcot."

Photos were taken, and Mrs. Marcot took her seat in the middle of the dais. The student body filed in, took their seats, and the ceremony began.

The scholarship was named the Marcot Award, and it would grant full tuition to five students displaying exceptional talent each year from this year forward. Matthew listened to the school praise the generosity of Mrs. Marcot as a benefactor and he heard her compliment the opportunity that the school provided the next generation of artists. Sitting just outside of the spotlight, Matthew struggled to keep his gaze on whoever was speaking, but his eyes kept creeping to the screens and the familiar symbol inside the Marcot family crest.

CHAPTER TWENTY-FOUR

C HARLIE AND KAABER WERE SEATED in a private alcove of Vivienne, the same place where they got engaged weeks earlier.

"I've heard the expression 'overnight sensation,' but I've never thought it was a literal description of how someone could become famous. I've heard interviews with emerging recording artists and they say that they've been living in their cars, doing bar gigs on the circuit, or playing in wedding bands for decades, but you're telling me your record drops tomorrow?"

"Crazy, right?" Kaaber laughed.

"Where's the PR buildup of the release date? Where are the TV appearances and radio interviews? How is anyone going to know the record is available?"

Kaaber leaned his elbows on the small table to lean closer to his beautiful fiancée.

"All of that will be micromanaged in such a way that chatter on social media looks like a grassroots push to spread the word about my music. People in the family will post about it, so their followers will know."

"The family?" Charlie asked.

"You know, the label. Adam and his band will post about it. Some of the other people in the industry who know how to feed the machine, and want the execs to owe them one, will jump on it."

The couple sat across from each other with a bottle of wine, stemless wine glasses, and plates of hors d'oeuvre between them. Kaaber had been to dinner with Charlie thousands of times before, but he felt like he was experiencing everything for the first time this week.

"I'm so fucking lucky. All my dreams are coming true. I get to marry the girl of my dreams. I'm going to have a record out tomorrow. If I wasn't me, I'd hate me."

Charlie laughed. "So, you're sticking with the engagement thing, for sure? What if you have groupies and Victoria's Secret models trying to steal you away from me?"

Kaaber studied her face for a hint of seriousness. "You gotta be kidding me. You were my dream girl from the first second that I saw you. I would have put up with a low IQ, shallowness, ahhh ... a militant hillbilly father or a domineering mother. I didn't care what baggage you had, I just wanted to walk beside you. And then I found out that you're smart, strong, and compassionate, and I love your family more than my own ... there is no improving on what we have, and nothing could touch it." He leaned forward a little to place his lips over hers for a few seconds.

"Okay, good. This is all happening so suddenly, I don't know what's real anymore. I mean, I didn't even know you were taking guitar lessons on Tuesday nights, or that you're a great singer. You never sang—not even along with Pandora. Everyone sings, even people who can't. I would think singing as well as you do, you'd want to be doing it all the time."

"Yeah, well, it made me sad, honestly. I thought I had to put those dreams behind me, but when I sold the place to Adam and got to know him a little bit, I grabbed my balls and decided to show him what I could do. I figured the worst thing that could happen would be him laughing at me, and then we'd never see each other again, which was likely anyway unless he bought another place in Manhattan in the near future."

"Well, you really are an inspiration, Sasha. I am so proud of you." Charlie smiled at him. She had tears in her eyes.

"Stop it. No crying. It's all good stuff. I'm happy for us because we're going to tour the country, we're gonna do good things for kids with cancer, and do benefits to raise money for public school music programs, and we're gonna give back like crazy all over the place."

Charlie raised her eyebrows. "Whew. I guess I'd better buckle up."

Kaaber's phone rang. He fished it out of his pocket, looked at the screen, and lay it face down on the table.

"You don't need to get that?"

"No one is more important that the person who has my full attention right now."

Charlie laughed. "We'll see if that's still true in twenty-four hours."

Kaaber raised his glass. "To promises made and promises kept. You will always be my top priority. Until we have children then you'll have to share top billing."

Charlie laughed and clinked her glass against his. "How about you let me get used to being engaged to a rock star before you knock me up? Things are moving fast enough, Kaaber."

"Baby, things are finally right on track."

———

It was well after midnight before Kaaber had the chance to listen to his messages. He left Charlie sleeping in his bedroom and snuck to the kitchen. Kelly Bailey called four times in the last six hours. Kaaber's stomach flipped around as he played the first voice mail.

"Hey Kaaber, it's Kelly. Just calling to see how you're doing. How the record is coming along. Ummmm, call me back, okay? Hey, my mom is home now. She's doing great, by the way, so, um, that's great. Ok. Talk soon."

Kaaber pressed "delete" and "play."

"Hey Kaaber, sorry to bother you again. Just wanted to say if you have a minute, I'd really like to talk to you, it's very important, so, even if it's late, please give me a call. Thanks."

Kaaber sighed, then proceeded to the next message.

"Hey, me again. Ah, could you call me? I think I'm losing it a little bit here. I need to talk to you. I, ah, tried to, ah, write a song today because I was feeling inspired and, well, it didn't, um … anyway, I think I just need to talk to someone who knows what I'm going through because it isn't like I can talk to many people about this, so … please call me, okay?"

Kaaber violently pressed "delete" and paced around the kitchen wondering if he should delete the last message before listening to it. His curiosity got the better of him, and he pressed play.

"Kaaber?" Kelly's voice broke. "I ..." He sniffed and exhaled. "I really need to talk to you. You were right. You were right. You said I shouldn't give this up and ..." he sobbed. "I'm so thankful that my mom is going to be okay. There's no comparison, but I don't even know who I am now. I gave the thing that defined me ... to you. And I can't live without it. I can't. I can't. I can't. Please. We have to talk, okay? I really need to talk to you."

Kaaber hit the delete button on his display screen ten times in rapid succession. He quickly paced around the island in his kitchen as he let out muted growls of frustration. He looked at the phone in his hand and whispered to it, "Fuck you, Kelly. Fuck. You. This is mine now. You got what you wanted; I got what I wanted—the deal's done. I fucking told you not to do it. You were the one who talked me into it, and you don't get to come back now and ruin this for me."

Kaaber walked and growled some more. He dialed the first three digits of Kelly's phone number to deliver the speech he had just spewed. He stood in the dark kitchen looking at the glowing screen and picked out the remaining numbers with his eyes. He growled again and turned off the phone. Kelly had nursed the talent that he now harbored. He had nurtured it, grown it, and developed it. Kaaber had only possessed it for a short time, and he already considered it the most valuable thing in his life. He would do anything to make sure that Davis was paid in full so that he would never be without this ability. It was priceless. He couldn't let himself imagine how Kelly must feel after losing it, but the sound of the teenager's excruciated voice gave him a taste of the pain.

"Fuck. You. Kid," Kaaber whispered as he blocked Kelly's number.

Kaaber took a deep breath, grabbed a bottle of water from the refrigerator, and went back to bed.

CHAPTER TWENTY-FIVE

CONSIDERING THE LARGE AMOUNT OF money involved, the sale was negotiated and closed very quickly. Twenty-four hours after Mauro bid on the ability to paint like the greatest contemporary artist of our time, he owned the rights to the priceless gift. His million-dollar deposit had been transferred from his account, and he was on the way to the meeting where he would take ownership. Wagner sat beside him on the subway.

"What if they recognize you?" Mauro asked.

"I been thinkin' about that. I can picture Davis's face—every detail. I imagined how he would look all these years later, but I bet he hasn't thought about me too much. Davis is the most neurotic guy you ever met. I'm sure I'm not a legend in the agency—maybe an urban legend. Davis will be at the closing today, no doubt. He loves this part where he gets to ride in on his chariot and seal a deal his agents worked to nail down. He likes being the hero who makes the dream come true. I'm sure there have been many generations of agents between my time and now. I bet he won't recognize me, but if he does, I'll see it in his eyes and I'll strike first."

"I say we don't give anyone the chance to recognize us. The second we see him; we go for his throat. If we have to tap dance a little with the lower-level guys, we can do that, but we can't let 'em take any blood from me or anything in case they can see the football stuff in there."

Wagner laughed. "What do think, they have some sort of scanner that's gonna tell them all about you?"

"Well, don't they? This is Space Odyssey meets NASA meets Dr. Jekyll meets Dr. Kavorkian … I don't know. What they can do is impossible, so why shouldn't I assume they can do everything?" Mauro wiped sweat from his forehead.

"They aren't looking at your genome. You're the mark willing to spend ten lifetimes of earnings to have something special. If you were already special, you wouldn't be a client."

The subway jerked to a stop and the two men got off the train. They didn't speak as they walked seven blocks to the clinic where they had been directed to go.

When they got to the door, Mauro pressed the combination he was given into the keypad. The door made a series of loud clicking sounds and Wagner grabbed the handle, pulling the door open for Mauro. "Wasn't too long ago we ran for our lives out of a place like this. You sure we wanna walk in there?"

Mauro walked past him into a large, open lobby. The area was well lit and white tiles gleamed from the walls. The flooring was hand scraped mahogany. There were no chairs, and no one came to greet them.

Wagner held the door open behind him until Mauro scolded him. "Shut it."

When the door closed, it made another series of clicks as it locked itself.

There was a long hallway straight ahead. Mauro scanned the ceilings for cameras. The bubbles of blackened glass told him that they were not alone. He walked directly under one and waved at it with a wide smile. "Fred Caruso here for my ten a.m."

Mauro thought he heard a motor inside the bubble, but he couldn't be sure.

"Some operation they have here," Wagner said.

The men turned toward the sound of footsteps that bounced off the hard surfaces. A young man wearing a doctor's coat rounded a corner that had not previously been discernible.

"Mr. Caruso, you are right on time." The doctor smiled and held his hand out to Mauro.

"This is my brother, Bill," Mauro introduced Wagner.

"I'm Dr. Johnson. Nice to meet you. Did you come for moral support, Bill?" The doctor asked.

"Yeah. Something like that," Wagner set his feet shoulder width apart and stood facing the doctor whom he outweighed by at least fifty pounds of muscle.

"You're a good brother," Dr. Johnson said. "Mr. Caruso I am very sorry to have to report that we have had an issue. Something that has never happened to us before."

Mauro and Wagner instinctively shifted their stances to be facing each other so that they could watch the full spectrum of the room by scanning the space at each other's back.

"You see, we do not yet have possession of the commodity." Dr. Johnson smiled again. "It was a matter of scheduling and I'm afraid that making your appointment for today was an error on the side of optimism."

"You don't have the commodity," Mauro repeated.

"No, sir. Not at this moment, but we expect to have it in our possession, perhaps as soon as tomorrow."

"Perhaps? I made a million-dollar deposit for an asset, not a hypothetical."

"I understand your concern, Mr. Caruso. Mr. Davis sends his most sincere regrets—as I said this has never happened in all the years that The Davis Agency has been doing business. That's why Mr. Davis has offered the use of his Park Avenue apartment and his car while you are here in New York waiting to complete the transaction."

Wagner shifted his chin slightly to the right. Mauro read "no" and agreed by tilting his head upward.

"That won't be necessary, but I would like to have the funds transferred into an account with both of our names on it until we are able close the deal."

I understand and I will send you the account information within the hour. The Davis Agency values the trust and integrity of our clients, and we maintain our spotless reputation by conducting all our business in a transparent manner."

Mauro had to stifle a scoff.

"Can you estimate a realistic time frame for rescheduling?" Mauro asked.

"I would hate to inconvenience you or embarrass myself by guessing. I held out hope that the delivery would show up this morning, but it has not."

"Is it on the way? Is it in transit, or—"

"Mr. Caruso, you are paying good money to avoid concern over such technicalities. I assure you that everything possible is being done to transport your purchase in the most expeditious manner. If you wish to reconsider Mr. Davis's offer to make yourselves comfortable at his penthouse, we will contact you there as soon as we have word."

"You know how to reach me." Mauro stared at the doctor the same way he used to challenge an offensive lineman to hit him. The doctor hesitated and then the phony smile crossed his face once again.

"You will hear from me very soon. I'll have your account information and update you on any new developments."

Mauro nodded. He and Wagner heard the door locks clicking at the main entrance. Mauro looked into the camera again—he hoped that Davis himself was watching on a monitor somewhere. He stared just long enough into the blacked-out glass bubble. Wagner took the first step toward the door and Mauro followed wordlessly; he had already said enough.

On the street, the men walked the opposite direction from which they had come. They waited ten blocks before either of them spoke.

"Now what?" Wagner asked when they were forced to wait for crossing traffic.

"The ad said that ability being offered was comparable to a certain someone's." Mauro faced oncoming traffic like everyone else pushing up against him and waited for an opportunity to walk against the light. "It's not comparable. It's *exactly*."

"Yeah, I know." Wagner was looking the same direction.

"So, if they don't have it, someone else does, and that someone is in a shitload of trouble."

The last car passed and walkers swarmed the street. Mauro and Wagner fought their instincts to stay in front of the pack and walked at a slower pace.

"What are you thinkin'? It was stolen?"

"How do you lose track of somethin' like that?" Mauro asked.

"You know they already have a team down there looking for it."

"Maybe we should be down there looking for them. Someone should be watching over the family. You know that's where Davis sent his guys first."

"Mauro, what are we? The FBI?"

"We were ready to take down whoever we encountered today, right?"

"We need to get to Davis. How does going twelve hundred miles away from where he is get us closer to him?"

"He could be anywhere. Just because this used to be his base doesn't mean he's here. That's why we gotta make him come to us."

Wagner was silent.

"You wanna finish this, right?" Mauro stopped walking and looked at Wagner.

"I wouldn't be here if I didn't."

"Well, let's finish it, then."

CHAPTER TWENTY-SIX

"**M**RS. MARCOT, MAY I HAVE a word with you?" Matthew called to the back of the woman's perfectly curled bob. When she turned to see who was calling to her, the wave of hair acted as one piece; every strand remained stuck to the one next to it.

"Mrs. Marcot, we haven't vetted any meet and greets," a man wearing a dark suit stepped between her and Matthew.

"It's fine, Mr. Kane. This young man doesn't appear to be a threat." She smiled at Matthew. "Can I help you? Oh, I'm sorry Matthew. I didn't recognize you at first."

"Um, it's okay. I have a question … about your family crest."

Matthew noticed three other men in dark suits coming toward them from the school's main foyer.

"I'm sorry. It probably seems weird that I followed you; I just thought if I could catch you—"

"Mr. Newcombe-Drake, shouldn't you be on your way to class?" Principal Evan's voice came from behind Matthew.

"Yes, Ma'am." He turned around, but Mrs. Marcot reached out and caught his arm.

"I understand how important it is to get back to work, Mrs. Evans. After all, that's why I felt the calling to establish a scholarship program here in my family's name, but if it isn't too much of an imposition, I would appreciate a moment to catch up with Matthew."

"Oh." Principal Evans looked embarrassed. "I didn't realize you knew each other."

"I knew Matthew's grandfather, Thad. I was on the west coast when he passed and haven't yet been able to offer the proper condolences."

"Of course, Mrs. Marcot. Please use my office. It's right through that door." Mrs. Evans indicated which of the row of featureless doors was hers.

"Thank you kindly, Principal Evans. Gentlemen, you can wait outside. Matthew and I won't be long."

The security team didn't look pleased, but they had been instructed.

"Have you ever been in here before?" Mrs. Marcot raised her eyebrows at Matthew.

"Only to drop things off, Mrs. Marcot. I promise."

"I spent an inordinate amount of time in the principal's office during my secondary school years. I was never the teacher's pet."

Matthew laughed. "That's hard to imagine."

"Oh, yes. I was too smart for my own good, and only too proud to show off. My energy was misdirected, of course, but one doesn't realize that until later."

Matthew pulled a chair away from the desk for Mrs. Marcot to sit down.

"Just like your grandfather ... a gentleman."

"Did you really know him or were you just saving my bacon out there?" Matthew asked.

"We were acquaintances," Mrs. Marcot answered slowly.

"What I really wanted to ask you about was the symbol in your family crest. The one in the upper right-hand corner. I've only seen that symbol once before today, and I was wondering if you could tell me what significance it has."

Mrs. Marcot's face didn't reveal any feeling or judgment regarding what Matthew's inquiry.

"Where do you think you saw the symbol?"

"I'm sure it's exactly the same. I'm an artist. I study lines, curves, and spatial orientation, so I'm absolutely certain."

"Where, dear?" Mrs. Marcot said slowly.

"My grandfather drew it on a letter he wrote to me before he died."

Mrs. Marcot seemed to be considering her answer carefully, but when she spoke, she only said, "I see."

"So, can you tell me what it means?"

Mrs. Marcot studied Matthew's face. "You must have been very close to your grandfather."

"Yes. He started teaching me to paint when I was little. About three, I guess. My mom was an only child, and she never showed an interest or an aptitude for art, so when I wanted to play with his brushes and slop colors on his canvases, he was thrilled. We kind of bonded over that. We were really similar."

Mrs. Marcot smiled. "My granddaughter and I have the same kind of relationship."

Matthew smiled and nodded his understanding.

"Your grandfather wanted you to know something about him. That's why he left you that symbol. Far be it for me to deny a man's dying wish, but I'm hesitant to provide you with information that might confuse your worldview."

"Some pretty confusing and scary stuff has happened to me since my grandfather died, Ma'am and if you could help me understand any of it, I'd be very grateful."

"I'd better advise my team that I might be a while."

CHAPTER TWENTY-SEVEN

"**S**O LET ME GET THIS straight. You were in a band in college?"

"Yes." Kaaber answered the late night TV host's question.

"And you guys were … good, bad, what?"

"We were okay, but the chemistry wasn't right, or the timing wasn't right … whatever that indefinable ingredient is, we didn't have it."

The show host laughed.

"But if they had a guy like you, how could it fail?"

Kaaber laughed. "The guys in my college band were good musicians. I just think it wasn't the right time and place."

"So, you move to New York, forget about music, and become a real estate agent? Knowing you in the capacity we do now, it's like picturing Michael Jackson showing properties to clients." The audience laughed at the seemingly impossible scenario.

"Yeah, I sold real estate until very recently, but it was really was good to me," Kaaber defended himself. "A little more cutthroat than the music industry though, so I like music better."

The studio filled with the squeal of girls happy to hear Kaaber's devotion to music.

"I bet you do," Jimmy laughed.

"Music is a disease really. Once you get the fever, it never fully goes away, so I started messing around with my guitar again, and I took lessons from a legit master, you know, rather than trying to figure it out by myself."

"That helps!" Jimmy laughed.

"It sure did. One thing kind of led to another as they say."

"You sold a house to someone in the industry …" Jimmy baited.

"Yeah, we all know Adam." Kaaber gestured towards the audience who cheered affirmatively. "I sold him a house and then I did something very unprofessional for a real estate agent, I sent him a demo." Kaaber laughed.

"And thank God you did, right? What if you had maintained your professionalism?"

"I wouldn't have the number one album right now."

The crowd cheered again.

"All right, we're going to pause and when we come back, Kaaber is going to perform."

The director signaled the host and Jimmy broke character.

"Okay, guy, go right over there where you did the sound check earlier. Just follow directions and they'll tape the performance segment. You'll come back here right after, no break in between, and we'll close the show. Okay?"

"Yeah, thanks." Kaaber looked for Charlie in the audience as he walked across the set. He stopped dead in his tracks at the sight of Kelly's face. For a moment he couldn't breathe. He blinked hard and realized that the boy he thought was Kelly was far older and had darker hair.

"Kaaber, need you on your mark," the director said over the P.A.

"Sorry, yeah."

Kaaber took several deep breaths.

"It's okay to be nervous, it's endearing. Just remember we're all pulling for you." The director's voice was in his in-ear monitors now. "I'm gonna cue your drummer and he's going to count you in, just like in rehearsal. Stand-by. Here we go."

Kaaber heard the click in his ears, and he closed his eyes. He immersed himself in the song and his performance was flawless. Before he knew it, his first national television appearance was over, and Charlie was in his arms congratulating him.

"Go home and watch it, you're gonna be happy." Jimmy shook Kaaber's hand quickly and disappeared into his dressing room.

"You were amazing!" Charlie's cheeks had trail marks from the waterfall of tears that continued to flow.

"Thanks, babe."

"How did it feel? For us, watching, it was like we were transported to a place where everything was perfect."

"It felt good."

"Good? That's all you can say? It was magic, Sasha. We all felt it. Don't tell me you didn't feel that."

"No, yeah, it felt great. I guess I'm still a little bit in shock." Kaaber laughed and kissed Charlie sweetly. "Let's get out of here, it feels like the walls are coming down around us."

The stage was being struck around them.

"Let's go celebrate!" Charlie suggested. "Hey, I have an idea. It's Tuesday. Where's that place you used to go after guitar lessons on Tuesdays? Where you went to see that kid perform. Go sit in with him! Wouldn't that be awesome? You could get him some publicity, I bet. Someone would tape you and put it on YouTube."

"I'm just breaking as an artist right now. I don't have the pull to help anyone else out yet."

"Oh my God, of course you do! You have the number one album in the country—"

"Jesus, I said no!" Kaaber snapped. "We're going home. Got it?"

The hurt showed on Charlie's face. "Why don't you go home?" She hurried to the exit and left Kaaber standing alone on the stage.

CHAPTER TWENTY-EIGHT

Matthew drew the symbol on a piece of paper from the principal's desk.

"See? It's exactly the same as your family crest."

Mrs. Marcot nodded. "Indeed. It is a symbol of an exclusive organization whose members have worldwide influence. Both your grandfather and I were involved."

"Organization? Like a secret society? Like the Illuminati?"

Mrs. Marcot let out a genuine laugh. "We are not nearly as sexy or interesting as the Illuminati."

"So, how long did you know my grandfather?"

"We attended many events together over several decades. I always found Thad to be an intelligent and conscientious gentleman."

"Yeah, that was Gramps." Matthew smiled. "Do you think that this organization that you are a part of could be ... dangerous in any way? I mean, I wonder if some of the problems I'm having lately are because he was part of this group."

"What do you mean?"

"This is going to sound crazy. I haven't even told my parents ..." Matthew stopped talking and pressed his fingers together, resting his pointers against his lips.

"I doubt that your parents know about our group, Matthew. I think your grandfather wanted you to know about us, so perhaps I am the perfect person with whom you should be talking."

Matthew looked out the window and drew in a deep breath. "All right. I need to know that this conversation doesn't leave this room."

"You can trust me, Matthew."

"Someone recently suggested that I might have inherited my grandfather's painting ability. Not like a genetic trait that was passed through DNA, but the exact talent he had. Like that it could be transferred from him to me." Matthew smirked and raised his eyebrows, but Mrs. Marcot's face became serious.

"I think you should tell me everything, Matthew." The older woman sat straighter in her chair.

After he was finished, Mrs. Marcot questioned Matthew several times about Thad's final wishes and arrangements. She suggested that he might have secretly requested that Mary carry out a task on his behalf after his death. Just when Matthew was sure that Mrs. Marcot hadn't heard the part of his story about him being abducted, she advised Matthew to go home and do just as the kidnappers had instructed—tell no one else what he told her. She left two of her security team in Miami to watch over Matthew's family, but she assured the young man that the worst was probably over. She reasoned that hurting Thad's family would serve no purpose. Rather, it would draw unwanted attention.

On the walk home from school, Matthew still couldn't help looking over his shoulder. There was no BMW following him, but after the day he'd had, it was impossible to relax. His shoes were finally beginning to dry; the South Florida heat was evaporating the remaining moisture.

Matthew pulled his ear buds from his backpack and listened to classical music as he made the habitual trek. Nothing looked familiar anymore. He knew every crack in the Coconut Grove sidewalk, but it all seemed new to him. He jumped off the walkway as a car backed out of a driveway—an embarrassing overreaction.

Matthew tried to concentrate on the music, but his mind was spinning, attempting to reconcile the events of the day. It had been terrifying to be at the mercy of those men, but he hadn't been hurt. Knowing they had violated the sanctity of his home while his mother was alone and defenseless made Matthew boil with rage. But that was just an emotion, and no physical harm was done.

Mrs. Marcot assured Matthew that his grandfather was a very wise and caring man, and that he would never put his family in any danger. It hadn't felt like that a few hours ago, but Matthew agreed with her now.

He knew it was important to act like everything was fine. He would go to school and work, as usual. Hang out with friends on the weekends, as usual. He would have to find a way to ignore the sci-fi thriller his life had become.

Matthew reached the end of his driveway, stopped at the mailbox, and went into the house. He locked the door behind him.

"Hey, you! How was your day?" His mother called from the kitchen.

"Good Mom, but it's better now." He gave his mother a big hug.

"Wow! This is like old times when you would come home from elementary school."

"Well, I forgot to bring home groceries, so I'm trying to divert your attention."

"Well played." Matthew's mother rose onto her toes to kiss his cheek. "We haven't ordered pizza in forever, so let's do that."

"I love you, Mom."

"I love you too, Matthew."

Mary picked up her cell phone and began placing the pizza order. Matthew walked to the front of the house and checked the front door; it was locked.

He looked at the sliding glass doors on his way back into the kitchen. "Hey, Mom, I'm going to take some of that PVC Dad has in the garage and cut it to fit the sliders. I saw on the news that there have been some home invasions around here."

"Having PVC pipe laying in the tracks is going to look weird, isn't it?"

"So, don't look at it. It'll prevent someone from lifting the door off the track and getting inside."

"You're such a worrywart, Matthew. Of all the houses in the Grove, no one is going to invade ours."

"It'll give me something to do after dinner, and that pipe has been laying there for years. Don't argue with me, little lady." Instead of walking past his mother to get to the stairs, he lifted her up and set her down in another location.

"Why didn't I have a daughter?" She laughed.

"Girls are nothing but drama," Matthew said over his shoulder. "Be thankful!"

Matthew went upstairs to take a shower.

CHAPTER TWENTY-NINE

THE FLORIDA HEAT ASSAULTED MAURO and Wagner as soon as they stepped onto the jet way.

"How can anyone live here? No one wants to go to Hell, and yet people live in Miami. Far as I can tell it's the same place." Mauro pulled his carry-on and stayed a step ahead of Wagner as they deplaned from their flight.

"Good news is, it's nine-thirty in the morning. It's only gonna get worse," Wagner said.

"I thought it was autumn."

"No seasons here, buddy. There's just Hell and Hell Plus. You were the one who had to get down here immediately, so don't complain or I'm getting on the next flight back to JFK."

"C'mon, Wagner, I'll make sure you get down to South Beach to see the chicks in bikinis, and have one of those girly drinks you like so much."

The two followed the signs to the rental cars and picked up a black Chrysler 200 from a company that didn't require a reservation.

They threw their bags into the trunk and headed toward Coconut Grove.

"So, now we're here, what're we doin'? Besides sweating our balls off?" Wagner asked as Mauro tried to stay with the flow of traffic.

The Chrysler narrowly missed being sideswiped by someone trying to make a fifth lane on the four-lane highway.

"Damn, you think driving in New York is rough, this don't make sense at all. These people are crazy!" Mauro leaned on the horn like a true New Yorker.

"You gotta be careful with that. Remember they shoot people on the Interstate down here all the time."

"No, I think that's phased out now, like killing the German tourists. Miami is just as safe as New York now. You got that address?"

Wagner began setting up the navigation app on his phone. After he promised that he was the passenger, twice, the automated female voice said, "Let's go."

The route took them to Coconut Grove where they easily found the Newcombe-Drake home.

"Pretty place," Mauro commented.

"Yeah. Doesn't look like anyone's here."

"That's a good spot to sit and watch the driveway at least. That hedge covers a lot of the front of the house, but if we parked there, we could see the comings and goings." Wagner pointed across the street to a Cuban coffee shop nestled into the neighborhood. The converted house was much smaller than most of the homes that surrounded it, but it looked like a busy place.

"Perfect. We'll hang out there right after we go to the school and familiarize ourselves with the area."

Wagner typed in the second address, and they covered the short distance in a few minutes. The school parking lot was full.

"The bell is at three-thirty and Matthew works at Publix today bagging groceries."

"How d'you know?" Mauro asked.

"Instagram. You can find out anything about anyone on Instagram. People are stupid; they post everything. *'We're on vacation in Tahiti—come rob our house!'* Stupid. Kids are worse. Matthew updates his status hourly—not hard to see a pattern."

Mauro shook his head.

"Where's the Hospice?"

"The one where Newcombe died?"

"Yeah. I want to go there next."

Wagner changed the navigation destination.

The perky female voice was as excited to go there as she was the last two addresses. "Let's go!"

"What do you think we're going to be able to find out at Hospice? They have laws about what they can say to family and we're not family."

Mauro smiled at Wagner. "I have papers in my carry-on that look exactly like a subpoena signed by Dade County Judge Herman Anderson."

"Your new internet buddies?"

"There's nothing you can't get, man. It's unbelievable."

When they arrived at Hospice, Mauro went to the trunk and got a tie from his luggage. He added it to the short sleeved button-down and dress pants that he already wore, and hoped that it would pass for Miami business casual.

Wagner stayed in the car with the AC running as Mauro rehearsed the lines that worked on an episode of CSI.

A young Latin woman behind the desk smiled when Mauro approached.

"May I help you?"

"Hello, yes, thank you. I need a copy of a medical file; I have a subpoena." Mauro held up his envelope.

"Ah, yes, for Mr. Newcombe. Your office called. I have it …" she stood up and walked to a tall file cabinet behind her. A manila envelope was sitting on top. "Right here." She handed the envelope to Mauro.

"Thank you very much." He turned to walk toward the door.

"Um, Sir, I need you to sign for that."

"Oh, right, I'm sorry. Of course."

The smiling receptionist handed him a clipboard with a little sticker indicating where he needed to sign. Mauro slopped some swirls on the line, handed the clipboard back to her and called over his shoulder, "Thanks again."

"Sir? Sorry, but I do need that paperwork. I'm going to need to show justification for allowing those file to leave the premises."

Mauro shook his head and laughed. "I don't know what's wrong with me today. Too much to do, I guess." He smiled at the young woman and handed her the envelope containing the counterfeit subpoena.

"Thank you very much, Mister ...?" She was looking at his shirt for some sort of ID.

"Melcher. And thank you."

Mauro made for the exit. The young woman looked down at the signature, then at the man rushing through the door.

A nurse came to the front desk. "Who was that?"

"Someone from the DA's office picking up a file. Some people really can't stand hospitals. He left skid marks on the way out."

"It's not the hospital that scares people, it's the death, and that's all we have here. I want to leave skid marks some days myself." The nurse smiled, helped herself to a cup of coffee, and went back to work.

Mauro threw the file in Wagner's lap and had the car in reverse before he closed the car door behind him.

"What the hell?"

"She had the file ready. Someone else must have called and arranged to come get it."

"Holy shit. And you just happened to get there first?"

"Yeah, and I don't wanna be here when Davis's guys come to get their file."

"Holy shit," Wagner said again.

"We're one step ahead right now. We just gotta stay that way and we'll be fine."

"Find us a place to go to look at that file."

Wagner put Starbucks into his map app and nine came up with five miles of their location. They followed directions to the nearest one. Mauro and Wagner went through the drive-through, ordered two grande iced-coffees, and parked the car.

Mr. Newcombe had only been at Hospice for two months. The file wasn't very thick. Wagner stumbled upon the information first.

"I know where the commodity is," he announced.

Mauro looked up from the page he was reading. "Where?"

"It went down the drain. Literally." He handed the last page in the file to Mauro.

"That smart bastard," Mauro marveled.

"So, you think he made a deal with Davis and then backed out this way?"

"He was terminal. If he made a deal with Davis, he got paid. Then he backed out this way," Wagner confirmed.

"You think Davis already paid Newcombe?"

"Davis would never advertise a product that he didn't have under contract. I know this sounds ridiculous considering who we're talking about and what type of business he runs, but he's very strict about protocol."

"You think the old man screwed him over?"

Wagner smiled and nodded. "I'd bet that's exactly what happened."

"Why would Newcombe kick the bee's nest like that? Didn't he know they'd go after his family?"

"Being a public figure like he was, he probably figured his suicide and the method of it would be national news. Davis should have found out that the spring ran dry."

"The talent's gone, but the money has to be somewhere," Mauro reasoned. "Newcombe would leave it to the family. Davis isn't going to let millions slip through his fingers."

"With all of your recent education in money laundering and hiding money, you can probably come up with a few ways to make millions disappear for a while."

"Speaking of millions, I'm gonna check that bank account Dr. Johnson set up yesterday," Mauro said, reaching into the backseat for his laptop. "Money's still there. No messages from Johnson."

"We came down to be guardian angels for the family so, with this much money floating around, we should probably get back to keep an eye on the house."

"Just one second." Mauro grabbed his cell and took a picture of the hospice document detailing Thad Newcombe's suicide. He airdropped it to his laptop, then began composing an email on the Tor Server, and attached the jpeg of the document.

Davis,

According to this, it will be impossible for you to fulfill my purchase. How did you let another one get away from you?

Salvatore Greco

He showed the email to Wagner.

"If I press send, I'm saving us a few days of sitting in this car in the blazing sun while we wait for 'em."

"They'll send an Army, Mauro. Right now, the odds might be more even. No doubt they have a team of sub-contractors down here, but maybe we can walk away from this thing if it's only a few guys. You send that and … talk about kicking the bee's nest."

"We don't want to sideline a few members of the team. We want Davis. This is how we make Davis come to us. He won't be able to resist."

Wagner looked down at his hands.

"We both knew what this trip could mean, Wagner. Living the lives we've had to live ain't living. If we don't stop this guy, what's it all for? He didn't get the chance to kill you and he didn't get my skills, but he took our lives. And he's taken lives every day since."

Wagner turned to face Mauro.

"Go ahead and sign my name too."

CHAPTER THIRTY

KAABER TRAVELED PAST THE SIRIUS XM studios at Rockefeller Center regularly, but since his career change, New York City landmarks had new meaning. He had access now, and the town he called home was revealing itself for the first time.

The Sirius XM studios were clean, bright, and massive. Unlike his first visit to a recording studio, the radio station lived up to his expectations. The green room looked like a luxury suite at The Four Seasons. Rafferty Blake, Kaaber's new publicist, got him there on time, leaving no room for nervousness.

"You're going to do fifteen minutes with the morning show and then they'll cue the performance, which will run three minutes flat. Don't forget to skip the solo and cut the second chorus at the end. Do that, and we'll be right on top of that three-minute mark that they want us to hit. With these guys, the time is the most important thing. You want to be invited back? Be a good guest and keep to the time." Rafferty handed Kaaber a very green liquid in a small glass.

"Shot?" Kaaber asked.

"E3 Live. Great for waking you up and keeping you focused. It's the world's most complete food. I'll give you some pure water after you slam that down."

Kaaber hesitated and then drank the thick fluid.

Rafferty gave him a fatherly nod in spite of being the same age as his client. Manbun notwithstanding, Kaaber trusted his teammate. He was well-known and unanimously liked by everyone in the industry.

His phone calls were answered, and his requests were granted. Rafferty was easy to be around, and Kaaber liked that he wore jeans and a bowtie every day. Anyone under age eighty who rocked a bowtie daily had to be made from good stuff.

"I gave them your backstory, so they'll probably spend most of the time on that. Remember to steer clear of relationship talk. Hit the record hard—get the title on-air every three minutes, at least. Other than that, just be your charming self. Have fun—people can tell when you're faking." Rafferty slapped Kaaber on the back. "Can I get you anything before you go in there?"

Kaaber held up the full bottle of water that Rafferty handed him seconds ago. "This will do it, thanks."

"I'll be right behind you. If they ask anything I want you to dodge, I'll tap your shoulder. The go to if that happens is—"

"The record and repeating the title like a well-trained parrot."

"You're a quick study," Rafferty laughed. "Okay, they're ready for you."

The duo made their way into the studio where they were greeted by three very enthusiastic morning show hosts.

"There he is!" Chrissy C. squealed.

"Oh my, he is even more handsome in person, not that I'm trying to make you feel like a piece of meat, Kaaber." Christina giggled.

"Ladies, you act like we keep you locked up in this room day and night, and you haven't seen a man in years," Eddie remarked.

"We haven't!" They said in unison.

Kaaber sat in the empty chair on the backside of the mixing board, put headphones on, and pulled the boom mic close to his mouth.

"Good morning, Good Morning Crew!" Kaaber laughed.

"Settle in—we're happy to have you here."

"Chrissy is the happiest," Eddie said. "She's single and looking."

"Well, hello Chrissy," Kaaber said in a sexy voice.

"Don't make the man pretend he wants ground beef when he has a steak at home," Eddie teased.

Kaaber laughed.

"Tell us—where you have been all our lives? How dare you keep this talent from the world while you sold real estate?" Eddie asked.

"You know, I never had the confidence to go for it, so I tried a different route, but it felt like I wasn't living an authentic life."

"So, would you go home from work and sing in front of the mirror like I do?" Chrissy asked.

"Actually, music was pretty absent from my life after college."

"How do you not do something you're so good at? Were you, like, amazing at real estate, so that filled the void for you?" Christina asked.

"Well, I was a good salesperson. I worked hard at it, and I was making good money—that felt good. You know, you hear stories about starving artists, and you start to think you made the right choice by having a career that provides well, I guess."

"No one can fault you for that," Eddie said. "But didn't you know? I mean, come on, you watch these talent shows on TV, and you see what's out there. Didn't you know in your heart that you were so much better than every other living, breathing musician?"

Kaaber laughed. "Ah, well, no. I have my own thing, but you're never one-hundred percent sure that what you do is going to resonate with the general public."

"Tell me what it was like in college. Your band must have been huge. Did you guys tour?" Chrissy asked.

"No. We were full-time students. We played at a local bar for fun."

"You make me wonder if I'm awesome at something that I gave up early in life. Like soccer. I quit that. And then I quit karate, basketball, hockey—"

"Why don't you just make the blanket statement that you gave up on any and all physical activity, Eddie? That would be faster," Christina said.

"The Eddie and Chris show can be done with one Chris, you know. Or we can just get two other girls and call them Chrissy and Christina. You know what the constant is?"

Eddie and Kaaber said in unison, "Eddie!"

The whole crew laughed, and Kaaber took control of the conversation.

"Regardless of how long it took me to get here, I'm glad I took the chance and released *Kaaber*. It's being very well received and I'm very proud of it."

"How long have you been sitting on these songs?" Chrissy asked.

"Wrote them all very recently. Music trends are very fluid, so anything I wrote before felt dated. This is all brand-new stuff."

"We have someone on the line who can attest to that, Kaaber. We have a little *This Is Your Life* moment in store for you. We have Billy McIntire on the phone from that college band we were talking about earlier—I think he wants a job. Billy, can you hear me? Say hello to your buddy Kaaber."

"Hey, man." Kaaber's headset delivered a voice that he hadn't heard in years.

"Wow! Hey Billy! How are you doin' man?"

"Not as good as you, bro, but it's all good. It's all good."

"Tell us about Kaaber as a young artist," Eddie prompted.

Billy laughed. "Well, I wouldn't use the word artist. Back in the day Sasha was more into chasing the pootang than rehearsing. I mean, we pounded out some recognizable stuff, but the band was awful."

Kaaber laughed and Rafferty moved from his position behind his client to alongside. Kaaber looked over his right shoulder and saw a question mark on his publicist's face. Kaaber nodded to let him know he could handle the situation.

"So, you guys sucked?" Christina asked.

"Pretty much," Billy said. "I have tapes that we made of live performances, and they aren't very good."

The morning show laughed and Kaaber faked a laugh.

"You have to start somewhere, and I did get a shaky start. Maybe my confidence was low for a very good reason."

Billy spoke up again. "The funny thing is how your voice has changed though, Sasha. Your tone is different, the tambre of your voice is different, not to mention the guitar work. It's like two different people."

Kaaber laughed and agreed with Billy, but his stomach was lurching, and he was beginning to sweat.

"Like I said, we all start somewhere. So, what are you doing now Billy?"

"Nothin' as good as you, brother."

"That makes all of us," Eddie laughed. "It's good to be king, right Kaaber?"

"I don't wanna be king, I just want to play my music. In fact, I'm going to do a song today if you want to hear it."

The girls clapped and begged. Rafferty shook his head; it wasn't time yet. He wanted the full seventeen minutes of on-air time that he negotiated for.

Kaaber stood up and reached for his headphones. "I go in there, right?"

"Can we come into the production room with you?" a Chris asked.

"You ladies stay here, or you'll distract me." Kaaber winked at them and pulled off his headset while the team filled the air with conversation and anticipation.

"Change of format? You want to go back in there and talk about the song after you play?" Rafferty asked as they walked to the studio next door.

"Nope. The interview is over. I'm gonna play and go."

Rafferty nodded. "Okay, the music speaks for itself, so knock 'em dead."

While Kaaber performed his song, Rafferty instructed the morning show team to wrap up the segment. They complimented Kaaber, plugged the release, and said good-bye from the programming studio. Kaaber waved through the glass as he and Rafferty walked down the hall.

Once they were out of the building, Rafferty called their driver and they climbed into the back of the Cadillac Escalade.

"You okay?" Rafferty asked.

"Yeah. I'm sorry. I guess I got nervous."

"You were fine until Billy came on the air and started talking about tapes. Is there anything I need to know? If I need to get ahead of anything, it's better that I know first."

"I guess I just got unnerved that there are tapes out there of me sucking. I bet they'll be on TMZ by this afternoon."

"We can spin that to give every kid hope. It's inspiring to see someone succeed after sticking with it and overcoming the learning curve."

"Still embarrassing."

"Don't sweat it. How bad can it be?"

Kaaber didn't reply.

"How bad is it?"

"I don't know, probably pretty bad."

"The important thing is what you just did in there. Live. And the live performance you gave on Jimmy's show the other night. You're not a studio creation. Embarrassment comes when you get caught lip-syncing or if you Milli Vanilli your way to a Grammy. You're someone who started out slow, stuck with it, and became a formidable artist who has the chops to hang with any of the industry's legends. In fact, that's what we're going to do. I'm not going to acknowledge this at all, and we're going to get you booked with a heritage artist for an award show performance. Who would you want? Clapton? He's very gener-ous with new artists if they have the talent."

"Jesus! Can you stop pushing for a second? I'm still processing what happened in there!" Kaaber yelled.

"Sure. We'll talk about it later."

Rafferty pulled his iPad from his messenger bag and began ma-nipulating the screen.

Kaaber looked out the window and watched the pedestrian traffic on Fifth Avenue. His eyes darted to a young kid with a guitar on the corner. It was Kelly. The kid lifted his chin and Kaaber sat up in his seat to get a better look. It wasn't Kelly. Kaaber's stomach began to roll again.

CHAPTER THIRTY-ONE

MAURO AND WAGNER SAT IN the Chrysler 200 with the engine running and the AC pumping. They had relocated to three different spots in the The Cuban Coffee Café parking lot before the prime piece of real estate that Mauro had been eyeing became available. From where they were now, they could see the Newcome-Drake home, and they had a good view of the street from both directions. There was a lot of traffic flowing in and out of the small coffee shop and the New Yorkers finally succumbed to the temptation to try the Caffe con Leche. With little else to do but look out the windows, they were each on their second little drink and polished off a full bag of torrejas.

"You ever have any second thoughts about selling the football ability, Mauro?"

"I wish I had never met you. No offense. I don't regret not selling, but whether I made the deal or not, my life was over. I just didn't know it at the time."

"I never understood why you didn't just go ahead and play in the NFL anyway."

"That would have kept me in the public eye—made me vulnerable. Davis wouldn't have let me live. I knew too much. I had to go off the grid just like you did."

Wagner checked his side view mirror to make sure no one was approaching the car from behind. "You and me both had promising futures," he said.

"You were making a lot of money, but your conscience wouldn't have let you go on much longer. If you hadn't parted ways with Davis over my case, you would have left him eventually. It was just a matter of time."

"So, you're sayin' my life was over the minute I took the job from him and yours was over the minute you met me."

"Pretty much." Mauro laughed.

"See, all these years I thought of us as each other's salvation."

"I never would have made it out alive that day without you. No doubt about that."

"But the lives we saved weren't really worth livin', were they?"

"We didn't know that back then. We thought we were savin' ourselves."

Wagner sighed and expelled a huge breath of air. "I ain't never been able to get close to a woman for any amount of time. I've put distance between me and my family. I don't have any friends ..."

"Hey! You're hurtin' my feelings."

Wagner laughed. "You know what I mean. All because this prick got us wrapped up his business."

"Once you knew about what they could do, did it make you question everything? I mean, do you wonder about everyone—*is it real*?"

"Man, I hope Michael Jordan was real."

"He didn't come from money. He was real." Mauro nodded his head in affirmation.

"Yeah, good point."

"You think Newcombe was real?"

"I think so. His parents were working people. I think when his wife got sick, he spent his savings, and then felt like he had nothing to show for his life's work. Other than his name, he had nothing to pass on to the next generation. A parasite like Davis probably had his financials and saw the opportunity." Wagner pointed to the street. "Get the tag number of that BMW. It's the third time that car passed by since we've been sitting here."

Mauro took out his phone and snapped a pic.

"Gotta be tons of black BMWs in a neighborhood like this. You sure it's the same one?"

"Yeah. Same flat black spoke wheels each time."

"Think it's them?"

"Yeah."

Mauro looked at Wagner. "However this ends, I'm thankful to you. For what you did for me all those years ago and for what you're doin' now."

"Yeah, well, as a pathetic as it is, you're all I got."

"A VW just pulled in," Mauro leaned closer to Wagner to get a better view. "Mark the time. It's 4:08."

Wagner wrote the time down on a pad of paper he pulled from the map cubby in the car door.

"She pulled into the garage. She's getting out of the car ... walking into the house. Screen door was unlocked ... looks like she went in through the slider there. So that must have been unlocked."

"Not smart Mrs. Newcombe-Drake," Wagner shook his head.

"How long before the son gets home?"

"He works at Publix until six o'clock today. His IG page says that he isn't looking forward to it."

"Stupid kids putting all of their movements online."

"How long do you think this place stays open, Mauro?"

"Yeah, I was wonderin' the same thing. I think their peak business is already over for the day. We're not going to be able to stay here much longer. You notice a sign on the door with their hours?"

"Wasn't one."

"All right. I gotta let out that leche anyway. I'll go in to use the can, but I'm gonna probably have to buy something. You want another bag of those torrejas? Those things were unbelievable."

"Yeah, I'll eat some more of those." Wagner got his wallet out. "You bought last time, so this round is on me. Get two more of those coffees too."

Wagner handed Mauro a twenty. He opened the driver's side door and slammed it shut. Before he reached the Chrysler's bumper, a white box van parked behind the car. Mauro looked to see if the van was waiting for a parking spot when the back door opened and four men burst out of the back.

"Wagner!" Mauro shouted as two of the men rushed him. Mauro felt a stab in his thigh, and he instantaneously felt like he was underwater. His vision was blurry, all he could hear was his was own heartbeat, and his limbs felt incredibly heavy. "Wa—"

Mauro thought he heard the voice of someone who sounded like home. He struggled to maintain consciousness, but it was no use. The last thing he heard before he passed out was a man with a Staten Island accent saying, "Bring the car."

A man dressed in Nike shorts and a sweatshirt ran past The Cuban Coffee Café for the third time that hour. His focus was the opposite side of the street on each of his earlier passes, but he arrived at the corner just in time to see Mauro and Wagner being heaved into the back of the white van. A black BMW traveled under the 30MPH speed limit on the street behind him. The runner paused to buy some time to evaluate the situation. He stretched his right quad, while drinking from a water bottle. When the van sped away from the coffee shop, the BMW picked up speed and followed.

The jogger retrieved a cell phone from his pocket.

"Kane, we have trouble."

CHAPTER THIRTY-TWO

M AURO FOUGHT THE URGE TO try to open his eyes. Instead, he listened. He heard a whirring sound, like some type of machinery or a large appliance was running. No voices. Someone was breathing in an offbeat and labored manner beside him. He felt cold, solid ground under his cheek and noted that he was lying, hogtied, on his stomach. The breathing was coming from the opposite direction that he was facing. Mauro lifted his eyelids so slightly that he hoped it would be imperceptible. Through his eyelashes he saw a very large warehouse, empty, except for a few hanging racks of clothes in dry cleaning bags.

Without turning his head, Mauro tried to see if there were cameras monitoring the interior of the empty expanse. He didn't see any, but he didn't want to risk attracting attention by changing positions to face Wagner.

"Wagner?"

No reply. The breathing continued at its unsteady pace.

Mauro tried raising his voice just a little. "Wagner?"

The breathing stopped for an uncomfortable minute, then continued.

"Wagner!" Mauro whispered loudly.

His partner moaned. Mauro tried resisting against his constraints, but they were secure.

"Wagner, can you hear me?"

"Yeah, Mauro."

Mauro whispered a silent prayer of thanks.

"Are you hurt?"

"I'm okay. Was it a taser?"

"I don't know."

"We aren't blindfolded."

Mauro considered Wagner's point.

"They're gonna kill us," Mauro confirmed.

"Can you get loose?"

"No. I'm bound so tight my limbs are starting to go numb."

"We'll wait for our opportunity, then."

Mauro closed his eyes and thought about his mother. The burden of not knowing her son's fate had shadowed her for so long. Would she finally get closure? Would someone find and identify his body? Mauro pushed the thought from his mind.

"How many did you see?"

"Two guys took you down and there were two more who came for me," Wagner answered.

"Davis must have gotten our email."

Wagner chuckled. "I wish I could have seen his face when he read it."

Footsteps echoed through the warehouse.

Mauro saw four pair of feet headed toward where he and Wagner lay.

"Welcome to Miami," a thick Staten Island accent said at a New York pace.

"You fly in just for us or do you live in this shithole?" Mauro asked.

"Winters down here are better. Summers are hell," the voice answered.

"Yeah, New York winters are rough." Mauro said. "What happens next?"

"It's gonna be pretty brutal. You two pissed someone off so good he's flyin' down."

"Do you feed your prisoners? All I've had all day is that Cuban coffee and those French toast things."

"You think you're at the fuckin' Fontainebleau? We ain't here to make you comfortable. We been ordered to kill you, but not until the big man gets here. He wants to watch."

"Cut the shit. I know you're working for Davis. He won't even come in this room. He'll watch on a computer screen. Could have done that from New York and saved us all some time," Wagner said.

A man with a Cuban accent joined the conversation. "I never seen him. I do contract work for him ten years and I never seen him once."

"Shut up!" Staten Island yelled in a clipped tone. He kneeled down next to Mauro. "You're gonna feel a little pinch."

"Don't hurt me before you kill me," Mauro said.

"You takin' my blood too?" Wagner asked.

"Nope. You get fingerprinted."

"I can tell you who I am. Davis knows me very well. I'm probably the only guy who ever crossed him and lived to tell about it. It's a great story if you want to hear it."

"I don't know why you guys are so talkative. I would think knowing you're gonna be dead soon would make you more … introspective. I think that's the word."

Staten Island finished drawing blood from Mauro. Then he pressed Wagner's thumb and forefinger over an inkpad and rolled it onto a sheet of paper.

"When I do kill you, it's gonna be horrible. That's what the boss wants and that's what I do best. I can get you sedatives if you want to take something now—it'll help you maybe accept it, and maybe be less aware. I mean, I won't knock you out so much that it takes the fun out of it for me, but …"

Neither of the hogtied men replied.

"Suit yourselves," Staten Island said. "I'll be back when the boss gets here."

CHAPTER THIRTY-THREE

MATTHEW DIDN'T RECOGNIZE THE MERCEDES Benz that pulled up next to him as he left Publix. Before he could turn around and run back inside, the window rolled down and Mrs. Marcot's bodyguard called out to him.

"Matthew, you need to come with me. There's been an incident."

Matthew's heart began to race. "Are my parents okay, Mr. Jacobs?"

"Yes. My partner has eyes on the house, but you're not walking home from work tonight. Get in and I'll explain."

Matthew opened the passenger door and slid onto the seat. He placed his backpack on the floor in front of him and the door whooshed shut almost silently as he pulled it closed.

Jacobs eased away from the front of the grocery store and waited until they were mired in street traffic to tell Matthew about what his partner had seen at The Cuban Coffee Café earlier that afternoon.

"What makes you think it's tied to my situation?" Matthew asked.

"You said there was a black 7 series BMW following you and that you were abducted in a white van. Both of those cars were at the scene today."

Matthew ran both of his hands down the front of his face. "So, they were still watching me. Who were the guys they grabbed? How are they connected?"

"I was wondering if maybe you could shed some light on that, Matthew. Did you possibly have any business with these two men?"

"Business? What kind of business could I have with anyone? I'm a high school kid."

"A high school kid who some people think may have something very valuable. Maybe something that you could cash in on and live on comfortably for the rest of your life."

"What are you talking about? I'm the person you're supposed to be protecting, not the one you should be interrogating. Maybe you should have gone after the bad guys so you could ask them these questions."

"My partner called it in to Miami PD. He has a contact there keeping us informed. The two men who were abducted were in a rental car that was stolen from the scene. Miami PD is tracing the car."

"Where are my parents?"

"Both home. Both unaware."

"Can I tell them about this now? About you guys and what happened to me? I mean … it's clearly not over. I've kept my mouth shut, but that isn't keeping them away."

"We anticipated that they would be watching the house. What they don't know is that we were watching them, or that Miami PD is involved now. We're in a good position. I don't think you have to tell your parents anything at this point, but Mrs. Marcot would like to talk to you."

Matthew got his phone out of his pocket and started looking for her number in his contacts.

"She said that she would like for you to wait for a time when you are completely alone. She wants a face-to-face call, if you don't mind."

Matthew set his phone in his lap. "I, ah … I guess that's okay, but it feels terrible keeping all of this from my parents. I mean, it's this big, huge thing and they could be in danger. It's irresponsible not to tell them."

"Rest assured that my partner is monitoring them while I'm with you. Phillips followed your mother to work this morning and saw her walk into the school. He went back to the house to watch while you were all away, then he followed her home. We don't feel like your dad is a target because he's so high profile in the community."

"Yeah, but these guys are obviously capable of taking down two grown men, so they could grab my dad the same way."

"I understand your concern. I'll ask Mrs. Marcot to fly another man in overnight. We will have one guard for each of you by the time you leave the house tomorrow morning."

Matthew smirked. "I can't believe this. I can't believe it's only getting worse. I don't have anything—I don't have what they're looking for and they know that now, so why don't they leave me alone? And who are these other guys?"

"We're finding out everything we can, Matthew. No one in your family has plans to go out tonight, right?"

"Not that I know of, no."

"Phillips and I will be watching the house and by morning, we'll have reinforcements and intel. We can reassess the situation at that time. For tonight, follow the plan. Go home and do what you normally do."

"Easier said than done, Jacobs. I don't *normally* keep things of this magnitude from my parents."

"I'll have more information for you ASAP."

"Yeah." Matthew picked his backpack up from the floor. "You better drop me here in case they're watching. I don't usually get rides home from work. I walk."

Phillips is on the next block. He's walking a dog on the opposite side of the street. I'm going to get you close to him before I let you out."

"Where'd he get a dog?" Matthew asked.

Jacobs didn't answer. He drove slowly down Matthew's street until they saw a man walking a dog coming toward them.

"Okay. You can get out here. Phillips is going to walk a little farther, then turn around so he will be following at your back. I'll go watch the house until you both get there."

Matthew climbed out of the car. Before he closed the door behind him, he leaned into the cabin. "Thanks. Sorry if I seem ungrateful."

"It's okay, Matthew. Don't worry, we're watching. No one is going to get to you or your parents."

Matthew closed the door and walked the rest of the way home with a yippy little mutt panting across the street and behind him.

He did his best to pretend that nothing out of the ordinary was going on as he engaged in conversation with his parents at dinner. After helping his mother clean the kitchen, Matthew went upstairs to his room to do homework, as was routine. He locked his door, got his iPad, and placed a FaceTime call to Mrs. Marcot, who picked up right away.

"Hello Matthew. Thank you for calling."

"Mr. Jacobs said that you wanted a face to face with me."

"Yes, dear. I wanted to make sure you were holding up all right under the strain. I was very concerned about you after I heard what happened today."

"Yeah, I don't know what to make of it."

"Jacobs and Phillips have contacts within the Miami PD. We will find out what they know. Until then, I'm sending two more men tonight. They flew out two hours ago."

"Thank you, Mrs. Marcot. As I was saying to Jacobs though, I really think it's time to tell my parents."

"That time may come soon, Matthew, but I want to leave them out of it for now."

A female voice came from behind Mrs. Marcot. Matthew looked more closely at the scenery around the older woman. The room she was in was as elaborate as he expected. He could see a high, arched doorway constructed of mahogany, and an ornate tapestry hanging beside it. A young woman with violet hair was entering the room.

"Gram?" She saw the iPad her grandmother held. "Oh, I'm sorry Gram. I didn't know you were on a call."

"It's okay, dear. This is the young man that I told you about. Matthew, meet my granddaughter, Cassandra."

Matthew smiled. "Nice to meet you," he said, but he was thinking, *Oh, so you can tell your family about me, but I can't tell my family about meeting you.*

"Nice to meet you, Matthew!" Cassandra gave a friendly wave to the image on the screen.

"Matthew and I haven't discussed you much, dear, other than in comparing his relationship with his late grandfather to my relationship with you. They were very close."

"Yes, I'm sorry to hear of his passing."

"Cassie?" Another voice came from the background.

Matthew looked behind Mrs. Marcot where he saw a young man enter the room. Matthew recognized him immediately. He gasped and the image of his face, filled with fear, momentarily froze on the screen after he hit "end." The man behind Mrs. Marcot had been in the driveway of the Newcombe-Drake home, and had stalked Matthew around Coral Gables in a black BMW right after his grandfather's death.

CHAPTER THIRTY-FOUR

KAABER AND CHARLIE WORKED TOGETHER like seasoned line cooks. The two prepared the Salmon Wellington recipe frequently enough to know their roles without direction, leaving time for non-food related conversation.

"How was rehearsal today?"

"Went great. These guys I'm going to be on the road with are beasts. I mean, they all read music, but they instinctively have the feel for the material as well. We've just started running these songs and I feel like we could play the first date tomorrow."

"And they have tour experience?"

"Yeah. The drummer was on Pink's last tour; the bass player was out with John Legend. They all know the drill."

"That's good for you—less pressure on you, right?" Charlie asked.

Kaaber placed a piece of salmon on a puff pastry.

"I don't really look at it that way. I'm still the one out front. I'm the one the ticketholder came to see, so I have to be perfect. These guys could mess something up and no one would probably notice. If I go off the rails, it'll be all over X, IG, Perez Hilton, TMZ …"

"I think your fans are rooting for you. They're not there to pick you apart. When our heroes show their human side, it's endearing. Remember when Jennifer What's-Her-Name fell on the stairs at the Oscar's? People loved that."

Charlie dabbed some lobster pâté on the salmon and then topped it with a delicious-smelling mushroom mixture. Kaaber pinched the pastry closed around the filling.

"I don't know. I don't really want to talk about it. What's going on with your work?"

"I quit, remember? It's been two weeks."

"Oh, yeah. I'm sorry. Just trying to change the subject."

"We could talk about setting the wedding date. My mother keeps asking."

Kaaber rolled his eyes and laughed. "You and your mother pick the date. It has to be after the tour though. I want to be able to enjoy the wedding prep, and I don't want to be working right up until the date."

Charlie placed the tray in the oven and set the timer. She turned to face Kaaber, leaned back against the cabinets, and folded her arms. "My Mom asked if you ever played music for me or wrote songs for me before you got this big record deal. I told her that you never did—not once. She wants to know what other secrets you're hiding."

"My music wasn't a secret; it was just a phase I had moved past."

Kaaber opened the door to the wine chiller and retrieved a bottle of pinot gris. He took two wine glasses from the cupboard and started opening the bottle.

"What other phases from your life might you revisit?" Charlie teased.

Kaaber laughed. "Why can't you just be happy that your fiancé, who loves you more than life itself, is going to give you a glamorous rock-star life?"

"I'm very happy for you. For us. But it's still weird. Still new. You must admit, it would feel more familiar tomorrow morning to go to your old office and try to move some property than it will to go to rehearsal."

"I don't know what you want me to say. I'm completely at home in the studio. Maybe the transition is tough for you, and I'm sorry if it is, but it's the most natural thing in the world for me."

"Then why do you have so many nightmares lately?"

"Nightmares?"

"C'mon. You know you're having nightmares. I sleep with you; you can't bullshit me about this."

"Maybe just subconscious anxiety about the tour. I don't know."

Kaaber went into the living room and turned on the TV. He sat down on the sofa and Charlie snuggled next to him. Kaaber flipped through the channels, unable to settle on anything. A few minutes passed before Charlie spoke again.

"You say music was a phase for you. Is it possible that relationships are a phase for you too? Could you see yourself revisiting any of the relationships you had before you met me?"

Kaaber turned his attention from the TV and looked at Charlie. "Of course not. My relationship with you is the cornerstone of my whole life. It's why I worked so hard in real estate and it's why I'm so excited about the future that I'm going to be able to provide for you and, one day, our kids."

Charlie looked down at her hands. "Then who is Kelly and why do you scream her name night after night?"

———

Charlie had been sleeping for hours, but Kaaber couldn't find rest. He paced the floor, flipped channels, and surfed the web, but he couldn't escape his thoughts. He rehearsed the call for twenty minutes before he picked up the phone.

Davis answered on the first ring. "What is it with you guys? You were the most high-maintenance prospects I've ever had, and you won't leave me alone now that the deal is cemented."

"Mr. Davis ... this is Sasha Kaaber."

"I know who it is. Your little buddy's been calling me non-stop, and I figured it was just a matter of time before he got you to intervene."

"I haven't talked to Kelly."

There was no response.

"Mr. Davis I would like to meet with you at your earliest convenience."

"I'll pick you up in thirty minutes."

"Um ... okay. Thirty minutes. Where? At my place?"

"Be in front of your building in thirty minutes."

Davis ended the call and Kaaber got dressed. The conversation hadn't gone as he had planned, but he would have the opportunity to present his offer to Davis in person, and sooner than he hoped.

It took Kaaber three minutes to dress and reactivate the product in his hair to his satisfaction. He looked presentable enough for the type of business meeting this would be.

He stood in front of his building for the better part of twenty-five minutes before the stretch Bentley pulled up to the curb. Kaaber heard the doors unlock from outside the car and he didn't wait for the driver to open the rear passenger door.

He slid onto the seat, and his eyes adjusted from the well-lit entry way of his building to the dark interior of the car. Davis sat beside him, and Kelly sat across from him. Kaaber could tell that Kelly had been crying.

"Thanks for coming—" Kaaber began.

Davis held up his hand and the car pulled away from the curb.

"We have a problem, gentlemen. I'm here to find out who that problem is. Kelly, you were in breach of contract when you contacted my office after the execution of our agreement. This has been explained to you several times, as I understand. Yet, you continue to call. Recently, you adopted the very unwise habit of calling my business cell phone."

"Mr. Davis, I just—"

"I'm talking!" Davis screamed. His eyed Kelly for a minute and chewed a piece of gum like he was killing it with his teeth. "I brokered a deal between you, which you both agreed to, and found mutually fulfilling on the day you signed the contract. I don't care if you have seller's remorse, Mr. Bailey. You and your parents made a decision that gave your mother a future. That decision altered your future, but that is the decision you made. You cannot come to me after the fact, in breach of our contract, demanding that the transaction be reversed."

"Mr. Davis, I'm willing to talk about doing that, too—"

"I. Am. Talking!" Davis yelled loud enough to ring Kaaber's ears.

"There are no takesie-backsies in my business. There is a non-disclosure agreement and a contract. You are in violation of the terms of the contract, which leads me to believe that you are a risk to breach your non-disclosure agreement. That is what we are here to talk about."

Kaaber looked out his window while Kelly looked down at his hands. Neither one of them spoke.

"You have overstepped, and in doing so, you stepped on the wrong toes. I now see both of you as a liability."

The car provided insulation from street noise. The tires hummed so softly that they could barely be heard traveling over the Manhattan streets. There was still traffic at this late hour, but the car traveled steadily between red lights. The Bentley's suspension absorbed surface imperfections, but the ride was unbearably uncomfortable.

Kaaber felt entombed in the silent cushion, and he began to feel as though oxygen was scarce. He wanted to demand to be let out of the car like he had done the first time he climbed into it. He closed his eyes and cursed the moment that he allowed himself to be seduced.

Finally, the car turned and came to a stop in front of a large rolling garage door in the garment district. The door lifted soundlessly, and the Bentley turned at a radius that seemed an impossible angle for a car of its size to execute. Kaaber looked at Kelly and his face reflected the panic that Kaaber was feeling. Kaaber tried to make eye contact with Kelly, but the kid's attention was fixed on Davis. Kaaber wanted to let Kelly know that it was two against one—or two against two if the driver pulled double duty, but it was useless. Kelly wasn't paying attention to him.

"Get out of the car," Davis ordered.

Kelly started to open the driver side door, so Kaaber went for the passenger door.

"No. Both of you get out of this door." Davis indicated the driver's side. Kaaber tried the handle of the passenger door anyway, but it was locked. Davis noticed his attempt and started to laugh. "You say so much without saying anything at all, Sasha."

Davis exited the vehicle first with Kelly at his back. Kaaber got out last and saw that two men in upscale dress attire were consulting with the driver.

They were inside a large warehouse that smelled like it was as a dye house at one time but stood empty now. Completely empty. The car, which had been turned off, was the only thing in a space as large as a basketball stadium and twice as high.

The men in fancy clothes retrieved three folding chairs from the trunk of the Bentley. They arranged two of them facing each other with the third alongside.

"Thank you, gentlemen." Davis gestured toward the chairs and Kelly and Kaaber sat across from each other. Two of Davis's men stood behind Kelly the third stood behind Davis.

"It seems that the terms of our agreement need some clarification and, perhaps, some revisions."

"I just want it back. Kaaber didn't want me to sell it anyway, so I'm sure he understands. I didn't realize how much of my identity was tied to my music. I don't know who I am anymore without it, I'm—"

"Shut up." Davis sneered as he said the words. He pointed at Kaaber.

"Rafferty says you're reluctant to book some of the media interviews he worked so hard to get you. You work for me. I accepted a measly million-dollar deposit from you to make this work. I'm carrying paper for four mil the first year, and you owe me fifteen after that. You realize you owe me nineteen million dollars, right?"

Kaaber nodded. He had no idea that his publicist was tied to Davis, and he was sickened by the revelation.

"Say it."

"I owe you nineteen million dollars."

"You have a few years of working your ass off for me, then you start making money like you've never seen before. The more media you to do, the harder you push this first drop, the quicker I get paid back, and then you're in business for yourself. When that time comes, you work as much or as little as you want. I don't care. But, until I get my payment in full, you follow the script. If Rafferty tells you to shave your asshole in Times Square and put it on YouTube, you go get your razor. Got it?"

"Yeah. You own me. I get it. I'm a slave working toward freedom."

"God damn mother fucking right you are." Davis turned toward Kelly, but then he glanced in Kaaber's direction again. "Curiosity is my weakness. When you called my cell phone tonight, what the fuck were you thinking?"

Kaaber looked Davis in the eye. "I wanted to let you know that I intend to make my second payment before the due date."

Davis scoffed. "Your eyes are brown for a reason, Sasha." He turned to Kelly. "What part of 'the undersigned parties agree that contact between them shall cease and desist upon execution of this contract and that payment for said commodity, heretofore referred to as musical abilities, represents payment in full' do you not understand?"

"Kaaber knew what the impact of losing my talent would do to me, but I didn't." Kelly looked at Kaaber with desperate eyes.

"You're selfish and weak," Davis said. "You were able to reciprocate the favor to the woman who gave you life, yet that isn't enough for you."

Kelly's chin started to quiver.

"When you signed this agreement, in the presence of your father, two other witnesses, and a Notary, did you understand the segment entitled 'non-disclosure?'"

Kelly looked from Kaaber back to Davis. For a moment it looked like Kelly was tensing to run, but one of the men who stood behind him placed a hand on his shoulder to dissuade him.

"I haven't said anything to anyone."

"Really?"

"I didn't tell anyone about you, or the deal we made."

"You didn't tell Jeff Adams that you, and I'm quoting now, '*would love to play at his place again, but are physically unable to do so?*'"

Kelly's eyes darted to Kaaber. "Um, I don't know if that's exactly what I said. I called him to tell him that I wasn't able to come back to work...as a courtesy, you know, and ..."

"You told him that you were physically unable to play music. When he asked you to explain, you told him that he wouldn't believe you if you told him anyway."

Kelly's light wash jeans darkened in the crotch, and he started to sob. "Kaaber ... please ..."

"All right. Enough. You have literally scared the piss out of him, Wesley. If we put things right, it takes the suspicion off Kelly and

I will still pay you the second million. That's two million for your trouble."

"And then what? What happens to the newest music sensation in the world? Kaaber just inexplicably disappears? Where do you think you're going to disappear to when every human on the planet has a video camera on their cell phone?"

"That could boost sales beyond belief!" Kaaber lowered his voice. "Think about it, Wesley. Kaaber comes out of nowhere, takes the music industry by storm and disappears after releasing what pop music deemed the most important contribution since the Beatles. The mystery surrounding the record and the artist would give it cult status for decades. It's better than James Dean!"

"The first time I met you, I was disgusted by your naiveté. Now I'm concerned that your idealistic tendencies could be harmful. To me. I'm going to show you how seriously I take my business."

Davis nodded, and the man standing behind Kelly pulled a .38 out of his pants and shot the teenager in the head. As Kelly's head exploded, fragments of tissue and blood showered Kaaber, but Davis remained unscathed.

"Ahhhhhhh … ahhhhhhh … ahhhhhhh …" Kaaber heard that the sounds were coming from him, but he wasn't aware of making them.

Kelly's body slumped from the chair and fell to the floor in a pool of blood.

"No … no … no … no …" Kaaber whispered. He turned to Davis. "What the fuck?" he screamed.

"Insubordination will not be tolerated." Davis spit. "You should be next, Kaaber, but you owe me money. You owe me tours and endorsements. You are my property, and you generate revenue, so you get to live today. But I want you to keep this in mind. You made a strong argument for your disappearance. That just might work. If you don't abide by the terms of our agreement, I will change course and your body will be dissolved in a barrel just like our poor friend Kelly Bailey."

Kaaber could barely breath. The smell of blood filled his nose and his own stomach bile pushed up his throat, filling his esophagus. He felt like he was drowning. His ears still rang from the gunshot. He closed his eyes to try to shut out the horrific scene in front of him.

Davis got up from his chair. "You might want to get cleaned up. You can't ride in my car with Kelly's insides dripping from you."

Kaaber leaned forward and emptied the contents of his stomach on the floor in front of him.

"Jesus ..." Davis rolled his eyes. "Scrub him up and take him home," he told his men. "Oh, and Kaaber, say hi to Charlie for me, will you?"

The garage door opened to reveal another stretch Bentley waiting out front. Davis checked the bottom of his shoes before he stepped into the car.

CHAPTER THIRTY-FIVE

MAURO THOUGHT IT WAS TOO coincidental that his captors happened to check on him right after he woke up and started talking to Wagner. It was clear they were under surveillance, so he and Wagner remained silent. In every scenario Mauro imagined, this was the last day of his life, but he didn't regret any decisions that led to this moment. He hadn't given up completely, he would still look for an opportunity to see the sunrise tomorrow, but he was at peace with the probable outcome.

Mauro closed his eyes and rested. He reasoned that sleep would give him strength, and he tried to get there, but his senses were too alert to allow it.

Time passed, and he heard footsteps again. Several pairs. He turned his head toward the noise and started counting. There were four men out front and three men behind them. Mauro chuckled at the amateurish imitation of the Secret Service. The suit in the middle of the back row was flanked by wannabes.

"Mr. Davis is here to see you, gentlemen," Staten Island said.

Mauro looked up toward the man with the good shoes, but the face was far too young to be Davis.

"Who the fuck are you?" Mauro asked.

Staten Island buried his boot in Mauro's midsection. "Speak to the boss with respect."

"I thought Davis was coming himself. Why did he send an errand boy? I thought we were so important to him that he wanted to see our suffering with his own eyes," Wagner said.

Staten Island stepped on his non-kicking foot to give the blow more leverage. Wagner let out an excruciating moan after one of his ribs produced a disgusting cracking noise.

"We were expecting someone else," Mauro said.

"I am Charles Davis of The Davis Agency. You sent me an email, I believe."

"Not you, buddy. We don't have any business with you," Mauro said. "Our beef with Davis is older than you are."

"Oh, you mean *The* Davis," Charles Davis laughed.

"The boss," Wagner said.

"We are all Davis and we're all the boss. Makes us a little harder to pin down, identify, arrest, or assassinate. That's privileged information, but it's not going to leave this room, so I feel safe divulging it to you. Think of The Davis Agency as an Army with many generals."

"I'm disappointed," Wagner said, which earned him another kick to his damaged ribcage.

"If it makes you feel better, I know exactly who you are, Reicher. You and your friend Greco cost The Davis Agency quite a lot of money once upon a time. We revamped many of our business practices after you exposed our weakness; even took a few years to regroup. I assure, you we have fortified our process. You're about to experience how good we have become at tying up loose ends. You should feel some pride in facilitating improved protocols." Charles Davis turned to the men standing behind him. "Let's get started. I want to be back at the airport before midnight."

Mauro didn't know what time it was, but he was somewhat relieved to hear that his torture would last hours rather than days.

"Do the treasonous employee first, but I want some questions answered, so don't complete the job until I give the okay," Davis said.

Two of the men unrolled a large sheet of plastic until they covered a twenty-foot square section of the cement warehouse floor. Mauro tried to watch Wagner's face, but his friend wouldn't turn to look at him.

"I'm sorry I involved you in this," Mauro said.

"I wouldn't be here if I didn't want to be."

"Shut up." Staten Island came over and stood between the bound men.

One of the grunts accompanying Charles Davis carried an office chair to the edge of the plastic, and Davis sat down.

Two men tried to carry Wagner to the center of the plastic, but he was too heavy, so a third helped.

"Make sure he's facing me and take his shirt off," Davis instructed.

Wagner looked him right in the eye. "You're nothing but a fuckin' footman."

"Well, you're about to take your last breath on the word of a fuckin' footman, so you must be pretty low on the totem pole of life. Who knows about your affiliation with The Davis Agency?"

"Only Mauro."

"Who's Mauro?"

"Greco," Wagner corrected himself.

"We sent a cleaner to your apartment. There were pictures of women."

"Just ladies I met online and maybe went out with once. No one knows anything, I kept to myself."

"Your parents are dead. Where's your brother?"

"I don't know," Wagner answered quickly.

"Hit him."

The man standing over Wagner shot a taser at him. The clamps attached to his back and Wagner soiled himself as the shock was sent into his body. His jaw clamped shut and his muscles tightened. Guttural sounds emanated from his throat.

Mauro tried to will his friend to look at him, but Wagner maintained eye contact with Davis.

"That's how this is going to go. You lie to me, and I order them to keep the charge going longer each time. That was five seconds. From what I hear five seconds feels like a year. Imagine ten. Where is your bother?"

"I don't know."

The trigger was pulled again, allowing the charge to travel through Wagner's body while Davis slowly counted to six.

"I'll give you ten seconds to rest, then I'm going to ask again," Davis said calmly. He counted to ten. "Where is your brother?"

"I told him … to leave New York. I gave him what I had … told him not to ask any questions … get as far from New York as he could … before the money ran out." Wagner's voice came in spurts, and it sounded like his tongue was swollen.

"I would ask questions if my brother told me to do something drastic like that."

"He did … didn't answer."

"So, where did he go?"

"I don't know."

"I find it hard to believe that you weren't in touch with your brother all along."

"I wasn't. Not for … twenty-five years. Leave him … out."

"Oh, you want us to leave him out of this? You should have said that yesterday. You see, your brother is a lousy listener. He didn't leave like you told him to. He got as far as Morris Park in the Bronx and stayed there. That's where he was this morning when we started looking for you. You know, after we got your email. We needed to know what he knew."

"You … fuckin' … he had nothin' … to do …"

"That's what he said too, but we had to lean on him to make sure. I honestly don't think he knew anything about The Davis Agency, but I don't like loose ends. Unfortunately, his girlfriend and his kid came home while we were there. The cops are gonna find a sickening mess."

Mauro couldn't see the eight by ten photo that one of the men held in front of Wagner's face, but the way Wagner flinched before pressing his eyes closed told Mauro all he needed to know.

"You soulless … bastard!" Wagner spit. "They … knew nothin' …"

"You did that, not me. I need to know what other loose ends I have to clean up after we formally terminate our business relationship here today. Where did the money come from for the deposit you made on the commodity you purchased?"

"Fuck … you," Wagner answered.

"Seven seconds," Davis instructed.

"Woah, woah, woah!" Mauro yelled "I placed the bid. I made the deposit!"

Wagner twitched and tensed as Davis counted while staring at Mauro. ". . . six, six and a half. And seven. The two of you worked together. I'm sure he knows as much about this as you do."

"I siphoned money off a deal I brokered between a drug dealer and an underground internet guy. It was a case of criminals fuckin' over other criminals. No loose ends there." Mauro said.

"Who knows you're in Miami?" Davis asked Wagner.

"No one."

"Hit him for eight seconds," Davis said. Wagner held his breath for eight seconds while his nerve endings stood on end. "Who were you meeting with in Miami?"

"No ... one."

"You expect me to believe that you and Newcombe's family didn't strike a deal on your own, eliminating The Davis Agency as the middleman? Hit him again."

Eight seconds passed slowly.

"Listen, man," Mauro raised his voice and tried not to sound desperate. "I engineered this whole plan. Wagner is here to watch my back. That's all. This is all me."

Davis turned nonchalantly to Mauro and said, "I don't care." He leaned forward, resting his forearms on his thighs, and snapped his fingers in Wagner's direction to get his attention. "Hey. Focus. Look at me. Who helped you disappear when you left the employment of The Davis Agency?"

"No ... body."

"Who's helping you now?"

"No one."

"You didn't think that you and Meathead could take down The Davis Agency by yourselves, did you? You can't expect me to believe you're that stupid." Charles Davis waited for a reply. He sat up straight again and shrugged. "Nine seconds."

Mauro willed strength for his friend as his body was ravaged with electricity yet again.

"How do you feel?" Davis asked.

"Can go … all … day," Wagner said. His words were much harder to decipher now, but Mauro could tell from the vowel sounds what his buddy was saying. "Don't worry Mo … tickles," he said. Then he made a groaning sound, and his jaw clenched tightly. "Oh, God! Oh …!"

"Wagner?" Mauro yelled.

The moaning continued for a few short intervals and then there a choking sound, followed by silence.

"What happened?" Davis demanded.

"I think … he's having a heart attack? I don't know." Staten Island kicked Wagner's midsection with such force that he listed lifelessly onto his back.

"I'll get 'em Wagner!" Mauro called out, hoping his friend could hear him. He never witnessed anyone have a heart attack—he didn't know what happened when someone experienced fatal arrest of the heart, but he guessed he was seeing it now.

"Check his pulse," Davis said.

"He stopped breathing and … no pulse," Staten Island reported.

"Well, that was anticlimactic," Davis said. He turned to Mauro. "I hope you give me more of a show than that loser."

Staten Island addressed the taser-happy wanna-be. "Help me get him out of here."

The teeth of the taser were removed from Wagner's back. Mauro blinked away tears of rage and said a prayer for the only person who had been in his life for the last quarter century. Four men were required to carry Wagner's body from the warehouse and, as they departed, Mauro saw that the taser gun had been left lying on the floor about five feet to his right. Davis was the next closest person to the weapon at twice the distance. Mauro didn't hesitate; he thrust his weight and propelled himself in an awkward commando roll toward the gun. In an unbelievable turn of luck, or perhaps it was Wagner acting as a guardian angel, Mauro was able to grab the gun with his right hand. He found the trigger, aimed behind his back and shot at the henchman closest to him. The teeth made contact and Mauro depressed the trigger. Davis began to yell for assistance and the army came charging toward Mauro. He wouldn't die without punishing at least one of them for killing Wagner, so he kept the trigger engaged.

Mauro was waiting to be tackled by at least six men when he heard the words, "Freeze! Miami PD! Nobody move!"

Mauro realized that his eyes were closed, and he opened them now. Nine police officers in combat gear had their weapons drawn. One of them shouted, "Put the weapon down!" Mauro realized they were talking to him, and he let the taser fall from his hands.

One of the officers instructed everyone to lay face down on the floor with their hands and legs spread. Everyone complied, except Davis. Who, Mauro noticed, was nowhere to be found.

"He's getting away! One of them is getting away!" he yelled.

"Calm down," a young Sargent commanded Mauro. "I'm going to remove these restraints and I need to know that you're going to be calm once I do."

"I want a lawyer," Mauro said.

"I haven't charged you with anything. You're the only one in here who's hogtied and I'm not asking how you got that way right now, okay? We'll get your statement at the hospital."

"No, I need an attorney."

"Kind of early to lawyer up," the cop said.

"Call David Drake. I need you to call him right now. Tell him I know his son, Matthew," Mauro begged.

"Patience, man. Everything's gonna be okay."

"David Drake," Mauro repeated. "I need you to get David Drake here as soon as possible. And you need to go after the boss. They killed my friend on his command."

"I'm getting you untied, and we'll talk," the cop said.

Mauro lay his head on the floor and closed his eyes.

CHAPTER THIRTY-SIX

Cassandra and Christopher reclined on two chaise lounges beside the Marcot Estate pool. It was a little too cool to swim, but the ten-foot Gowen Cypress trees around the perimeter of the pool deck cut the breeze, leaving only the warmth of the late afternoon sun and a pleasant lemon fragrance.

The wicker stretched and complained under Chris as he changed positions. It was quiet for a moment and then the high-pitched squeaking started again.

"You suck at relaxing," Cassie whispered.

"Yeah, I guess I do."

"Are you ready to go inside?"

"Is it the time of day that we usually go inside?" Chris asked sharply.

"Go ahead and say what's on your mind. I can almost hear your thoughts, but your squirming is drowning them out."

"Okay, well, I really enjoyed staying here while your grandmother was gone, but now that she's back I feel like a teenager visiting my girlfriend at her parent's house." Chris kept his eyes closed while he talked. "I just had the instinct to put my hand in your bikini bottoms, but then I remembered I was under surveillance. So, what's on my mind is ... how much longer are you planning on staying here, Cassie?"

"I'm sorry if you're unhappy. God, I feel like all I do lately is make you unhappy." Cassandra sat up and slid her sunglasses to the top of her head. Chris turned and squinted at her.

"I'm just asking what the plan is."

"I guess I'm taking it day by day," Cassie replied shrugging her shoulders.

"Taking what day by day? We don't do anything. We lay in the sun, read, play tennis, watch movies … I'm worried your grandmother is going to think I'm some kind of mooch."

Cassie wrinkled her nose. "I feel like the two of you have been well aligned since your first meeting. It seems like you both want the same thing—for us to rejoin a society we wanted to correct."

"Mrs. Marcot said the point of us staying here for a while was to regroup and think things through. Plan our next step. Maybe we should repay her hospitality by doing that."

Cassie moved her sunglasses back to her nose and made the attempt to twist her hair into a topknot like she used to when it was long. The short hair slipped from her grasp and fell around her face in a blunt frame. "So, what do you want to do, Chris?"

"I want you to tell me what you want, Cass. Do you want to go back to the house? Do you want to get an apartment together and start living again? Do you want to get a job?"

Cassie stared at the waterfall that cascaded into the swimming pool. "I don't know. I don't think so. I don't think I want to do any of those things."

Chris was quiet, waiting for Cassie to continue.

"When we were in school, I was working toward a degree. Then we both decided that an undergraduate degree wasn't enough, so we got our Masters'. Now I feel like I don't have a goal. I really wanted to stop the waste and the excess. Maybe because I have guilt for all the excess I haven't earned." Cassandra threw her arms out wide to emphasize her point.

"I don't know about your parents, but your grandmother seems open to supporting you in anything you choose to do. She just wants you to do *something*. That's the impression I get anyway."

"Why do I have to know what I want to do with the rest of my life right this moment? Don't plenty of people backpack through Europe and 'find themselves'?"

"Do you wanna do that?" Chris sat up and rested his forearms on his thighs. "Let's do that!"

"Just us and our backpacks?" Cassie asked sarcastically. "If I mentioned that idea to my Gram, she would fuel the Gulfstream and arrange five star hotels across the EU. That wouldn't do much to alleviate the guilt I feel about what I haven't earned."

"You don't have to rebel against who you are or any of the privileges you have. You're an intelligent, pretty, funny, charming girl who enjoys the finer things. What's wrong with being that girl?"

"You make me sound very shallow."

"No, no. Not shallow at all. Sophisticated."

"Do you remember the first time we met?" Cassandra asked quietly.

Christopher smiled. "I remember the first time I saw you. I thought there was a supermodel loose on campus. I stalked you on your way to the Commons."

Cassie laughed. "You never told me that!"

"Yeah, I was on the way to class, but you were walking across the quad, and I took a massive detour."

"That's adorable. Somewhat creepy, but mostly adorable."

Christopher picked up the pitcher of iced tea that sat on the table between them and refreshed Cassandra's glass before filling his own. "Is it adorable that I got all dressed up the following week to catch you there at the same time?"

"That was the day you introduced yourself?"

"Yeah." Christopher smiled. "I set the trap and you ran right into it."

"It should be illegal to be as good looking as you are. The fact that you're also brilliant and compassionate makes you an alien."

Christopher laughed.

"When you asked people about me, did they say that I was a stuck-up rich girl?"

"We were at Harvard—weren't they all stuck-up rich girls?"

"Before you came along, I kept to myself … you know that. I wasn't in a sorority, so I didn't have a ready-made friend base."

"I take full credit for making your senior year and your grad years more memorable than they otherwise might have been."

"I feel like I've had the opposite impact on your life. After we met, you spent all your time alone with me."

"Who else would I need? I met a girl with an IQ that is probably double mine. Anyone else I hung out with prior to you bored me within an hour of meeting them."

"You found a way to kill an hour though, huh?" Cassie teased.

Christopher laughed. "See? That's what I love, and I can't seem to stop following you—even when you to go to the weirdest places."

"Did you ever feel like our relationship cemented too fast?" Cassandra said, taking a sip of her tea.

"What do you mean?"

"We met and then, boom, we were together. All the time. Inseparable."

"When it's right, it's right."

"You've said that all along, but there are times that I feel like you should have asserted yourself more."

"So, I'm too easy-going?" Chris laughed.

"I didn't date very much before you, but in every sitcom or movie where a romantic relationship is featured, there's a lot of turbulence. We don't have any. Doesn't that raise a red flag for you?"

Christopher took a deep breath and leaned back in his chair.

"I don't know what answer you want to hear."

"That's exactly what I'm saying. I feel like you always give the response you think I want, and maybe part of you that isn't being a hundred percent authentic."

Chris shook his head and sprang to his feet. "I'm going to go take a shower. I'll see you at dinner. After you go to your own room and take your own shower." Chris retrieved his T-shirt from where it hung on the back of the chaise and hung his towel around his neck. Cassie watched him power walk toward the house. Once he had disappeared from view, she slipped into her cover-up and followed the stepping-stone path Chris had taken.

Cassie noticed that the height of the soft green lawn was flush with the stone walkway. She wished for a single piece of grass that dared to be longer, but there wasn't one. The main house loomed overhead, and Cassie began to climb the stone staircase to the patio that ran the entire back of the home. Three sets of French doors opened to the foyer and Cassandra let herself in through the set on the far left. She almost made it to the main staircase when her grandmother's voice floated out of the library.

"Cassandra, dear, is that you?"

Cassie paused for a moment. "Yes, Gram it's me. I was just coming in from the pool."

"Can you come in here for a second, darling? There's someone I want you to meet."

Cassandra changed direction and flip-flopped to the library where Mrs. Marcot sat across from a middle-aged man in a three-piece suit.

"Cassandra, this is Wayne Preston, he is with Habitat for Humanity."

Cassandra nodded and smiled. "I would shake hands, but I'm sure I have SPF all over me. I was out getting some sun."

Wayne Preston's genuine smile made his dark eyes sparkle. "Good for you."

"Mr. Preston has a very interesting idea that would positively impact many needy families in Culver City. He is looking for an investor, and I am inclined to get involved. My only hesitation, no offense to you Mr. Preston, is that I would like to have a representative on the board to make sure that the money is used for the intended purpose, and that the project is seen through to fruition. I was thinking that you would be the perfect liaison, Cassandra."

Cassie raised her eyebrows questioningly at her grandmother.

"Perhaps we could discuss the details at a better time. Say, tomorrow? You could come to my office and see the renderings," Mr. Preston stood up and handed his business card to Cassandra.

"I'm afraid I'm not in a position to make any long-term commitments at this time." Cassandra smiled at Mr. Preston.

"Cassandra, you haven't heard what the project entails. This is something that you could really put your heart into. Why don't you meet with Wayne tomorrow and then you can make an informed decision?"

Cassandra walked a few steps to her grandmother's desk and set the card down. "My grandmother knows how to reach you." She nodded to Mr. Preston and quickly exited the room. As she left, she could hear her Gram's apology bouncing off the marble walls of the foyer.

CHAPTER THIRTY-SEVEN

KAABER CLOSED THE DOOR TO his apartment and reached for the deadbolt. His shaking hand slipped off the slim piece of metal twice before he managed to grip it between his thumb and forefinger and twist it into place. He stripped to his boxer briefs. The moment when Kelly's head exploded played on a loop in his mind as he walked on shaky legs to the kitchen to retrieve a garbage bag. Kaaber rolled the end of the bag between his fingers more than a dozen times before he realized that he was attempting to open the wrong side. He turned the bag over, opened it, and threw his clothes and shoes inside. A suitable hiding place didn't reveal itself, so Kaaber dropped the bag in the middle of the kitchen. The words that Davis spoke to him less than an hour ago bounced around his dizzy head, *"Say hi to Charlie for me."* Kaaber stumbled to the bedroom where Charlie was sleeping. He turned on the overhead light, opened the closet door, and pulled a suitcase off the highest shelf, letting it slam to the ground.

"Sasha? Are you okay?" Charlie sat up in bed, squinting to protect her eyes from the harsh light. "What are you doing? Did you have another nightmare?"

Kaaber stepped to the back of the walk-in closet and started pulling Charlie's clothes from hangers. "You're leaving, Charlie. Right now."

Charlie scoffed and put her face in her hands. "Come back to bed, Sasha."

"Go get the suitcase from the hall closet, this one isn't big enough for everything."

"Are we going on a trip? What did I miss while I was sleeping?" Charlie reached to the bedside table and picked up her phone. "We have two hours before the alarm goes off. Why are you awake right now?"

Kaaber stormed from the closet to the foot of the bed and spoke through bared teeth.

"You're leaving. Right. Now. I want you out!"

Charlie's face reflected disbelief and confusion. "Baby, you're scaring me. Please just sit down and we'll talk—"

"Get the fuck up!" Kaaber shouted. "Get the fuck out!"

Charlie choked on her breath and started shaking. "Wha—"

"Wha?" Kaaber mimicked. "I said get out!"

"What are you doing? Why are you doing this?" Charlie shrunk against the headboard as tears spilled down her cheeks.

Kaaber allowed himself to look into her eyes and his body unwittingly exhaled a sob. He loved her so much. If anyone else in the world dared to treat Charlie this way, he would have beaten them within an inch of their life. But this is what he had to do to save hers.

"I'm about to embark on the greatest opportunity I've ever had, and I don't need you and your mother clinging on, and trying to shift my focus from the tour to flavors of fucking wedding cake."

Charlie shook her head. "You're not making sense, Sasha."

"You want to fast forward past the tour to the wedding, that's all you care about, but I have a lot of work to do between now and then."

"I know. I'm not pressuring ... how can you say ...? I don't understand."

"I don't want to be with you anymore. Is that simple enough for you to understand? Do I have to fuck someone in front of you to convince you that I don't want to be with you anymore?"

Charlie's eyes hardened and she sat up in bed. "What did you just say to me?"

"I'll oblige you, Charlie. I can have a gorgeous fuckbuddy here inside of ten minutes. Some nameless chick who will be satisfied with one encounter with *Kaaber* and not try to put a leash around my neck afterward."

"Who do you think you are?" Charlie unfolded her long legs and got out of bed. Chest to chest with Kaaber, she looked at him with hatred in her eyes. "Whoever you *think* you are, I guarantee you're a hell of a lot less without me."

Charlie walked into the closet and pulled out her full-length wool coat. She thrust each arm into a sleeve like she was throwing a punch. As she stepped into a pair of knee-high boots, she said, "Have my things delivered to the Beekman today. Today! I won't be there tomorrow."

Charlie stood face to face with Sasha as she pulled the giant emerald and diamond ring from her left hand. She tossed it nonchalantly on the bed and added, "I don't want anything that you ever gave me, so don't send over a single item that will remind me of the time I wasted with the pathetic, insecure asshole with whom I almost made the biggest mistake of my life."

Kaaber watched Charlie walk defiantly out of the bedroom. He heard the deadbolt retract, and the front door beeped as she opened it. The moment seemed to linger, and Kaaber wondered if she was considering turning around. He knew he wouldn't have the willpower to hurt her again. He wanted to run after her and beg her forgiveness. Tell her everything that happened that night and run away with her to some place the Davis Agency couldn't find them. But he knew that was just a fantasy. He sold his soul, but he wouldn't lose Charlie's.

The door beeped again to signal that it closed. Kaaber melted to his knees, lowered himself onto his side, and cried.

CHAPTER THIRTY-EIGHT

D AVID DRAKE SAT BEHIND THE desk in the dry cleaner manager's office. He heard some ridiculous stories over the course of his law career, but the one he just heard from Mauro Giordano, or Salvatore Greco, was the most far-fetched.

"I still don't understand how you know my son or how he fits into any of this," Drake said.

"As I said, I've never actually met your son. I told the police to mention Matthew's name when they called you because I knew that would get your attention. My associate and I didn't want to interfere, but we suspected that your family might unknowingly be in danger, so we came here to keep an eye out."

"You were stalking my family."

"Protecting."

"And the bad guys who were watching us took you down."

"Essentially."

"So, I'm supposed to believe that you have nothing to do with them. You're just a good-hearted guy who flew across the country on your own dime, to guard a family that you've never met."

"There's still stuff online about me from my BU days. Some guy has a web site that blames me for the dismantling of the BU Football program. My parents sued Boston University when I disappeared after an away game. Instead of getting on the bus and going home, I ran. Earlier that day was when everything went down between Wagner, Davis's guys, and me. Anyway, this web guy's a fanatic, he has pictures of me and stats and stuff. It'll prove that I am who I say I am. Look it up."

Drake took his phone out of the inside breast pocket of his suit jacket. He Googled "Salvatore Greco Images." The young Salvatore had the same features as the older man who sat across from him. Drake clicked "web" and spent a few minutes looking at different web sites that recounted the story that Mauro had just told him. He put his phone back into his jacket pocket.

"You aren't being charged with anything. The cops would like to question you, of course, but you're free to go."

"I didn't ask for legal advice. I asked for you to have the opportunity to tell you that you and your family are in danger."

David Drake stood up and retrieved his briefcase from the desk. "I don't think we have anything more to talk about."

"You have to stay, I retained you as my attorney. I gave you a dollar."

"You borrowed that dollar from me, and you don't need an attorney."

Mauro stood up and blocked the door. "Please. I know how crazy this sounds—how freakin' impossible it seems, but your family is in danger. These guys are real. They killed Wagner. They were watching your house. These guys, the ones who killed my friend, were hired guns and they were across the street from your house."

"How do I know they weren't there for you? You were watching my house too."

"I bet one of these guys approached someone in your family all nice and slick-like before they resorted to this. That's what they do. They send a broker. A handsome young guy wearin' a designer suit and layin' on the charm. But, if the guys with corporate haircuts and million-dollar smiles don't get the business done, the second unit comes in and the second unit guys have a whole different skill set. This MO ringin' any bells?"

Drake locked eyes with Mauro. "How do I know you didn't send that guy to accost my wife in the driveway?"

"I was the one who was hogtied."

"Deals go bad between criminals."

"All I'm guilty of is having a fake ID. Your father-in-law made a deal with these guys. They paid him, but they didn't get what they paid for. This won't be over until they have the commodity or their money. That's the best-case scenario. The more you know about them, the more of a liability you become, and they don't leave loose ends. That's why Wagner's dead right now."

"My father-in-law didn't leave any money. I handled his estate. He was broke; in fact, my wife and I supplemented him the past few years without him knowing."

"I believe you're not hiding the money, but I'm not the party you have to convince."

Drake stared at Mauro's face, studying his expression. "I've been a trial attorney for over thirty years. I know bullshit when I hear it."

"Then you know I'm telling the truth. That ball in your stomach that's been getting bigger and bigger since I started talking—that's fear. You're afraid because you know I'm not lying."

"Where are you staying in case I want to contact you?" Drake stepped back and perched on the front of the dry cleaner manager's desk.

"I haven't even thought about it. I'm sure everything I brought with me is evidence now."

"And you're not going to change your mind about talking to the cops?" Drake asked.

"What part of this can I tell them without starting the process that puts me on an involuntary psychiatric hold?"

"You don't have to talk to them." Drake looked up at the ceiling as if he would find an answer up there. "Stay at my office tonight. There's a shower and a sofa bed that I sleep on when I'm pulling all-nighters. We'll stop at Wal-Mart and pick up what you need. We can talk more tomorrow."

"Are the cops watching your house tonight?" Mauro asked.

"Yeah. In light of recent events, they're going to keep a squad parked in front."

"Good," Mauro nodded. He swung the door open and stood back. "After you."

Drake walked out into the hallway and toward the storefront where bags of clothes were hanging, cleaned and pressed, waiting to be picked up by their owners. "You could probably find something nice in your size right here," he said.

"That would be stealing," Mauro replied.

Drake cast a glance inside the warehouse where the murder scene was being photographed. He thought about the men who were being questioned at the police station and considered Mauro one more time.

"Let's go before I change my mind."

CHAPTER THIRTY-NINE

MATTHEW WAS SITTING ALONE IN the kitchen waiting for his father to come home. The rectangular table made of solid wood had a long bench on one side and three chairs on the other. Matthew started out sitting in one of the chairs. It proved to be comfortable for only slightly longer than a standard mealtime, and Matthew moved to the padded bench where he was laying on his back studying the ceiling when he heard the garage door open.

He got up, grabbed two coffee cups from the cabinet, and selected two coffees from the Keurig carousel. By the time his father came through the kitchen door, the aroma of freshly brewed coffee filled the room.

"Hey, son." David Drake set his briefcase on the floor inside the door and sat down at the table.

"Can I talk to you, Dad?" Matthew placed the coffee in front of his father.

"Thanks." He took a sip. "I need to talk to you, too, but you can go first."

"This is hard because I tell you everything; even stupid little things that aren't important. And I've been keeping something really, really big from you. I thought I was keeping you and Mom safe by keeping my mouth shut, but those guys across the street tonight … I think that had something to do with me."

David Drake removed his tie and cufflinks and unbuttoned the top two buttons of his dress shirt before he spoke.

"Tell me everything, start to finish, and don't leave out any detail regardless of how small you might think it is."

Matthew talked for nearly twenty minutes with very few interruptions from his father. He told him about being forced into the van, how the men had been in the house while Mom was home alone, and all about Mrs. Marcot and her men. When he had finished confessing, he tried to sum it all up neatly, but he couldn't.

"So, does Mom have what they're looking for?"

"No. We don't have it, but I'm not sure that strengthens our position." The elder Drake got up from the table and popped another K-cup into the coffee maker. "You told Mrs. Marcot everything you told me?"

"Yeah, but I wish I hadn't because since I saw that guy at her house, the guy that was in our driveway, I don't think we can trust her."

"There are easy ways to test her loyalties. You want another cup?"

"No, thanks."

Drake brought his freshly brewed coffee to the table and sat back down across from Matthew. "What if we lead Mrs. Marcot to believe that we have what these men are looking for?"

Matthew smiled. "Her reaction would tell us a lot."

"It might."

"But, Dad, she has four men watching us now and it's just you, me, and Mom. Are we going to involve the police?"

"No." Drake took a long drink. "We have a garbage man on our team as well. He knows a lot about the operation. He might be helpful."

"Your turn to tell me some stuff," Matthew said. "From the beginning."

CHAPTER FORTY

THE REHEARSAL STUDIO WAS SMALL, thus requiring an isolation booth for vocals, and that's where Kaaber stayed as he ran the musicians through the show from start to finish. When the last chord of the last encore hit, Kaaber used the mic to talk to the band.

"Sounds good, everybody. We ran just a little short of that ninety-minute mark that we want to hit, but the staging will probably run us over, so I'm not going to stress about time. Take a tight thirty for lunch, and we can run the whole show twice more before we break for the day."

Kaaber removed his in-ear monitors and scrolled on his phone until the last of the musicians left the room. Rafferty tapped on the booth's window and gestured for Kaaber to go with his band, but Kaaber ignored him and kept his attention on his phone.

"Hey, man. If you have some posts for soc, I'll get those up for you while you have lunch."

"Close the door, Rafferty. If I need you, I'll let you know."

"Okay, yeah, but I'm here to take that off your shoulders so that you can bond with the band and focus on the music."

Kaaber shook his head dismissively.

"When you have a good relationship with your band off stage, it shows on stage. Fans really like knowing the bands they love are living the life together. Like the Stones, right?" Rafferty's tone was that of an elementary school teacher.

"I'm not here to make friends."

"They're a great group of dudes though, and if you want them to have your back on tour, you have to cultivate—"

"Go to the Green Room and bring me a salad, a sandwich, and a fifth of whiskey."

Rafferty laughed. "That's the rock-n-roll attitude. Seriously though, go have lunch with your band." He left the door to the booth wide open when he left the studio.

Kaaber made his way to one of the mismatched plastic chairs that sat haphazardly around the space. He put his new motorcycle boots against the wall and balanced the chair on its back legs. He took a picture of the boots and posted the shot on his Insta with the caption, "*How stupid are these boots? I don't even have a motorcycle*" with the hashtag Rock'n'roll. Then he watched the likes multiply. It reminded him of years ago when the national deficit ticker was in Times Square, and the numbers climbed so steadily the last digits were a blur.

Charlie hadn't blocked him, and it was obvious that she was using her page for revenge. She scrubbed all the photos of them together and posted an inordinate number of sexy selfies daily. Today she was laughing in a coffee shop. Kaaber expanded the shot to zoom in on her face. She was superficially flawless … and she had truly loved him. He would never have that again. As he had done a hundred times since their break-up, he contemplated liking her photo. Maybe she would see it and interpret the message that he loved her still, despite his actions and absence. Kaaber threw the phone into the wall, but the soft soundproofing prevented any satisfaction.

"Hello? Is anyone nearby?" He yelled.

"Hello? Oh, hi Kaaber." Someone's young female assistant answered his call.

"Hey, yeah, could you bring me a salad and a sandwich from the Green Room?"

"Sure," she answered eagerly. "Any preferences or allergies?"

"Nope. Just want food." He closed his eyes as he rocked the chair back and forth.

"My pleasure. Be right back."

A minute later, Kaaber's chair landed hard on the floor, and he reacted by grabbing the seat with both hands. "What the—"

Rafferty stood in front of him. "I told you to go eat with the band and you sent Sara to get your lunch and bring it in here?"

"Why does my PR Guy care where I eat?"

Rafferty smiled apologetically at Kaaber. "I care about everything you do. I care about you being a huge success. And I've done this before, so I know the formula."

Kaaber lifted himself out of the chair and stood uncomfortably close. "How many times have you done this before?"

"You want to see my CV?"

"You're not a PR person, you're a mole. And probably an accomplice to first degree murder. How many times?"

Rafferty's face changed above his signature bow tie. "Enough. I've done this enough."

"I liked you better when you were a PR Guy."

Rafferty sat down in the chair that Sasha had vacated. "You knew what you were getting into, and you made that decision before we ever met, so don't take your buyer's remorse out on me."

"Yeah, well, things changed when the kid got shot in front of me and the next thing out of Davis's mouth was a thinly disguised threat against my fiancé."

Kaaber placed his boot on the chair between Rafferty's legs and leaned toward him. "I know what I have to do and I'm doing it. What I'm not going to do, is endanger anyone else by involving them. I'm not going to be buddies with the band. I'm not going to have a genuine relationship outside of photo ops. All I have to do is make music and pay my debt."

"How much fun you have, or don't have, is up to you, but if you play the game and do what I tell you to do, the windfall will come faster and heavier than if you isolate yourself and post stupid photos of these ridiculous boots." Rafferty shoved the boot off the edge of the chair and stood up quickly, causing Kaaber to flinch. "Your tour is sold out. You're the hottest musical act in the world right now. You're living the dream. Don't forget who made that happen for you, and don't be ungrateful. Now, go grab lunch with your band, or I'll have to call Wesley and tell him we're having problems."

Kaaber scoffed and looked at Rafferty. "I hate you."

"I don't care. Go have lunch. And be charming. Make them like you."

Kaaber did as he was told.

CHAPTER FORTY-ONE

TWELVE SHOWER HEADS ENSURED THAT Cassandra was as immersed in warmth as she would be in a bath. The strong jets kneaded her muscles as she rotated slowly to take full advantage of the massaging effect. She turned on the overhead rain nozzle and washed her hair, letting herself become completely drenched. As the water and the suds carried away the SPF and sweat from her day at the pool, Cassandra began to regret the behavior she displayed a few minutes ago when her Gram introduced her to Mr. Preston.

Cassandra ended the warm-water deluge with the press of a single button and retrieved her towel from the warmer. She quickly dried off, combed her hair back, and threw on a sundress.

She hurried past Chris's room, toward the main staircase, and descended with quick, light steps.

"Gram?" Cassie stepped into the library. "Gram, I was hoping to catch Mr.—" Golden sun lit the empty library. "Shit," Cassie muttered to herself.

She walked to her grandmother's desk to see if the business card was still there, but the desktop was clean. Cassie opened the top drawer. It slid more easily than she had anticipated, and the contents of the manila folders in the drawer shifted, spilling out of their covers. She opened the file folder on top and began to straighten the papers inside when she saw her name printed on the top of the first page. It was the original report of the first time Cassie's IQ had been tested in second grade. The full-scale score was 167. Cassandra flipped to page two and saw the report from her first IQ tests at Harvard. She had been selected by the Psychology Department to help them with a study. Her score had been considered a mistake or a fluke, so they asked her to take a different test to eradicate the anomaly. The result was the same ... her score was immeasurable but estimated to be 202. Cassandra scanned the documents that were attached and stopped at a note in her grandmother's handwriting.

> *An Intelligence Quotient in this range is exceptionally rare; about 6.67 standard deviations above the mean. To possess an IQ this uncommon secures a future of success, contribution, and untold wealth if the owner should choose.*

"She's writing my resume?" Cassie mumbled to herself. She sat down in the desk chair, staring straight ahead. Cassie gathered herself and decided that there was only one way to find out. She would ask her grandmother. She placed the papers in the file in the order she found them and closed the file. Only then did she notice the phone number written in pencil across the bottom of the cover. Crossed out with a single line was: *Christopher W. (516) 774-3973.* Cassie recognized this as the cell phone number Chris had when they were in school. Beneath it was a new phone number. Cassie grabbed a pen and wrote the number on her hand. She quickly placed the file folder back in the desk exactly as she had found it, and went back to her room to think.

CHAPTER FORTY-TWO

MATTHEW AND HIS FATHER SAT close together and waited for the FaceTime call to be picked up on the other end.

After several rings, Mrs. Marcot appeared on the screen. She was dressed in an emerald green sweater and a silk paisley scarf was skillfully looped around her neck. Her hair was styled, and she seemed wide awake, although it was only six in the morning on the west coast.

"Mrs. Marcot, I'm sorry to bother you so early. We had an eventful night and—"

"No need to apologize, Matthew. I've been very worried about you. I inquired with my security team several times overnight. It's wonderful to see you with my own eyes. And I imagine the handsome man whom you so closely resemble to your right is your father?"

"Hello, Mrs. Marcot, I'm David Drake."

"It's a pleasure to meet you Mr. Drake. I can't imagine what you must think of me after I colluded with your son to keep information from you. Please accept my apologies and understand that I never imagined that it would go this far."

"You didn't expect my family to be in any danger and yet you left a security team to watch over us?"

"Out of an abundance of caution, which later proved to be practical."

"Mmmm. Well, we can't have yesterday back, can we?" David Drake watched the older woman's face closely. "Matthew told me what you discussed when you visited his school. I have some information to add, and I'd like to ask your advice on how we should proceed."

"I would be more than happy to help you in any way I can."

"Mrs. Marcot, Matthew was not aware of this because there seemed to be no need for him to know, but I have what these men say they're looking for."

Mrs. Marcot nodded.

"My wife was with her father when he died. We managed to keep that and his suicide out of the news in an effort to protect her father's reputation, and to prevent her from having to answer questions that would force her to relive that horrific event."

"I see. So, Thad gave her ... or instructed her to collect ..."

"A vial of his blood. Yes. And I'm willing to give it to the men Thad sold it to if it ensures the safety of my family."

"I think that is the wisest solution," Mrs. Marcot nodded solemnly.

"Do you know how I could reach out to them—the brokers?"

"I'm afraid that possessing this commodity puts you in danger. I could have one of my men take it off your hands—"

"Thank you, but I want to do this myself," Drake regained control of the conversation. "I will deliver the product so I know, without question, that the terms of the agreement were met, and we can put this behind us."

"I know who could guide us. Thad was very close to the President of our organization. If Thad told anyone about this business arrange-ment, it would have been him. Give me a few hours to track him down; he could be anywhere. Will I find you at home today?"

"We're all here and the item in question is here as well. We'll stand-by and wait to hear back from you," Drake said.

"Very good. I'll get started. Matthew, you did the right thing by talking to your father."

"Yes, Ma'am."

"We'll talk soon, then," Drake said.

"Yes, soon. Stay put and try not to worry." Mrs. Marcot smiled sweetly, waved, and then ended the call.

"And now we see if that lady is a nice little grandmother or a devious bag of bones," Mauro said, coming out from behind the scope of the iPad camera where he had been standing.

"What are her men doing?" Drake asked.

Mauro looked out the window at the Drake house next door.

"Still sitting in the cars, watching the main house. They haven't moved since you smuggled me into the garage and told them you were in for the day. They have no idea we moved next door through that hedge maze."

"I still don't fully understand what we're expecting them to do." Matthew's mother looked past Mauro through the same window.

"Whatever they do will tell us if Marcot is really on our side. From what Matthew said, she keeps some shady company."

"So, this used to be the guest house for your house?" Mauro walked into the hallway and looked around the second-floor landing.

"It was part of the property when we originally bought it. We rent it to a lovely couple of snowbirds."

"All four men are heading to the house," Matthew reported.

The group huddled near the window.

"We don't have much time to get to the car," Mauro said walking toward the door.

"I'm watching … shit, they have guns drawn. They just opened the door and went in with guns drawn," Drake said.

The foursome enacted the plan they discussed while they were packing bug-out bags an hour earlier.

"Fuck you, Mrs. Marcot," Matthew said under his breath. He was the last person to leave the room, and the first person to reach the car.

CHAPTER FORTY-THREE

ASSANDRA HAD THE ADVANTAGE OF knowing that Christopher was a heavy sleeper. When he was out, he was out.

Cassie opened the door to Christopher's room without making a sound. She walked over to the bed and watched him sleep as she had done countless nights before. The soft sheets clung to his tall, muscular frame creating an outline similar to that of a Greek sculpture. His dark hair stood out against the pillow and his face looked relaxed. Cassandra knew that she could run her fingers through his hair without waking him, but she didn't. Instead, she walked to the landline phone that sat on the bed stand. She dialed the number from the palm of her hand and heard the phone ring very close by. She disconnected the call after one ring and held her breath as Chris's breathing varied slightly. Cassie waited for his steady rhythm to resume before returning the telephone handset to the base and began to search the nightstand for the source of the ringing. Chris placed the phone in the top drawer by habit. The missed call message illuminated the contents of the drawer. The sight of the gun sitting next to it turned Cassie's stomach. She glanced at the sleeping figure and considered confronting him with the phone that he wasn't supposed to have, and the weapon he was hiding, but she wanted the truth, and she assumed Chris would lie. Cassie grabbed both items and slipped from the room.

Cassie locked her bedroom door behind her, then went into the en suite bathroom, locking that door as well. She flipped the lights on, and sat on the edge of the bathtub looking at her boyfriend's secret cell phone. This was the moment she always feared was inevitable. She tried to suppress it, but the nagging worry that her perfect boyfriend was too perfect had been with her since she started seeing Chris. Cassie looked straight ahead and caught her reflection in the mirror. She looked disheveled and desperate. "Ready to cross another person off your Trusted List?" she asked herself. "I bet it's password protected anyway," she mumbled. She pressed the home button and a picture of Chris standing next to a beaming blonde appeared on the screen.

"Well, who are you?" She asked. She pressed the home button again and the screen for the passcode appeared. Cassie tried the six-digit pin number that she used for her apartment security system in Boston. The home screen appeared. "What a dumb ass," Cassandra whispered.

Cassandra's thumb hung in the air for a moment as she decided which app to invade first. "Let me see who your contacts are, Christopher ..." There were four. *Mrs. M* and *Kane* were two that jumped out at her. She didn't recognize the other names, so she selected *Mrs. M*. Her grandmother's cell, home phone, and an email address were there, but the email address ended in .onion and Cassandra didn't recognize it. She started to send the contact card to her own device before she remembered that she didn't own a cell phone anymore. It was easy enough to commit to memory.

Cassandra navigated back to the home screen and touched the camera app. She swallowed hard as the camera roll opened, but there was only one photo there—the one from the lock screen. The date on the picture indicated that it was taken while Chris was visiting his sick grandmother in Boston. Cassie expanded the photo and analyzed the background. It was dark; she couldn't find anything to indicate where it was taken. Chris's expression was one that she recognized but hadn't seen in a long time—he looked happy and relaxed. Tears welled up in Cassie's eyes and she hit the home button again to make the image go away.

There were three emails waiting, so Cassie opened Chris's inbox. Along with the new, unread mail there were hundreds of old messages and most of them were from her grandmother's .onion account. They dated back to her senior year at Harvard. Cassie decided to start at the beginning.

Dear Christopher Weston,

Going forward, this is the name you will use in your new position at The Davis Agency. After much consideration, it is my pleasure to inform you that I have chosen you to carry out the duty that I consider to be the most important role within the purview of the agency, and for me personally.

My granddaughter, Cassandra Marcot, presently attending Harvard University, possesses the most valuable asset of the company. The intellect embedded within her is the origin of the company itself. The genius that discovered the process by which to exhume talent and ability from one human and transplant it in another, lives on in Cassandra. She will be fully in your charge. You will protect her, and the treasure she carries, while directing her towards useful purpose. You will have a team at your disposal, but the personal relationship that you will forge makes you the pinnacle. This position replaces your former duty as an acquisition agent, but you may be called upon to provide support as needed in other capacities beyond safeguarding Cassandra. You will report directly to me and take direction only from me.

I look forward to working with you to provide Cassandra the perfect conditions within which she will thrive to her fullest potential.

Congratulations,

Mrs. M

As Cassie read, chills ran down her spine. Disbelief became enlightenment as more details and evidence were revealed with each email she opened. Tears flowed freely and Cassie gasped for breath between sobs. Her grandmother's last email, sent four hours ago, answered any questions that remained:

Cassandra showed no interest in attaching herself to the community redevelopment project that I offered to fund. I concur with your conclusion that she has been given every opportunity to use her gift in a way that would serve both her personal interests and the greater good. Therefore, it is my determination that the best course of action is to reassign her ability. The commodity can be harvested without her knowledge, and I will advise you on how to proceed. Rest assured that your commission will be paid upon closing. Your services will be retained, and your salary paid for as long as Cassandra cares to maintain a relationship with you.

The realization that the world Cassandra lived in was a fallacy made her want to run screaming from the house, but she knew the evil wasn't confined to the house. Based on what she just learned, the evil that created the nightmare she was living existed inside her.

Cassie beathed deeply to regain her composure and focused on packing a few necessities while she formulated a plan. When she was ready to act, she called Kane from the phone in her bedroom.

"Mr. Kane, could you please bring the car around? I'm going to need a ride. Yes. Right now. Thank you."

She hung up and looked out her bedroom window. When she saw Kane leave the guard house, she started down the rear staircase—the one the staff used. Once on the first floor, she used the path that she and her cousins mapped out as teenagers when they wanted to evade the detection of adults. The carefully planned trail fell outside the scope of the property cameras and required an almost comical combination of zig zag steps. Cassandra was headed to the property line but changed her mind when she got as far as the guesthouse. She needed time to think, and she knew that no one would look for her there. After all, someone with an IQ as high as hers wouldn't choose to hide something of such tremendous value in a place so obvious.

CHAPTER FORTY-FOUR

THE OPENING ACT WAS A band Kaaber would have purchased tickets to see. Charlie loved their latest release and played it non-stop just a few months ago. The familiar songs now felt like the soundtrack of a movie far too depressing to watch, so Kaaber muted the monitor is his dressing room.

Playing Madison Square Garden was the goal of every musician across the globe, and Kaaber dreamed of it himself while he watched Billy Joel and Elton John grace the stage here. It was his turn to add to the legacy of the magical venue, but there was no sense of awe, accomplishment, or joy in the moment. Former friends and co-workers requested VIP Access backstage, but Kaaber offered no invitations. His parents still weren't fully aware of the scope of what was happening to him, apart from expressing anxiety over quitting real estate. Instead of being surrounded by loved ones excited to share and witness his success, Kaaber was alone in a cold room, framed by four walls of painted concrete blocks that reminded him of a middle school cafeteria. When Kaaber glanced at the monitor on the wall, he was jealous of the band on stage—they were having the time of their lives, just like they seemed to do the night before.

Kaaber picked up the guitar that he used to write the songs he was about to perform and mindlessly noodled the strings. His guitar tech would have his show axe ready when it was time, but he liked the feel of the guitar he held now. The one he bought right after he bought

Kelly's ability, back when he thought it was possible to embody super-stardom and remarkable talent without debilitating guilt.

A song came out of him and Kaaber let it happen. He knew the chords and could hear the melodic lyrics in his mind. It happened sometimes; Kelly's skill remembering what it created when it still lived in the teenager. Kaaber realized it was the song about loss Kelly wrote while his mother was sick. He stopped playing, grabbed the guitar by the neck with both hands, and swung the instrument into the concrete wall. The impact caused an explosive crashing noise, which attracted security.

The guy on the other side of the door sounded appropriately concerned. "Mr. Kaaber, is everything okay in there?"

"Doing rock-star shit!" Kaaber yelled back.

Suddenly exhausted, he laid on the couch and wondered who had occupied it before him. When he closed his eyes, he saw Kelly on stage in the Village. He remembered how confident he was as he performed, knowing that his skills were special. Kaaber could envision what Kelly would be doing at this moment as he was getting ready to perform at MSG. His parents would be here. Probably neighbors or classmates. Jeff, the bar owner would be here bragging that he gave Kelly his big break by giving him a set at his club. Kelly would be basking in his mother's pride. Maybe he would invite her up on stage to do a song with him for the encore.

There was a knock on the door. "Fifteen minutes."

"Yep!" Kaaber yelled, not moving.

After a few deep breaths, Kaaber stood up and walked to the full-length mirror. When he was selling real estate, he dressed impeccably, even though he would only see a few clients each day. Tonight, he would be seen by tens of thousands, and he hadn't showered, washed his hair, or shaved. He wore the clothes the wardrobe department provided. For the first night at MSG, it was light blue silk joggers and a loose white T-shirt with a strategically stretched V-shaped neckline. The two pieces probably cost more than his best suit, and they were comfortable, so he didn't care. The PR team never consulted him about his image. He wore the same dingy T tonight with jeans and his stupid motorcycle boots.

"Pre-show huddle!" Rafferty opened the door and leaned into the dressing room. "What did the guitar do to piss you off?"

Kaaber opened the door the rest of the way and walked past Rafferty to the area where his band was waiting for him.

"All right, my musical brothers!" He clapped his hands together a few times before placing his arms over the shoulders of the guys standing on each side of him. The band followed suit until they were a tight circle. "Thank you, God for the talent you have bestowed upon us and for bringing us together. Thank you for the opportunity to entertain these people by sharing our gifts. Thank you for the ability to give them an escape from their troubles for the next ninety minutes. Bless the love that will be shared here tonight in your name."

Rafferty captured the private moment on his phone and posted it before the group could chorus, "Amen!" Kaaber added his own exclamation under his breath, "Bullshit."

The stage crew set the headlining act in fifteen minutes, hitting the mark they practiced for. Kaaber inserted his in-ear monitors and strapped on his guitar. As the band began to take their places, the audience roared. The opening chord rang out and an omniscient voice cut through the noise.

"Ladies and gentlemen, please give a huge Madison Square Garden welcome to New York City's own ... Kaaaaaaberrrrrrrrrr!"

Kaaber's ear monitors were noise cancelling, but the screams bled through the open mics on stage. His head was filled with shrieks, and he flashed back to the night Kelly was shot. The gunshot had caused his ears to ring, dampening the sound in the same way his monitors did now. The crowd noise was like the sound he made as he cried out in terror. Kaaber knew he would relive that event every single time he stepped onto a stage and these conditions repeated.

He waved to the audience and approached his mic. "I am the greatest musical artist of all time!" The crowd noise raised another ten decibels. "And tonight ... I'm playing just for you!" Kaaber started playing the opening riff of the first song on the set list and hoped the night would fly by quickly so he could go home and be alone.

CHAPTER FORTY-FIVE

MAURO SAT AT THE UNSTABLE round table that was positioned next to the motel room window. He tapped on his laptop while the Drakes stood around him watching.

David cleared his throat and broke the silence. "Let's think this through again. If I can talk to my partners, we could contact the proper authorities and resolve this without going to the extremes you're suggesting."

Mauro continued to scroll and click. "I know exactly how you feel right now. This is the second time I've started over. Experience doesn't make it easier."

David Drake started pacing, and his wife and Matthew instinctively sat on the bed to get out of the way. "No offense, Mauro, but I'm walking away from more than a Waste Management job and an apartment in Jersey City."

"No offense taken," Mauro said without looking up from the computer screen.

"I'm not in the habit of making huge life decisions based on the word of strangers."

"No offense taken," Mauro repeated.

"I don't even know if what you've told me is true."

Mauro leaned back in his chair and pointed toward the seated Drakes. "Unfortunately, the only proof that what I'm saying is true leaves one of these two, or both of them, dead. You found out that Miami PD turned five murder suspects over to the FBI and no one's talking. They don't even have names for the assholes that killed Wagner, may he rest in peace. It's my fault he's dead. He knew we had no chance against Davis, but he had my back because I was determined to watch over your family, and I was convinced that I could somehow capitalize on the trouble they were having …" Mauro laced his fingers together and placed his hands on top of his head. He closed his eyes. "I was wrong. Wagner paid the ultimate price for my arrogance. I can't let them kill you too."

"There has to be another way for us to stay safe," Drake said.

Mauro's laptop sounded an audio alert and he looked at the screen.

"We've got someone. He says a thousand dollars apiece for US Passports and driver's licenses. He can meet us now. How far is Liberty City from here?"

"I can't just walk away!" Drake yelled.

"Keep your voice down," Mauro said evenly. "You're starting over with more cash than most people accumulate in a lifetime. Do you want your stuff and your law firm, or do you want to live the rest of your life with the people you love? Because if you stay, your family, and maybe you if you get in the way, won't make it through the day. It might end with you dead anyway, but I want to try to keep you alive."

"God damn it." David Drake sat on the bed next to his family. "We can be in Liberty City in twenty minutes."

CHAPTER FORTY-SIX

MAURO WATCHED THE FAMILY PASS through airport security with their bug-out bag carry-ons. The Davis family's possessions had been consolidated to three duffel bags, but the cash they transferred out of the country would provide for new belongings to go with their new identities.

On the other side of security, David Drake turned around and nodded at Mauro who returned the gesture. He placed his arms around his family and guided them to their new beginning.

Mauro left the airport terminal and got into the second rental car that he had acquired since his arrival in Miami. He started driving toward the Drake residence without having been aware of the moment he decided to do so.

As he suspected, there was still a car parked in front of the house with two hired guns inside. Mauro parked his rental nose to nose with the car, having to drive on the wrong side of the street to approach the vehicle from the front. He held eye contact with the driver. As Mauro got out, he held his hands where they could be seen and walked to the passenger side of the security team's car. As he approached, the window slid down. Mauro slapped the roof of the car twice with his left hand and reached through the open window with his right to unlock the car doors. He opened the door to the back seat and slid into the car.

"I need a meeting with your boss. Take me now."

The two men exchanged glances and the driver picked up his cell.

"We have Greco. He would like to talk to you in person." The driver listened for a moment. "We're on the way."

The security guard had to put the car in reverse to avoid Mauro's rental before he pulled out onto the street. Mauro looked at the Drake home as they pulled away. *Such a beautiful place to grow up*, he thought with Matthew's face in mind. He hoped that they would be okay. If they were smart, they would be fine. He knew from experience that it was possible to avoid Davis's detection and he wasn't a man of the law. He was just a dumb kid from Jersey. Certainly, David Drake would see to it that his family stayed safe.

The security guard in the passenger seat made a phone call asking someone on the other end to be ready to go in fifteen minutes.

Mauro watched through the window as the car drove to Signature Aviation at the Miami Airport. Since he had been a young boy, Mauro wanted to fly on a private jet. He smiled to himself that he was checking things off his bucket list right up until the end.

The gate leading to the ramp opened when the driver punched a code into the keypad outside. As the car drove slowly in front of the parked jets, Mauro guessed which one would be his ride. He was focused on the planes and the elaborate paint jobs, so he didn't see the four men following the car on foot. When the car stopped, the door he was leaning on burst open and his face was covered with a cloth that smelled horribly sweet.

When he woke up, the taste of vomit was fresh in his mouth and his face lay in a puddle of chunky liquid. Mauro was hogtied again. This was not how he imagined riding in a luxury jet, but he mentally clicked the box anyway.

"I need the head" he said loudly.

Six men, all dressed in variations of the same designer navy suits were seated around him. Four sat in leather chairs that resembled La-Z-Boys facing each other and another two sat on either side of a long leather couch.

"Take him," One of the men barked. Now Mauro knew who the lead guy was.

The two men from the couch got up and walked to where Mauro lay in the aisle.

"I'm going to untie you and let you walk to the head. We all have tasers and we can spend the rest of the flight showing you how they work if you want to start any shit. Don't do anything stupid, and we might belt you into a seat like a human being for the rest of the flight because we're sick of stepping over your fat ass every time we want to walk around."

"I got it. I don't have beef with you. I'm outnumbered and I'm not stupid, but I do have to piss. Really bad."

Mauro felt pressure on his hands and then they fell free. His feet followed. He stood up very slowly and rolled his head, first one direction and then another. "Is it back there?" He pointed to the back of the plane.

"Yeah. I'm coming with you and you're gonna leave the door open."

Mauro walked down the short aisle to the rear of the plane. He unlatched the door to the lav and let it swing all the way open. He couldn't help but let out a sigh of relief as he released the contents of his bladder. When he finished, he washed his hands in the sink and used the foam to clean his face. He rinsed off and swished some water in his mouth to rid himself of the taste of bile.

"That's enough. You didn't say you were going to take a sponge bath." The grunt watching over him had grown impatient. "Let's go. Grab a seat on the right side and fasten your seatbelt."

The conversation in the cabin came to a halt when Mauro reappeared. He nodded at the security team and wondered if they were Blackwater types. He belted in and tried to enjoy the ride. The chatter resumed, but Mauro couldn't hear much. He stole glances at the guards. All were younger than he was by at least twenty years and most were his size or bigger. Mauro looked out the window to see if he could see the ground. They were still above the clouds, so Mauro figured they had a ways to go.

"Excuse me, can I lift the leg support and lean back?" he asked the number one guy.

The lead chuckled. "Sure."

Mauro heard one of the team say something about how most guys would be shitting their pants to be in Mauro's shoes right now. Another guy replied that ignorance was bliss.

Mauro closed his eyes. One thing he couldn't claim to be was ignorant. But he felt peaceful. He was in the eye of a hurricane that he had been anticipating for over two decades Flying on the G 450 was far better than the commercial flight from JFK to Miami. Even the air was better. Fresher. The seat was wider by half and the legroom was adequate for a man his size. Mauro wanted to be ready, so he slept.

CHAPTER FORTY-SEVEN

ROLLING STONE
The meteoric rise of Sasha Kaaber
By M Gijbels

Six months ago, Sasha Kaaber was not a household name. But his isn't a rags to riches story. He was a successful real estate agent who enjoyed a luxurious Manhattan lifestyle. Sasha was charming, good-looking, and he had a secret ... he was the most prolific songwriter the music industry hadn't heard of yet.

A chance meeting, or perhaps it was destiny, with Adam Stone changed the trajectory of Kaaber's career. He found Stone a new NYC home, and, once the deal was closed, Kaaber asked for a favor.

"It was the most unprofessional thing I've ever done," Sasha told me. "Totally out of line. Adam's a very generous guy, and I kind of had the feeling that he wasn't the type to call my boss and get me fired but sending him that email with the mp4 attached was a big risk. I'm grateful that it went the way it did."

From the moment that Adam heard the demo, Kaaber's music career rocketed.

"I'm fortunate to already be generating sales equal to musicians who have been at the top for the last decade," Stone

said. "It's easy to forget that there's unmatched talent all over the world, but we will never know those names because they never crossed paths with the person who could help them fulfill their destiny. It's intimidating as fuck, actually, because I know there's some dude in Nonameville, Wisconsin that can play circles around me, is technically a better vocalist than me, and could knock me off my perch if he ever got that Golden Ticket. I'm simultaneously jealous of that guy and happy to provide the introduction he might need to get where I am in my career."

I met Sasha Kaaber at the Beekman Hotel in lower Manhattan. He answered the door to the suite himself, greeting me with a firm handshake. The head of his PR team, Rafferty Blake, deeply engrossed in his laptop, barely acknowledged my arrival, which is atypical for a PR guy. The atmosphere was tense. This was the rare artist whose team was not going overboard to give a music journalist the impression that their brand was made of sunshine, rainbows, and naturally flowing waterfalls of Dom Pérignon. The tone was set for an interesting interview.

Kaaber wore a black dress shirt with charcoal gray dress pants for our meeting, looking more like the real estate agent he used to be than the rock star he is now. He wore two pieces of jewelry; a Breitling watch and a silver chain around his neck, from which hung a woman's emerald and diamond ring. We sit on upholstered velvet couches positioned across from each other with an antique-looking coffee table between us. Kaaber leans back into the couch, positions his right ankle atop his left knee, and clasps his hands in his lap before flashing a smile that invites me to begin.

MG: Let me start off by congratulating you on your amazing success. It's been heady to watch from the outside. How are you doing after being shot out of a rocket?

K: (Politely laughs.) I'd be an ungrateful prick if I said it's been anything other than awesome.

MG: We all know the story of how you were discovered. I'm curious about how you're making the transition from being unknown to being thrust into the public eye. And how are the people in your life handling it?

K: Everyone in my world is happy for me, obviously. I'm lucky to have a lot of support, but right now the people I'm closest to are the guys hitting the stage with me every night. I'm looking forward to spending time with those dudes as we tour. They're amazing on stage and off. I'm gonna learn a lot from them.

MG: How about the people in your personal life? Is there a girlfriend somewhere in this suite who might want to give her perspective?

K: (Laughs) No, there's no scoop to be had on that front, unfortunately. I'm very single.

MG: Where do the love songs come from? There were a couple on the release.

K: I'm not in a relationship right now, but I've had my share of joy and heartache on that front. I'm no different than anyone else.

MG: You were seen with a gorgeous blond when you appeared on Jimmy—

K: (Smiles and shakes his head as he gets up from his seat across from me and walks to the bar.) Can I get you anything? We have a good selection here, but we can call downstairs if you want something special.

MG: So, no dating talk at all?

K: I don't want to talk about my personal life. There isn't one special woman. Know what I mean?

K: (Returns to the couch with a rocks glass.)

MG: What does a day in the life of Sasha Kaaber look like these days?

K: I get up around eight, hit the gym for an hour or so, eat breakfast, go to rehearsal, and go to bed.

MG: That's not very Rock-n-Roll.

K: Maybe once the tour starts, I'll be more interesting. Our shows at MSG went well. I was happy with the crew and the band, but I want to feel more comfortable on stage. I want to give people a show that sticks with them long after they leave, so I like rehearsal mode. This routine makes me feel ready.

MG: I attended the first night at MSG and I thought the show was flawless. What do you think you have to work on?

K: I used to go to the Village to watch this kid play on Tuesday nights—

MG: What was his name?

K: Sorry, I don't remember. It was a long time ago. I only saw him twice; maybe three times, but he embodied the music in a transformative way. I'm not sure I've mastered that.

MG: It would be cool to give this kid a shout out in Rolling Stone. Where did he play?

PR GUY: This is an article about Kaaber. Do you mention random club acts when you write about Harry Styles?

MG: What do you want your fans to know about you?

K: That I'm not special. I'm really not special. But if you have a gift, nurture it. Take care of it. Cherish it. Don't sell-out to anyone. Treasure your gifts because those abilities are the essence of who you are.

MG: Well, there will be a lot of people who will disagree that you aren't special, but I love the rest of that message.

At this point, Kaaber's PR Guy told me that my time was up and Kaaber walked me to the door himself. Before he closed it, he whispered, "The kid's name was Kelly Bailey. Look into him."

I wish I could say that I found Kelly Bailey. I didn't. But I found the club where he used to play on Tuesday nights and the bar owner who hired him. He agreed to talk to me off the record and confirmed the legend of Kelly Bailey whose talent impressed Sasha Kaaber. The bar owner gave me the name of Kelly's mother, which led me to an address on Canal Street. The occupant of the apartment has only been living there for a few months and had no knowledge of the previous tenants. Neighbors didn't provide any useful details. So, Reader, I pass the quest on to you. Kaaber wants us to know Kelly Bailey and I want to find him. Talent can't hide—let's find it. There might be more Sasha Kaabers out there and the world needs their music. In the meantime, we are satisfied with the one we have, and look forward to watching his star burn brightly for years to come.

CHAPTER FORTY-EIGHT

BEFORE THE CAPTAIN OPENED THE passenger door, the number one guy gave Mauro a speech about walking slowly, letting the men surround him, and walking straight to the car that would be parked outside the FBO terminal. Mauro reminded him that he was the one who requested the meeting, and assured him that he had no second thoughts.

The entourage wasn't unusual for the private airport in Van Nuys. One man being escorted by six didn't even turn a head. Mauro was guided to a white Rolls Royce, and he sat in the rear of the car after Number One opened the door for him. Two men in suits and a driver were already inside, and the lead closed the door after Mauro.

"Six guys to cover me on a plane at forty-thousand feet and just two guys and a driver on the ground?" Mauro's New Jersey accent and New Jersey cynicism oozed from his words.

"You are in good hands, Mr. Greco, I assure you," the older of the two men said.

Mauro resisted the urge to reply with sarcasm and chose to look out the window instead. He had never ridden in a Rolls, and he had never been to California. Two more boxes checked. The ride took just under a half hour and there was no more conversation until the older man spoke to the driver.

"Please use the back gate. We're going to the guest house."

"Yes, Mr. Kane."

Mauro saw wrought iron gates with a huge capital "M" in script across the center. The car followed a circular road, made a sharp turn toward the property, and paused outside another set of smaller, prison like gates. They opened more quickly than Mauro thought possible, and the car entered the grounds. Mauro saw a swimming pool and bathhouse, tennis courts, and a huge mansion ahead. Off to the right stood a bungalow that would have swallowed whole the shaker style house that Mauro's family owned. That was their destination, and the driver parked in front.

Mr. Kane opened the car door and got out, waving his hand military style for Mauro to follow him. There were more suits at this location than had been on the plane.

"You guys own stock at Brooks Brothers?"

Mauro counted six guys. With the two from the car, that made eight. Mauro got a look at the driver through the windshield and factored him out immediately. He should have been forced to retire long ago.

"Right this way, Mr. Greco," Kane pointed toward the double doors being held open by two of his men.

Mauro entered the dollhouse-like knock-off. It looked like a page from an architectural magazine had been printed in 3D. The pillows on the couch were perfectly fluffed, as if they had never been used. The tables were overly accessorized—a remote control or a coffee mug wouldn't fit among the bowls of seashells and stacks of large photo books. An area rug in the center of the living room had three inches of pile, uniformly standing at attention.

There was a full kitchen, dining room, and what looked like a split floor plan on either side of the great room. Mauro walked toward the right side where he guessed the master bedroom would be.

"Can I use a bathroom? It's been a while."

Mr. Kane stared at Mauro in reply.

"Of course, you may use the restroom, Mr. Greco. There is one off the hallway to your left." The authoritative voice came from a woman, and Mauro swiveled his head to find her. When he made eye contact with her, the hair on the back of his neck stood up. She was beautiful for a woman in her later years, Mauro couldn't pin the decade—maybe sixty, maybe seventy. She had bobbed hair, perfectly coiffed, and she was dressed in a very expensive looking cashmere track suit. She was more intimidating in person than she had been on the iPad screen.

"Thank you." Mauro reversed direction and went toward the bathroom. He had been correct; this side of the house was the guest wing. The master would be on the other side. Mauro used the facilities with the door open and with an audience of one suit. He looked out the glass door at the pool, wondering if it was heated. He washed his hands and joined the others in the great room where everyone remained standing.

"I understand that you wanted to speak with me, Mr. Greco," the older woman said.

"With all due respect, Mrs. Marcot, I asked to speak to Mr. Davis, the head of The Davis Agency."

"I think you've been made aware that there is no one specific 'Davis.' If your intent is to speak with the person at the helm of The Davis Agency, that is me."

"How long have you been in charge?"

"Long enough to remember the case that changed many of our protocols, Mr. Greco. It brought me satisfaction to hear that karma finally caught up with Mr. Reichert. It's both a frustration and a relief to learn that you were personally responsible for precipitating the only two gaffes to blemish our agency in recent history. Once we settle our business today, I have every reason to believe that we will return to business as usual with no detractors."

As Mauro laughed his eyes sparkled. "I'm glad to know that I've been a thorn in your side all these years," he said.

"I'm sure my life changed very little compared to yours after your encounter with our organization. You weren't there to comfort your mother when your father passed away. You haven't married, had children of your own, or used the talent you so foolishly coveted. Hindsight being what it is, do you regret not trading your gift for the millions that might have saved your father? He might have avoided heart disease and stroke, had his lifestyle been different. At the very least your parents' standard of living would have been improved."

The suits remained standing on the periphery of the conversation, but Mrs. Marcot opted to make footprints in the pile rug and make her impression on the perfect looking couch. She gestured toward Mauro, "Please, sit. There will be plenty of time for your discomfort later."

Mauro remained standing. "I came to make you an offer. It's one-sided in your favor, so I think you'll like it."

"Amusing that you think you are in a position to bargain, but I am curious."

"You will never find the Newcombe-Drake family and they don't have Thad's ability anyway. They had no idea that his talent was quantifiable. That Face Time phone call was a set-up to test your loyalty. I was in the room while you talked to Matthew and Drake. In exchange for your promise to leave them alone, I'll give you what you wanted from me many years ago when you were willing to pay an obscene amount of money for it to cover your loss on the Newcombe deal."

"How generous of you, Mr. Greco. But you're offering me something that is already in my possession. I have you, so I have your genome. How I handle my business with Thad's heirs is none of your concern."

"They don't have it. He bled out. Straight into the drain. The coroner completed his exam and sent the body to the crematory. Certainly, you know this. You have ways of knowing everything."

"Why did you bid on his ability? Of all the listings available, you chose the one with which there was a problem to exploit. You were obviously working with the family, perhaps even with Thad himself."

Mauro shook his head. "You think you're so infallible, but your arrogance is what's going to be your downfall, lady. The idiots you have posting online are braggarts—they show no professional discretion." Mauro pointed at Christopher. "You have that kid running his game in Miami and then showing up in your house while you're video chatting to Matthew. You have money changing hands before the commodity is received; your buyers are ignoring your non-disclosures. That tech guy was on TV lettin' the world marvel at his newly unveiled musical ability ... I hate to break it to you, but you have problems with more than one listing."

"Things have gotten more difficult for us in recent years. News travels quickly over both social and mainstream media, and our clients are eager to cash in on whatever notoriety their abilities may bring. But these developments can be used to our advantage. Our commodities are worth more than ever, and we can locate our business partners quite easily by cruising YouTube. You needn't worry about the future of my endeavors."

Mauro left his size 13 footprints on the carpet and moved toward Mrs. Marcot, animating the suits that were standing at attention.

"I'm just taking the lady up on her offer to sit down, boys. My back is killing me."

Mauro lowered himself onto the far end of the couch, leaving a deferential gap between himself and Mrs. Marcot.

"My plan, well, my hope was that the deal I was offering would get me in the room with Davis, so I could cut the head off the snake. I thought I could kill The Davis Agency by killing Davis. That's why I asked your goons to bring me to you."

One of the suits lunged at Mauro, grabbing his arm, and pulling it behind his back in an awkward position. Mauro looked at Kane. "Really?"

Kane nodded for the young security guard to release Mauro, but he and the rest of the security team kept a hand on their weapons.

"There are many capable people within the organization who could step into my role at a moment's notice. I'm afraid that makes me more insignificant than I care to admit." Mrs. Marcot's voice was steady and confident.

"You steal lives."

"We market attributes that were formerly only attainable through the genetic lottery. We make the lives of those who can afford our services far better. I think you will agree that we provide safekeeping for the most valuable assets on earth. Would you rather have the world's most dazzling singing voice belong to a responsible person who will provide it the finest care, or would you rather see that gift in the hands of a crack-addicted degenerate who will burn it up before it can reach its full potential?"

Mauro laughed so hard that his shoulders shook, causing the rest of the room to tense.

"I guess you have to rationalize that you're breaking about half the commandments and all of society's laws of ethics."

"I don't expect you to understand, Mr. Greco, but answer this question for me. Was your talent utilized for the good of all mankind or was it hoarded by an immature and selfish boy?"

"I would have used it. I could have made a lot of people happy over the course of what promised to be a long career. I could have been a role model for kids. I could have given hopeless people something to believe in ... if Greco can pull out that win, maybe I can get that promotion ... stuff like that. I would have made a difference. I would have used my platform for good. You took that away from me."

"You came to cut off the head of the snake, yet you'll settle for making me feel guilty?" Mrs. Marcot raised her eyebrows and inhaled sharply. "I'm afraid I have to disappoint you. I'm quite proud of my role in reassigning ownership of this world's most valuable possessions. I've been rewarded both financially and personally. My family will have lives of privilege for many generations to come before the well runs dry thanks to the work I've done in my lifetime."

"Prosperous family businesses generally get passed down. You tellin' me you're the last Czar?" Mauro's accent was thick with sarcasm.

"She has no heir. Her sons want nothing to do with her. They must know her secrets." Cassandra appeared in the doorway of the master bedroom, holding a gun in her shaking right hand.

The small army of security guards aimed their weapons toward Cassandra's voice. Kane held his hand up like a crossing guard, directing his men to halt.

"Miss Marcot, I'm going to walk over to you and you're going to hand me that gun."

Cassandra pointed the gun at Kane. "Not another step. Gram, tell your dog to sit."

"Cassandra isn't a threat, Mr. Kane, and she is going to put that gun down because she is making everyone nervous."

"I imagine that you're as surprised to see me with a gun as I was to find it in Christopher's drawer—next to the cell phone that he uses to communicate with you." Cassandra scoffed. "I thought that I introduced the two of you, but his phone history indicates otherwise."

Christopher looked at Mrs. Marcot, but her focus never left Cassandra.

"You refused to allow me to provide a bodyguard for you, dear. I wasn't about to let the love of my life run around this world unprotected."

Cassandra laughed. "Oh, I must have misread the whole situation. You hired Christopher to pretend to fall in love with me so he could carry out the job you hired him to perform as my bodyguard? Or, rather, my intellect's bodyguard?"

"No, Cassie." Chris shook his head. "I mean, maybe at first, but then after being around you, I had to admit to your grandmother that I broke the first rule of personal security."

"Stop the bullshit, please. Both of you. Don't insult the intelligence that you wish to reassign. What did you do to get promoted from an agent to a boyfriend, Chris? Can I still call you Chris? I wonder what those interviews entailed. And I'm curious to know how much the commission is for selling the thing that makes me tick."

Mrs. Marcot spoke softly, "Cassandra—"

"No, Gram. I read all the emails that went back and forth between the two of you. A dot onion account server is secure, but if you don't delete your emails and empty the trash; if you just leave the emails in your inbox for anyone to find, it doesn't really matter."

Cassandra held up Christopher's cell phone.

Mrs. Marcot barked at Kane, "Your team was supposed to be watching her."

Kane knew better than to speak. Instead, he held out his hand to Cassandra.

"I'm not giving you the gun, Mr. Kane, but you don't have to worry. I'm not shooting my Gram with it either." Cassandra pointed the gun at Mauro. "You came here to cut the head off the snake—to hurt my grandmother? Well, you can't hurt her. There's nothing ... you can do ... to her." Cassandra's voice cracked and she started to breath in short sobs. "But there's something I can do. Gram, I believe what you said just now ... that I'm the love ... of your life. And you ... were mine. At least that's what I thought, or my borrowed brain thought. What do I know? I don't even know who I am."

As Cassandra spoke, no one dared to move, to exhale, or to make eye contact. The room was charged with a tangible form of electricity that came from knowing something monumental was about to happen. Cassandra looked at her grandmother with eyes that displayed the agony of her broken heart. She took a deep breath and her voice regained strength.

"Exactly when did you decide to sell me out, Gram? Protect me, my ass! You ordered Chris to harvest me."

"Don't be so dramatic, Cassandra. You were determined not to utilize your gift to its full potential. The intellect you currently possess has been passed down and cultivated for centuries. It was a gift that I gave you when you were a child, but you don't want it or need it. You have more money than a lifetime of work in the highest position could provide. You may have noticed a decline in your ability, but I'm convinced that you would have been relieved. The constant motion of your mind burdened you, and that was my fault. By removing the genome, I simply intended to correct my mistake. I have always taken care of you and this particular situation would have been no different."

"Except that you didn't value me enough to love me as I was. Do you love me or your creation? Are we so close because you built me?" Cassandra looked pleadingly at her grandmother, but Mrs. Marcot remained silent. "Removing my intellect, maybe my memories, or my ability to reason ... it's a pretty big risk, don't you think? Obliterating an integral ingredient of my personality? Do you know, with absolute certainty, what that would have done to me, or were you more concerned with the asset? How could you possibly justify stealing the essence of a person? You look at what there is to gain, but you conveniently look away from what's lost. Well, see how it feels when something you love is taken from you, Gram."

In one swift motion, Cassandra placed the gun barrel in her mouth and pulled the trigger.

Mrs. Marcot screamed in terror as her granddaughter slumped to the ground. The older woman stared and searched the air around her with empty hands. She began to breath rapidly, as if hyperventilating, then she collapsed on the floor in front of the couch. The security team divided their attention between their boss and Cassandra's body. Mauro slowly rose from his position on the couch and inched away from the scene. He noticed that his boots were leaving a trail in the thick carpet. He calmly walked backwards to the bathroom he had used earlier, and let himself out the door that led to the pool.

EPILOGUE

Michael Allen Douglass blew out the candles on his cake. His girls lined up to hang from his neck and give him kisses.

"Buon compleanno, Papa," Chiara shouted too loudly for their proximity. Michael laughed at the beautiful six-year-old. He ran his fingers through thick, curly black hair that hung far below her shoulders.

"Grazie, bambina."

"Don't call me baby, Papa. I'm almost as grown as Isabella. I fit into all her shoes!"

"You have a little way to go," Isa laughed. "Buon compleanno, a day early, Papa. I hope you like your cake. I baked it with Mama. It's the chocolate flourless you used to have in America. The one your mother used to make you."

"Grazie! I can't wait to dig into it." Michael hugged his sixteen-year-old daughter. He had been exactly her age when his life changed dramatically.

He winked at his wife. He loved her deeply, but she would never fully know him. It helped that she wasn't naturally curious and, perhaps, a little self-centered. When they met, in college, she asked the necessary questions about his background, but she preferred to tell her stories. Adalina had a negative view of Americans in general, even an ex-patriot who had forsaken his homeland and chosen hers. The less she reminded herself of the fact that he was from the states, the easier it was to view him as a prospective mate. Now, as the American's wife, she infused their lives with as much Italian culture as possible. She did make exceptions, like chocolate flourless cake from a recipe that her deceased mother-in-law left to her son.

"This is the most special birthday celebration I have ever had!" Michael said, smiling.

"Papa, you say that every year!" Isa laughed.

"Every year, you outdo the last!" Michael hugged her close.

"Why can't we come with you to Switzerland? I've never been apart from you on your birthday before!" Chiara shouted.

Adalina shushed the young girl. "We've been over this, bambina. Papa has business. Don't ruin tonight because he has to leave tomorrow."

"Dance with me, Papa?" Chiara asked sweetly.

"My pleasure," Michael answered.

Adalina poured the remainder of the wine into three glasses, Isa getting only a few ounces. Chiara selected a song from her iPad, and the sound filled the room.

"Mama said this was one of your favorite artists from when you were a teenager," Chiara said proudly.

Michael smiled at his daughter. "You are correct, bambina. This is a singer and songwriter named Kaaber. He was very good—wrote some of my favorite songs back in the day."

Chiara stepped onto the top of her father's feet and held her right hand out for him guide her through their dance.

"Does Kaaber still write songs, Papa?"

"Not anymore," Michael replied as he covered every square foot of the kitchen with his large, wild dance steps. Chiara held on and squealed with delight.

"Why doesn't he make songs anymore, Papa?"

"Because he's dead, Stupida. Don't you know anything? He was driving his McLaren in California, and someone pulled out right in front of him. He died at the scene, but the music he recorded before he passed away was released as a love letter to his fans from the great beyond. Isn't that tragic?" Isa said dreamily.

"Enough, young lady," Adalina warned.

"Oh, yeah! Kaaber's picture is on the poster you have in your room, and the T-shirt you wear, and the poster that you kiss at night!" Chiara yelled above the music. "Papa, I'm getting dizzy!"

Michael lifted his young daughter into his arms and walked back to the table where Isa and Adalina had set out cake plates.

"Thank you for a truly wonderful birthday, signores."

The little party kept the girls up past bedtime, so Michael cleaned the kitchen while Adalina rushed them through their nightly routine.

Tomorrow was the milestone birthday that Michael had waited twenty-four years for, and he was terrified. The second page of Thad's letter instructed him to use the attached key on his fortieth birthday. The address in the lower right-hand corner of the blue stationary was for a bank in Switzerland. Matthew, now known as Michael, had been monitoring the solvency of the bank for twenty-four years, and tomorrow he would go in person to find out what was waiting for him there.

As Michael dried the wine glasses and placed them back in the cupboard, he thought about his parents, who hadn't lived long enough to discover what Thad had left behind. He wished they were with him, but he was glad he shared Thad's secret with each of them before they died. David passed away first, then Mary a year later. They were Michael's only connection to his past. His parents knew his story, the life he left behind, and why he started over. Even though they rarely discussed the reason they fled the United States, it helped to exchange knowing glances and thoughtful winks with people who shared his history.

After the rest of his family drifted into sleep, Michael settled into his favorite chair with a familiar book … he knew he wouldn't be able to focus on new material. He half read; half daydreamed until it was time to get ready.

Michael departed for the airport before his girls were awake, so he left a note on the kitchen counter like he used to do for his mother when he was young. He drove himself, passed through security, and boarded his flight without incident. The one time he would have invited a disruption, everything went smoothly. During the flight, Michael tried to imagine every scenario that might occur at the bank, and developed a defensive plan for each possible obstacle. Michael knew all too well that other people might have had this day marked on their calendars as well. This might be the day that The Davis Agency finally took possession of what they believed was rightfully theirs.

The taxi driver encountered no traffic delays on the way to the bank and Michael reached out to open the door just as a bank employee unlocked it from the inside.

He didn't noticed the elderly man approach him from behind until his large hand rested on his shoulder.

"Matthew. You made it."

He trained himself not to react to that name, but the familiarity of the voice made him turn around. The eyes were exactly the same—kind, but hard at the same time. His skin was looser, the tufts of hair that remained on his head were now grey, and the giant man seemed to have shrunk a few inches—perhaps Matthew's perception had changed—he hadn't seen Mauro since he was a sixteen-year-old boy.

"I can't believe it!" Matthew smiled.

The two men embraced, slapping each other on the back.

"It's just us, Mauro."

The old man nodded his understanding. "I know."

"Dad would be glad that you're with me."

"Someone has to look after you if he can't." Mauro choked on the last few words and began to cough uncontrollably.

"Who's watching over you?" Matthew asked.

The older man regained his composure. "You'd be surprised what I could still do if I had to. They'd have to get past me to get to you, kid, and ain't nobody getting' past me." The New Jersey accent hadn't faded. "Let's go see what Thad made you wait more than two decades for."

The men entered the bank and were escorted to the secure room that housed the safety deposit boxes. Box 4448 was among the largest, on the lowest row. The bank teller had to kneel to insert her key into the lock and Matthew did the same. Once the door was opened, the teller tried to slide the box from its vault, but it wouldn't budge. Matthew and Mauro teamed up to lift the box to the table in the middle of the room and the teller excused herself, closing the door behind her.

"That was a hundred pounds easy," Mauro said. He rolled his shoulders a few times and arched his back. "You gonna open the lid?"

Matthew exhaled. "I guess we've waited long enough. But I'm not ready for what might be in there."

"Oh geez ..." Mauro flipped the lid open. The box was full, a cotton cloth covered the contents, and a canvas sat by itself on top.

Matthew lifted the canvas by placing his fingertips on the edges. It was a watercolor portrait of Mary sitting in her favorite chair on the lanai of their Coconut Grove home. Matthew involuntarily made an "oh" sound as he exhaled, and tears welled in his eyes. "It's amazing." He cleared his throat and studied the details through blurry vision.

"Beautiful painting of a beautiful woman," Mauro agreed.

"Wow. Thanks, Gramps," Matthew whispered.

Mauro looked into the open box. "There's a lot more in there, kid."

Matthew set the canvas down and removed the cloth that was tucked into the sides of the box.

"Oh ... boy." Matthew lifted out a stack of bills bound together. "It's all hundreds. He unpacked the top layer and confirmed his finding again. "It's all hundreds!" He laughed in astonishment. "Mauro, I want you to have half of whatever's here."

Mauro smiled. "Son, that's your family legacy, not mine. My legacy was gettin' you to it alive and I did that."

Mauro picked up the canvas and brought it to his face to study it closely. Until he was forced to look at the back of the canvas, Matthew hadn't noticed the envelope taped there. His name was written on the outside in his grandfather's perfect handwriting.

Matthew carefully removed the envelope and stared at it for several seconds.

"You gonna open it? I feel like a broken record over here ..." Mauro gestured wildly with his hands as he spoke.

"Yeah, yeah, yeah ..." Matthew slid his finger along the seal and removed a piece of his grandfather's stationery. He recognized the blue paper with the unusual crest on it. He unfolded the single sheet of paper and started reading.

Dear Matthew,

I hope that this letter will provide you with the answers you deserve.

First, I want to tell you that I love you. Everything I did, I did because I love you and your family. Because my ego was bigger than the sky, I thought that I could play with fire and not get burned. My greatest fear was that the people I cared for most would suffer to pay my penance. I know that burden will be on my heart when I die, but I hope and pray that my plans worked out, and that you are standing in a vault in Switzerland reading these words. I wish that I could tell you how sorry I am for involving myself and, thusly, involving you with the horrible thugs to whom I sold my artistic ability. It was my last attempt to be justly compensated for my body of work. Before I could go through with it, I realized that all treasures not bestowed upon us by God come from the other one, and I did not wish to be in business with him. Mine was a God-given ability as yours is, Matthew. I could not dishonor that gift by conceding it to His detractors. Stealing is number seven and I'm sure I will be held accountable by my creator. Hopefully, what I've stolen can help compensate for what was taken from you. There is no way to place a value on what you may have been through, and I shudder to ponder the misfortunes you may have had to suffer because of my decisions. I tried to leave no loose ends that would point to my family, which is why my will contained no provisions. You have finally claimed your inheritance. Do with it what you will. I know you will find a way to change my shameful actions into blessings. Be sure to take the other keys with you and factor in the contents of the other nine safety deposit boxes. You will find those keys in an envelope at the bottom of box 4448.

*You are my legacy, Matthew. You possess a gift far
greater than mine. Please forgive me for my selfishness.
I am infinitely proud of you.*

With love,

Gramps

Matthew wiped his eyes several times as he scanned his grandfather's words. Mauro waited patiently for Matthew to absorb the letter,
but his eyebrows had been on alert since Matthew exclaimed "Whoa"
two full minutes ago.

"Looks like you are going to have to take some of this money,
Mauro. I'm going to be in a logistically impossible situation if you
don't." Matthew moved the bundles of money in box 4448 aside and
searched the bottom until he found the envelope. He lifted it out of
the box and opened it. Matthew laughed heartily and he held up four
more keys.

"Holy shit," Mauro whispered. "My hat is off to you, Thad
Newcombe. You stuck the bastards for the whole lot of it!"

"How much do you think is here?" Matthew asked.

"They were asking twenty million," Mauro answered.

"There's a lot we can do with twenty million, Mauro."

"You can, son. I'm an old man. I don't have many more years to
live."

"The way I see it, you stopped living at twenty-two. You have a lot
of catching up to do."

"I'm free now, Matthew. I got you to this point. I followed through
on the promise that I made to your dad, and now I'm free. At my age,
that's winning my own kind of lottery."

"Well, a couple hundred thousand can't hurt. Dad always wanted
to be able to repay you for saving our lives." Matthew filled the pock-
ets of Mauro's overcoat with as many stacks of hundreds as he could
fit.

"Okay, that's enough, Matthew," Mauro laughed. "These old ladies
I date, if they find out I have money they're gonna pressure me for
marriage, and I can't have that."

Matthew smiled at Mauro. "What do I do now? I can't exactly transfer this to my bank in Italy."

"It's been here for twenty-four years, son. It'll be safe here. Maybe you buy a vacation home nearby—gives you an excuse to come here every so often when your sock drawer runs out of currency."

"My girls want to come here. I have two girls, Mauro. They're beautiful. I have a wife and two girls because of you." Matthew's eyes welled with tears again.

"Don't blame me because you got snared in some broad's net!" Mauro deflected. He smiled at Matthew. "I'm really glad, kid." Mauro hugged Matthew and slapped him on the back three times. Matthew unwittingly expelled air from his lungs. "I have to go."

"Can we grab some lunch, at least?"

"Nope. Sorry. I got things to do."

"Okay. Will you come see us sometime? I'll give you the address."

"274 A Venezia?" Mauro smiled and winked. "Maybe I'll drop by sometime."

"All right. I'm gonna unlock the rest of the boxes. See if Gramps left any other artwork."

"You do that. Take care, Matthew."

Mauro pulled the door closed behind him until he heard the lock click into place. He nodded at the bank teller who had opened the safe deposit vault, and told her that Matthew would be a while.

Mauro pushed the heavy door open and stepped out onto the street. He scanned the sidewalks surrounding the bank. Nothing seemed out of order, and no one looked suspicious. He walked over to a young man who was playing guitar for tips a few paces from the bank's main entrance.

"No one followed you, Sir, and no one has been loitering around the entrance of the bank."

"Thanks, kid." Mauro let a hundred-dollar bill float into the guitar case that the young musician had open on the street. "Looks like it's been a slow morning." Mauro gestured toward the nearly empty case.

"That's all right." The kid grinned widely. "I just love playing. If someone appreciates listening, that's cool, but the joy I get from playing is priceless. Can't buy that with money, so what good is it?"

Mauro smiled and began walking back to his hotel.

ABOUT THE AUTHOR

Photo: evokestudio.io

Marci Giebels is a professional singer, compulsive writer, labradoodle butler, yogi sailor, pilot wife, and dedicated mom to two exceptional college kids. Her inspiration and purpose are named Bailey and Rafferty.

www.ingramcontent.com/pod-product-compliance
Lightning Source LLC
Chambersburg PA
CBHW011517240626
47154CB00010B/3059